Iris Rainbow

by

Ilona Fridl

Iris Rainbow

Cover Art by *Rae Monet, Inc. Design*

The Wild Rose Press, Inc.
PO Box 708
Adams Basin, NY 14410-0708
Visit us at www.thewildrosepress.com

Publishing History
First Mainstream Historical Rose Edition, 2014
Print ISBN 978-1-62830-214-1
Digital ISBN 978-1-62830-215-8

Dedication

To the love of my life,
Mark,
who helped make this story sing

Prologue

At the words "Ladies and gentlemen, KRLA is pleased to present The Beatles!" sixteen-year-old Teri Darden was engulfed in a wave of noise from the crowd. She could just make out their new song, "Help." She looked over at her close friend, Evie Campbell, and their eyes caught as they joined in the frenzy. To Teri, the audience seemed to have a life form of its own, seething and writhing.

Screaming from the audience echoed off the dark hills behind them, and she could barely hear. The Hollywood Bowl had never seen its like, she was sure. It was hard to believe the Fab Four were in the same area as she. It had been love at first sight when she stared at *The Ed Sullivan Show* and was bowled over by this English group. Now here they were in front of her, looking even better in person, especially Paul, on whom she had a crush.

Too soon, the Beatles left the stage. Teri and Evie sat next to their respective boyfriends, David Kelsey and Ken Barnes, waiting for a break in the large mass of humanity blocking the aisle next to them.

"David, you got great seats!" Teri rasped, hoarse from screaming. "So close, and what a view!"

He smiled. "My dad got them for me. Working for the entertainment section of the LA *Times*, he gets tickets for just about everything."

"What a great way to freeload off your father." Ken laughed.

"You'd better be nice to me, since I paid for your date tonight."

"I drove, sucker. You owe me gas, then." Ken patted David on the head.

David retorted, "It's your dad's car, so you're a freeloader, too!"

Trying to clear their throats, Teri and Evie made a vain attempt to talk. Teri's ears were still ringing.

"Come on, we'd better start back to the car." Ken took Evie's arm and guided her into the moving column of people, then Evie grasped Teri's hand, and David brought up the rear. *We must look like a snake winding its way through the crowd.* Finally, they made their way to the blue Chevy station wagon.

Ken and Evie climbed into the front seat while David and Teri slid in behind them. Teri suddenly was very tired and put her head back, closing her eyes. Not hearing the car start, she opened them again and saw the traffic in the parking lot was at a standstill.

"Might as well wait for some of the cars to clear out." Ken put his arm around Evie, and she turned to him and they kissed with passion.

"Sounds good to me." David put his hand on the back of Teri's neck and drew her over for a kiss, making a move to caress her breast, but she laced her fingers through his.

"I'm not ready for that yet."

"Let me know when you are."

Teri snuggled into David's arms for a few minutes before Ken turned the key in the ignition. They were on their way.

****

Looking out the window of John Simon's black Ford pickup, Tim Olson sighed. Slouching down on the passenger side of the cab, he put his arms behind his head, dreaming of girls screaming for him. Glancing over at John, who was leaning on the steering wheel with his chin on his hands, watching the cars not moving in front of them, Tim poked John on the arm.

"Do you think we'll ever be that popular with our band?" Tim warmed to the idea. "Wouldn't that be cool to have all those chicks throwing themselves at us?"

John chuckled. "You're beginning to sound like Luke. I don't think we'll get anywhere without a manager or an agent. Since we got out of high school, all we've managed to get bookings for is high school dances and weddings. It seems pretty dead end to me."

"Maybe we can ask around. We're good enough. I'm sure of it. Four years out of high school, we should be doing better than this. My dad is starting to bug me about going to college."

"Yeah, I told my dad I would give it a five-year try, and I've got one year left. Let's get Roy and Luke next week and find someone who'll represent us. Who knows, we may get a record contract someday."

Drifting off, Tim stared out the window and into the night sky, dreaming of riches and fame. The roar of the pickup engine startled him out of his reverie. Cars in the parking lot were moving, so John pulled out into the line. Tim turned on the radio and resumed his thoughts.

Chapter 1

Teri and her mother were setting the table for dinner. Teri glanced up to comment, "It's hard to believe it's been a year since the Beatles concert. They're supposed to be back this year, but I don't think we can go." As her gaze came to rest on the car pulling up in the driveway outside, she added, "Oh, here's Dad."

Her father, a flight instructor at the nearby airport, breezed in and greeted her mother. "Well, we didn't lose any students today," he added, then turned to Teri. "Pixie, when are you going to learn to fly?"

Rolling her eyes, Teri sighed. "Dad, please don't call me that anymore, I'm seventeen. I told you I don't want to fly a plane like Laura did."

"Did I hear my name mentioned?" Teri's sister entered the room with a grin.

Embracing his oldest daughter, Father smiled a welcome. "Laura, it's good to see you! How long are you home from college?"

"For a few days. I don't have classes for the rest of the week."

By this time, Mother had brought the pork roast out and everything else was on the table. Sitting, they passed the food around, and when they started eating, Father turned to Teri. "Pix—er, Teri, do you have plans this weekend?"

"Yes, Dad, why?"

"I need you to mow the lawn."

"Sure, I'll do it Sunday afternoon."

"Do you have a date this week?"

Teri looked at him. "Yes, Saturday. I'm going to the Scene to see a brand-new group called Virgin Ram. It's their first appearance at the club this weekend. Bud Tyler is going to introduce them, and they'll be in Alhambra once a month."

He was silent for a moment. "Who are you going with?"

Biting her lip, Teri ventured, "Evie, Ken, and...David."

With a stern line to his mouth, he remarked, "Didn't you go out with David a couple of weeks ago? I told you, I didn't want you going steady in high school."

"Daddy, I do go out with other boys that ask me. It's just that David asks me out a lot."

"I don't want you to get too serious about this boy. I'm concerned that if you only date one boy, things might get out of control. I worry about you getting too deeply involved."

She smiled sweetly at her father. "Dad, I know. Don't worry about me." *Just get off my back.*

Concern wrote on his face. "I do all the time."

Laura glanced at Teri. "That's the same rule I had. You'll survive." Teri snorted.

Picking at her food, she thought about the sandy-haired surfer dude she'd dated since she was sixteen. Knowing David for the last five years, Teri liked him a lot, but she didn't know if she loved him. *I feel good with him. We like the same things, but why don't I feel*

5

those fireworks that are supposed to happen?

Saturday evening, Teri had just finished combing her long auburn hair when her mother called, "Teri, David's here!" Teri made sure her white lace blouse and green mini skirt were straight and went to greet David. They were meeting Evie and Ken in the club's parking lot.

Teri walked into the Scene teen club with eager anticipation. She dug her elbow in Evie's side. "I hear Virgin Ram is popular all over Los Angeles."

Evie nodded. "I've never seen them before, but I know the reports are all good."

The four friends squeezed onto the dance floor to get a good view. When Bud Tyler, the owner, walked on stage, David chuckled. "That guy really looks out of place in his own club, with that dark gray suit and his hair in an out-of-style pompadour." Bud looked at the eager crowd through his black horn-rimmed glasses.

Ken put his arm around Evie. "He may be out of date, but he sure knows how to find talent."

"We are pleased to have with us this evening," Bud said with a flourish, "a new group from Encino that has caused a stir around the area. We will have them here once a month at the Scene, and I hope you will welcome them. Here is John Simon on drums." Coming out to cheers, John settled on the stool behind the drum set, waving to the crowd. "On the keyboard, Roy Gardner." The cheering continued as Roy stood behind the electric keyboard, bowing. "On the bass guitar, Tim Olson." Tim came out, picked up his bass, and smiled at the audience, while Teri felt her heart skip. *What a dreamboat!* "And lead guitar and singer, the most popular, Luke Knoll."

When Luke came out into the spotlight with his guitar, the girls in the club went crazy. Evie's eyes grew large. "Wow! He is every inch a rock star. See how tight his clothes are? He just oozes sex."

Bud yelled out, "Let's hear an Alhambra welcome for Virgin Ram!" Everyone went wild as the group launched into "Shout."

When the band took a break, Teri and Evie went into the restroom. When she heard the heavy green door shut with a thump, Teri grabbed Evie's hand. "Did you see him?" Teri fanned herself.

Evie grinned. "You mean Luke? Isn't he fabulous?" She leaned toward the large mirror behind the white porcelain sinks to check her makeup, then smoothed out her shoulder-length brown hair.

"No, I meant Tim, the bass guitarist. The one with the smile that just melts me." Both turned to look as three more girls came in, chattering.

Evie pulled a folded piece of paper from her purse and waved it under Teri's nose. "I found these fliers about the group on a table in the front lobby, and it says here that a fan club is forming. We could sign up. It would be the first one we've joined for a local group."

"I'm with you." Going into the small lobby, Teri took one of the fliers off the table and put it in her purse.

Their boyfriends were waiting for them by the dance floor, and David grabbed Teri's arm. "We have time for one more set before we have to go."

Teri pointed to the stage. "They're coming back!" Almost breathless, she watched the group ready their instruments.

The next set started with a slow tune. David and

Teri danced, and she discreetly maneuvered toward the stage, getting a good look at Tim. He had dark thick hair, down to a little past the nape of his neck, and a handsome face with very striking green eyes. She judged his height at about six feet, and he looked well built. He wore the same outfit as the rest of the group: a red shirt with white collar and cuffs, open to his mid-chest, and silver herringbone hip-huggers with a white belt. Black boots completed the uniform. Tim looked very—was sexy the right word?

All of a sudden, she heard, "Teri—TERI! Are you listening to me? The music stopped."

She stared at David and felt her face go warm. "I—I'm sorry, David. I was daydreaming. What did you say?"

Watching her, he sighed, then laughed, and repeated, "I said, let's go sit with Ken and Evie for a couple of numbers."

Teri followed him to one of the tables on the side of the dance floor. Evie giggled as she dug her elbow into Teri's side. "Your next crush?"

Teri stuck her tongue out. "Shut up!" she hissed, but her face burned again. She absentmindedly traced the wood grain in the old table with her fingernail.

During every dance after that, Teri snuck peeks at Tim over David's shoulder. She couldn't remember ever being this flustered before. A couple of times, Tim looked like he was watching her and smiling.

After the second set finished, the four friends said their goodbyes in the parking lot, and David and Teri got into his old white Chevy. At Teri's house, he pulled to the curb and shut the engine off.

"Thank you for the fantastic evening, David."

He gazed at her for a moment, his face glowing green in the lights from the dashboard. "Teri, I want to go steady with you." He clasped her hand tight.

"David, you know what my father said. I can't go steady in high school. That's his number one rule," she said, squeezing his hand back. *Anyway, I don't know if you're the one.*

"It stinks. Why can't we go steady anyway? Your father doesn't have to know." He took both her hands, looking at her intently.

"I can't lie to my father. I never have, and I'm not going to start now." Teri steeled her spine. "You know I care about you. We'll still see each other."

A shadow seemed to pass across his eyes. "It's just that I'm afraid I'll lose you to someone else," he said in a low voice.

Letting go of his hands and lifting his chin up, she studied his face for a moment. "David, no matter who I date, I'll always come back to you, I promise." They kissed tenderly. "I have to go in. Goodnight, David."

"Goodnight, Teri." She got out of the car and walked up the driveway to the house, then turned and waved. He waved back before he started the engine and drove off down the street. *Why does it feel like I lied to him?* She sighed, opening the door.

****

At the Scene, members of Virgin Ram were ending their last set, with the audience applauding wildly before getting ready to leave. Tim Olson scanned the crowd, wondering where that girl went that he'd noticed earlier. Coming up behind him, Luke slapped him on the shoulder.

"Looks like we're a hit here in Alhambra." Luke

grinned. "Hey, Tim, are you looking for somebody?"

"Yeah, I saw a gorgeous redhead here earlier, but I don't see her now."

"You mean the one in the green mini skirt? I was checking her out, too. Maybe she'll be here next month."

"I hope so. I'd like to meet her."

"Hey, quit drooling." Luke gave Tim a sleazy smile.

Hitting him on the arm, Tim smirked. "Look who's talking, you with the notches on your dick. Come on, we'd better start tearing down and loading up."

Luke muttered under his breath, "It's sure going to be nice when we get roadies to do the grunt work for us."

Unplugging the amps and starting to coil the cable, Tim was thoughtful. "You know, we've really come far since we hired Mel as our manager. He's gotten us better gigs than we could ever come up with on our own. It's about time."

Luke nodded. "Sure is. With him taking our original songs to record companies, I hope we get something out of that, too. Roy told me our high school friend Dolores is offering to start a fan club. Hey, maybe we can get a break on a local teen television show."

"I remember trying to convince my parents that I wanted a music career instead of college. They didn't like it at first, but they did agree. It looks like the tide is finally turning."

Tim pushed the last amplifier up the ramp of the van and closed the double doors. John was already behind the wheel, and the other two followed in Roy's

Ford sedan.

Glancing at Tim, John beamed. "The gig went great tonight, didn't it?"

"Sure did. I like the Scene, it's a cool club. There was a gorgeous redhead I would love to meet."

"Whoa, Tim, what about Dana? A girl friend's got rights. You two on the outs?"

Tim was quiet for a moment, thinking about the brown-haired, brown-eyed beauty he'd dated since high school. "Dana started to put the wedding moves on me. I told her I wasn't ready for that, not with the music career."

"In other words, you dumped her."

"Not really. Just put her on hold for a while."

Shaking his head, John retorted, "I swear, between you and Luke, I don't know whose dick is going to get them in more trouble. Why don't you find a cool chick like my Carol?"

Tim smiled wickedly. "Are you offering?"

John smacked Tim on the back of his head, and they both laughed.

By now they had reached the shed behind John's parents' house, where the guys stored the van with the equipment. They finished putting things away, and then John and Tim climbed into John's pickup and headed to the apartment the two shared in an older section of Burbank.

Chapter 2

Teri and Evie pored over the Virgin Ram fan club material when it came in the mail a few weeks later. At Evie's house, they sat in the middle of her double bed with the warm sun streaming through the window. The girls had spent much of their childhood at each other's homes, sharing secrets and dreams, and now was no different. They studied the bio sheets of their respective loves.

Waving Luke's bio under Teri's nose, Evie declared, "It says here that Luke likes romantic walks on the beach and watching old movies. Doesn't he sound dreamy?"

Teri laughed. "You sound as smitten as I am." Looking at Tim's bio, she remarked, "It says Tim's favorite color is blue. So is mine."

Evie snickered. "Good. You're compatible." The girls ended up giggling as Evie came across a list of appearances Virgin Ram was signed to do. "Oh, Teri, I wish we had a car to go to some of those gigs, especially the battle-of-the-bands challenges."

Teri bubbled over. "Well, that won't be a problem for long. I've almost got my father talked into the Ford Fairlane that one of our neighbors is trying to sell."

Evie's eyes grew large. "How are you going to afford it?"

"I've saved a hundred and fifty dollars from

babysitting, and our neighbor is selling it for three hundred, so I asked my dad for half, promising I would pay him back. Keep your fingers crossed for me."

There were two loud pops on the other side of the closed door and the girls nearly fell off the bed. "Sam and Andy! I'm going to get you for that!" Evie cried as she whipped open the door. Her two little brothers were already hightailing it out of the house as she leaned over to pick up the red and blue rubber pieces that once were two balloons. "Those little brats!" Evie turned and showed two open safety pins to Teri, and they both started laughing.

At dinner that evening, Teri picked at her food. With Laura away at college, she was experiencing what it was like to be an only child. "Dad?" she said tentatively.

Looking up from his plate, he responded, "Yes, Teri?"

"Did you think about what I asked you yesterday, about the car, I mean?" She tapped her fork on her plate.

"You need one hundred fifty dollars, right?"

"Yes. I'll pay you back."

Glancing at Teri's mother, he ventured, "What do you think, May?"

Her mother winked at Teri. "I think she's good for the money."

"Teri, I will take three dollars a week out of your allowance until the loan is paid off. You will get five dollars instead of eight. You can give me a portion of your babysitting money, if you want it paid off faster. Is that a deal?" He held his hand out across the table.

"Deal!" Teri cried as she pumped his hand with

both of hers. "Thank you, Daddy!" She noticed her father trying to suppress a smile.

The following Saturday morning, Teri drove to Evie's house, showing off her new car. "Well, what do you think?" she called out the open window as Evie came bounding out.

"Far out! We got wheels!" Evie shouted as she jumped in next to Teri. "Where are we going?"

Reaching into the glove compartment, Teri pulled out the Virgin Ram info. "There's going to be a battle-of-the-bands competition at the Pasadena Auditorium. I told my parents we'd probably be there today. Wanna go?"

"How much?" Evie said, finding her wallet.

"Two bucks."

"Got it. I'll go tell my parents, and then let's go cheer our boys to victory."

The morning was bright and shiny, with no hint of the smog that usually covered the valley and mountains, as they drove to the auditorium. Colorful banners and flags streamed against the blue sky, announcing the band contest, and the line of people at the entrance was already long. The girls decided to buy lunch before they went in, since the acts started at one o'clock. They had time to kick back and talk. As the cool of the day gave way to the warmer afternoon, they found their seats in the second tier up, where they had a good view. Scanning the program, they saw Virgin Ram was second to last. Smells of stale popcorn, cola, and sweaty bodies permeated the place.

Teri sighed as a band exited the stage. "It seems to take forever to get through the fourteen bands ahead of them."

Evie nodded. "Some are very good, some are so-so, but all seem to have their legion of fans." She pointed to the stage. "The Big Balloo is back."

A deejay from a local top-forty radio station, The Big Balloo, as he called himself, was stylishly dressed in a dark blue Nehru jacket and black slacks. Now was the time the girls had waited for.

"And," he said with a sweeping gesture, "here is a band that has been shaking up the Southland. From Encino, I give you...Virgin Ram!"

A thunderous roar came from the crowd, while Teri and Evie jumped up and down and screamed. At the end of the song, there was an explosion of cheers. The girls clasped each other's hands, yelling, "They've got it!" Teri was truly sorry for the last band to play. They were good, but Virgin Ram was a hard act to follow.

When all sixteen bands came out for the voting, Evie grabbed Teri's arm and said, "Come on. Let's go down to the ground-floor level. They won't be checking tickets now."

Traveling down the middle aisle, they noticed a number of fans had the same idea. The band members came out with the Big Balloo. The girls were thrilled. Virgin Ram was only about forty feet away, and Teri couldn't take her eyes off Tim. The Big Balloo went down the line and gauged the cheers they generated. He registered the polite enthusiasm for the other groups, but when he got to Virgin Ram the crowd went wild and there was no doubt who won. Teri and Evie cheered as the group received their trophy. Teri swore Tim looked directly at her, waving. She glanced to see who was behind her and turned back to see him smiling directly at her. *No, Teri, you're seeing things.*

In the car going home, Teri told Evie what she thought she saw.

"Teri, think about it. With all those people there, he saw just you? He probably saw someone he knew behind us."

Teri was silent for a moment. "You're right. I'm seeing things. Bummer." Giggling and heading to Alhambra, the girls turned up the radio and sang along.

Teri and David went to the drive-in that night. She half-thought of the contest that afternoon while she watched the movie.

Meanwhile, David put his arm around her shoulder and nuzzled her neck. "David?"

"Teri, you turn me all kinds of on," he whispered. "Let me love you." Moving his hand up her sweater, he caressed her breast, and her nipple hardened and her breathing came in gasps.

"Mmm, David, that feels good," she moaned.

They kissed deeply. When David moved his hand to her stomach, she quivered, became warm and wet—and then a warning light went off. "David, stop it. We keep up like this, we're going to go too far." She fought for breath.

"Teri, I need you. Just a little more." She saw fire in his eyes.

"No, let's just cuddle. Or you can take me home."

Slumping in his seat like a little boy in a pout, David put the speaker on the rack and started the engine. "Suit yourself." He took her home.

Silence hovered in the air as David stopped the car in front of her house. He sighed. "I'm sorry I acted that way. I shouldn't have pressured you." His hand kept a steady rhythm on the steering wheel.

Taking a breath, she put her hand on his arm. "That's okay. You're forgiven."

He kissed her. "I'll call you tomorrow."

"Goodnight, David." As she opened the front door, she was conflicted. *Why don't I feel the same way when I see David as I do when I see Tim? David doesn't give me that wonderful feeling. Yet I've never met Tim. What's the matter with me?* She tossed and turned in bed that night, wondering.

****

After the contest in Pasadena, Tim was helping John load the equipment van when he heard footsteps.

"Hey, Tim, you guys were fabulous today."

Turning around, Tim put on a weak smile. "Hey, Dana, I didn't know you were going to be here." *I don't want to deal with her now.*

Dana leaned into the van and said to John, "Can I drive Tim back to your apartment?"

John nodded. "Sure, Dana, we don't need him anymore. See you later, Tim."

Tim reluctantly followed Dana Stanley to her Volkswagen Beetle. When they had slid into the small car, she started the engine.

"Tim, I wanted to talk to you about us," she said, pulling out of the parking lot.

"What about us?"

"We've been going together for seven years. When are we going to get married?"

"Dana, look, with all that's happening with the group, I don't think being tied down would be a good idea right now."

She bit her lip. "You told me you would consider it when the group was up and flying. Well, it looks like you're doing pretty well now. My parents have been bugging me about the two of us getting married."

Tim turned to her. "Dana, I'm really sorry, but I'm not ready."

Her voice got lower. "Tim, do you remember Steve Marshall from school?"

"Do you mean that jock who used to make those moves on you?"

"Yeah. He asked me to marry him. I haven't given him an answer yet."

Tim stared straight ahead, not answering. From high school on, Dana was a convenient screw when he couldn't get another date. He liked her, but he didn't love her. They could probably end up killing each other.

Dana glanced at him with flashing eyes. "Well, you don't seem to be putting up much of a fight. Do you even care?"

Drawing a breath, he answered, "You know how I feel, and this doesn't change things. You would have to wait until I was ready. The answer is up to you." Tim suddenly realized what she'd said before and turned to her. "By the way, when did you start seeing Steve? Or are you lying to me?"

"God damn you, Tim Olson! Don't go acting so high and mighty with me! Where have you been all those weekends you've been off work? What back-street little whores have you been with?"

"I notice you didn't answer my question."

Pulling into a parking lot a few blocks away from Tim's apartment, Dana turned on him with tears of hatred. "You bastard! You god-damn bastard!" She pounded the steering wheel with her fist, then sobbed.

Tim's cool facade was breaking, and he put his hand on her shoulder. "Dana, listen..." He was cut short when she slapped him hard.

"You son of a bitch, I invested seven years in you because I thought you loved me."

Tim's ears rang from the slap. "Dana, I do love you in a way..." His voice trailed off.

"What way?"

"Not like a husband should love a wife."

Dana screamed, hit the steering wheel with her fist again, then flew out of the car and pulled the door open on the passenger side. "Well, if that's the way you feel, you can get out and walk the rest of the way."

"But Dana—"

Grabbing him by the arm, she yanked him out. "Get out of my car and out of my life. I'll get you one day for this, Tim Olson." She slammed the passenger door shut and got in again on the driver's side.

He rubbed his sore cheek as he watched her pull away, and grumbled, "Women! Go figure." John was already at their apartment when Tim came in feeling grim.

"What happened to you?" John said, and eyed Tim's face.

"Dana dumped me. Literally!"

"Why?"

"Because she got a marriage proposal from Steve Marshall and I wouldn't change my mind about marriage."

"You mean that stupid jock from school?"

"Yeah."

"Bummer. Tough luck, man." John slapped Tim on the back, then wandered into the kitchen. "Let's get a beer." As John came out with two bottles, he stopped for a moment. "You look almost relieved."

Popping the top off his beer with the bottle opener, Tim raised the beer toward John. "I am."

Chapter 3

The weeks passed, and the girls were able to get to most of the gigs, appearances, and band contests that Virgin Ram was scheduled for. Some of the time, Teri thought she saw Tim smile, waving in her direction. She would freeze and tell herself, "No, you're imagining things."

Ken Barnes purchased a Volkswagen Microbus, the right size to haul surfboards to and from the beach. The four friends planned a Saturday at the seashore, with a bonfire in the evening. Teri had just finished packing her picnic basket when Ken's gray vehicle pulled into the driveway. Reaching into her duffle bag, she quickly shrugged into her white cotton lace cover-up to hide her new blue string bikini.

"Your friends are here," her father called from the front door. "When are you going to be home?"

"Around eleven." Teri moved the large wicker basket around him.

Laying a hand on her arm, he ventured, "What are you wearing?"

She smiled sweetly. "I have my new suit under the cover-up." She tried to leave.

He frowned. "I don't see much material through the lace. Let me see it."

Teri chewed on her lower lip, then relented.

He studied her critically. "I want you to change

into your old one-piece bathing suit."

Rolling her eyes to the heavens, she explained, "Daddy, I outgrew that one, so I bought a new suit."

Gritting his teeth, he shook her gently. "Teri, that is not a suit. It's two postage stamps and an envelope."

She set the basket down and refastened the cover-up. "Does this help?"

He looked at her sternly. "Leave it on!"

Picking up the basket and the bag, she waved. "Bye, Daddy," and was out the door. Teri climbed in the back with David and the surfboards.

"Hey, Sweet Stuff, what took you so long?" David moved the basket behind him.

"Oh, my dad threw a fit about my new bathing suit."

"I told you he would." Evie turned around in the front seat. "String bikinis always seem to set fathers on edge. That's why I had to settle on this two-piece." Teri had seen it a few days before when Evie bought the conservative red-striped suit.

The ride to the beach was a little cramped. When they got there, Ken and Evie opened the back and guided the boards out while the other two pushed.

It was a perfect day. The blue sky and sunshine made the water glitter a blue-green with a white lace of foam as the waves raised in a graceful arc that came crashing down with a roar. An ever-present breeze blew the loose sand and blasted it against Teri's skin. Greasy cooking odors came from the weathered stands on the pier and mingled with the ocean's seaweedy smell and a sweet aroma of suntan lotion lingering in the air.

Ken and David carried their smoothly lacquered boards while the girls toted the land provisions. Like a carefully measured safari, they marched through the soft sand to a spot near the water. As the girls set up camp, the boys wiped the boards before going to war with the waves. Many other girls were lying out in the sun while their boyfriends surfed.

Teri sat cross-legged on the beach blanket as Evie opened the blue umbrella behind them and then carefully rolled down the waistband of her conservative red two-piece into a bikini look. That done, she plopped on her stomach beside Teri, watching in silence as the boys waded into the surf with their boards. A number of surfers were out, already dotting the waves over and under.

"I heard you had a date with Tony last night. How'd it go? From what you told me, you were just following your father's rules to go out with other guys," Evie finally said, breaking the silence.

"Horrid." Teri wrinkled up her nose. "We went to see some dumb war movie at the drive-in. His hands were all over me, and he wanted me to give him a blow job."

"Did you?" Evie looked disgusted.

"Oh, ick, no. He made me appreciate David a lot more." Teri sat, thoughtful, after she pulled the suntan lotion out of the duffle bag. "I wonder if that's why my father didn't want me to go steady. I'd never know about the guys that come out from under rocks." While Teri was spreading the lotion on her shoulders, she glanced at Evie. "Has Ken ever put pressure on you to go further when you make out?"

Putting her chin on her hands, Evie gazed out on the water. "Yes, he has. We've been fooling around, but I'm a little afraid to go further. Has David been pressuring you?"

Teri nodded. "It's funny, Evie. I know I have to control the situation, but I end up enjoying the feelings myself. It seems I'm trying to control David *and* me." Teri stretched out.

"Yeah, I enjoy it, too. If it wasn't for babies, I would probably let myself go. It's too bad we're too young for the pill." Evie chewed on her lower lip. "I honestly don't know how long I can resist him."

Teri sighed. "I know what you mean."

Evie turned on the small transistor radio to their favorite top-forty station, KRLA. The Beach Boys' song "Fun, Fun, Fun" wafted over the salty air. The girls lay on their stomachs, singing along, watching the boys ride waves.

The lovely summer day was spent eating, sleeping, wading into the surf, and wandering the pier with a number of wolf whistles sent in the girls' direction. They glanced at each other and shared a giggle. As the sun went down, they found a fire ring. The boys took supplies to the Volkswagen and brought back an armload of firewood. The blankets were used to take the chill off the evening when the sun went down at the edge of the world. After starting the fire, the young people huddled in the blankets, listening to the voice of the Doors' Jim Morrison singing "Light My Fire" through the tinny speaker. A few other fires dotted the beach on either side of theirs, flickering in the twilight glow of the sky as a few stars began to show.

Under the blanket, David rubbed Teri's back and nuzzled her neck. She shivered, in spite of the warmth of the blanket and the fire. She glanced at Ken and Evie, and they had disappeared under their blanket. She kissed David on his neck and ran her hands down his shoulders as he moaned, "Oh, Teri, you're beautiful." Then he freed a breast from her bikini bra and the cool air caused the nipple to tighten. Teri let out a small gasp as he kissed it, and the voice in her head shouted a warning, but the tingling of her body took an edge over her brain.

Teri lay under the blanket, her mind reeling from the new feelings as David teased her belly button and kissed it, then slipped down beside her. Next to her thigh, she felt a hot, hard bulge when David stretched out, and they continued to pet, with Teri panting and moaning. Taking David's hand, she put it on her wet bikini bottom, and he shook as he untied one side of the bikini, caressing her, running his fingers along her slit. Taking a deep breath, he slipped his fingers down the front. Teri exploded in a new wave of emotions. Her heart was racing and her breath came in spasmodic pants. When her body started to sweat all over, she wanted to feel David deep within, and she instinctively spread her legs, but suddenly something inside made her stop.

With David's breathing quickening, Teri felt him shudder. "Oh, god," he moaned.

"David?" Teri whispered as she reached for him and curled her fingers into his shoulders.

In the darkness, he sat up beside her and, along her leg, she felt a warm sticky substance. "I'm sorry, Teri, I lost control."

Sitting up, she wiped her leg with a towel. "I think we'd better go, before we do something we'll regret." She retied her bikini, then tossed him the towel, and he wiped off his bathing trunks. When they stood, they shook out the sand from their blanket and Teri put on her cover-up as Ken and Evie looked out from under their shelter. In near silence they piled wet sand on the fire, packed the Volkswagen, and headed home.

All four of them remained quiet on the way. Teri was the first to be dropped off, and she thanked Ken for taking them, then said goodbye to Evie. David walked her to the door, carrying the picnic basket while Teri carried the duffle bag. Placing them by the door, they kissed goodnight, and she felt a warm glow.

David smiled. "I love you, Teri."

She gazed at him. "I care for you, too. Goodnight, David." Unlocking the door, she picked up her things and went inside. Her parents were watching television.

Her mother looked serious. "Hi, sweetheart, how was your day at the beach? It looks like you got a little sunburned." She came to inspect the damage.

"I'm okay, Mom, it's not painful."

"Teri, you know that suit is not the one I approved of. Why did you buy it?"

"I like it, and it covers up everything that needs to be covered. Mother, everyone is getting a suit like this. Why couldn't I?"

"Because your father and I don't think it's appropriate for a seventeen-year-old. We'll go shopping next week and get you a new one. Usually you don't defy us like this, so we've decided to ground you for only a week."

"A week! But, Mom, I—"

"Two weeks!" Her mom set her mouth in a tight line.

Glancing at her father, sitting silent in his chair, Teri sighed. "All right, you win. Goodnight, Mom and

Dad." She slammed the door to her bedroom. *Parents just don't understand fashion. Well, I've served time before.*

Lying awake a long time, Teri thought about how she felt about David and whether she wanted to go further. *He seems to be the only boy who cares about me, and I guess that's important.* Rolling over, she tried to get some sleep.

****

It was March of '67 when the four friends double-dated at the Scene and Virgin Ram played their monthly gig. Teri and David were dancing a slow number near the stage when Teri looked at the band and saw Tim watching, and he smiled, winking at her. Teri's jaw dropped and after the song finished, she flew across the dance floor to grab Evie's arm. "We have to go to the bathroom," she hissed, dragging Evie behind.

"What is going on with you?" Evie said as the door shut.

"I'm not crazy. When David and I were dancing near the stage, I looked up and Tim smiled and winked at me. I swear to god."

Staring at her friend a moment, Evie started to laugh. "Teri, I have never seen you this delusional. You have really gone ape over this guy."

"I haven't lost my mind, but I can't seem to convince you." Shaking her head, Teri checked her watch. "Come on, we're just about at curfew."

The friends said their goodbyes in the parking lot, since the boys had driven separately. David pulled up in front of Teri's house, turned off the motor, and gazed at her in the glow of the dashboard.

"We have five minutes before you have to go in.

Teri, I love you." Putting his arms around her, he kissed her.

"David, I—oh!" she said as he put his hand under her sweater, caressing her breast, making the nipple pucker, and a thrill went down her body. "I have to go in. Goodnight, Tiger." Laughing, she gently disengaged herself.

"Goodnight, Sweet Stuff," David called as she closed the car door.

Walking to the front door, Teri was a little ashamed because once again David had told her he loved her and she couldn't return it. Not when she was thinking about someone else. Turning, she waved, and he waved back as he drove down the street. She rested her head on the cool surface of the door for a moment before she went in.

****

A few days after the gig at Alhambra's Scene, Tim and John rested in the apartment on one of their rare evenings off. Slowly strumming his acoustic guitar, Tim sprawled on their green overstuffed armchair by the window, and John had his feet up on the matching couch, reading a copy of *Reader's Digest* by the dim light of the pole lamp.

"Damn it, John," Tim finally said, "I still haven't been able to meet that redhead at the Scene. She seems to disappear before the gig is finished."

"Maybe she's spoken for." John looked up from the magazine.

"There's no ring on her finger, so that means she's fair game." He chuckled. "You should have seen her face when I smiled and winked at her. She's hot for me. I know it."

John threw a pillow at Tim's head, and the old green satin pillow went bouncing off, but Tim caught it. "What an ego!" John said as the phone rang. A few seconds after answering it, John suddenly let out a whoop.

Tim mouthed, "Who is it?"

John mouthed back, "It's our agent," and, in his normal voice, continued, "Yes, we'll be at the office at nine o'clock sharp." He pushed the receiver button down, then let go and quickly began to dial. After a moment, he said, "Roy, go pull Luke off whatever woman he's on and get your asses to our apartment, NOW!" When he hung up, he waved his hands in the air and yelled, "Yippee!"

Throwing the pillow back at John, Tim hissed, "What the hell is going on?"

Bouncing the pillow again off Tim's head, John exclaimed, "We got it, you fucker!"

"What?" Tim was getting exasperated.

"A recording contract, you asshole! We did it! We're going to be rich and famous!"

Jumping up, Tim threw the guitar against the ceiling, and it rang loudly. "Let's get drunk!"

John shook his head. "We're meeting with the corporate execs tomorrow, so let's not be hung over."

Tim went to the fridge and pulled out two bottles of beer. "Beer, then." He opened them and they clinked. "Here's to fame and fortune!"

After taking a swallow, they grinned at each other. "Yeah!"

Ten minutes later, Roy and Luke showed up. Luke plopped on the couch. "This better be good." He pouted. "I have a horny woman waiting for me."

John went behind the couch, putting his hands on Luke's shoulders. "Would you consider a recording contract as good as a horny woman?"

Both Luke and Roy shouted as Luke jumped up. "You aren't messing with us, are you?"

John punched Luke. "We're to be at our agent's office at nine sharp tomorrow."

Tim asked, "You two want a beer?"

Both said "Sure" at the same time.

John cast an amused look at Luke. "What about your horny woman?"

"She can wait," he threw off.

Tim raided the fridge for two more beers.

Chapter 4

After Easter vacation, Evie called with big news. Virgin Ram had signed a record contract. "And that's not all! We've been invited to the group's introduction to the press and autograph-signing party!"

"Fab, Evie! How'd you manage that?"

"I called the fan club secretary and got us on the list."

"After all this time seeing them at the Scene and cheering them at band contests, we'll really get to meet them? How great is that!"

"I know what you mean. I'll pick you up about eight Saturday morning. Be ready!"

"Oh, I will!" Teri hung up the phone, catching her breath. *Oh, god, I'm actually going to meet them, especially Tim. I wonder if he really noticed me all those times, or am I losing my mind? Well, I'll find out Saturday.*

"Mom! Dad! That was Evie on the phone." Teri bounded into the living room. "Virgin Ram, you know, the group I like? They just got a record contract, and Evie and I are invited to a press introduction and an autograph-signing party, and we get to meet them, and Evie is picking me up on Saturday morning at eight, and can I go? Oh, please, please, please, please…!" She bounced in place, clasping her hands in a plea.

The corners of her father's mouth twitched while

he tried to be stern. "Will that cut into your study time for your finals?"

She shook her head. "No, no! I'll have plenty of time to study, I promise!"

"How did you get to be invited to this press event?"

Teri told him what Evie had said.

"This seems to be a once-in-a-lifetime chance. I guess you can go."

She gave her father a bear hug, saying to her mother, "Isn't he just the greatest?" Going into her room, Teri lightly touched the poster of Virgin Ram hanging on the inside of the door. Since Laura had left for college, Teri enjoyed having the room to herself for the first time in her whole life. Looking at the empty bed, she missed someone to talk to about things she didn't want her parents to know, though.

Saturday morning, Teri appraised herself in the bathroom mirror. She wore her pink plaid miniskirt topped with a poor-boy ribbed top. Her hair flowed down to her waist, and Teri shook the tresses back and held them with a black John Lennon cap. Slipping on her flat pumps, she gave her makeup a quick check and was ready to go.

"Teri, Evie's here!" her mom called from the front door.

"See ya, Mom!" And Teri jumped into the old Buick Evie had purchased a week ago. They both waved to Teri's mother.

At the record company's location in Hollywood, they parked a block away and walked to the building. They traversed the large reception lobby awash with sunlight streaming through the huge window panes and climbed a blue ceramic tile staircase circling a concrete fountain to arrive in a dark blue carpeted room with glass walls. Evie asked a well-dressed blonde at the front desk where the press party was for Virgin Ram.

"What are your names, please?" the receptionist questioned as she picked up a list.

"Evie Campbell and Teri Darden."

The receptionist checked off their names and handed them a couple of plastic identification cards. "Take the elevator to the next floor, then go all the way down the hall to your right. That will take you into the conference room. Put these IDs on so there will be no questions."

"Thank you," said Evie, and the girls pinned on the tags.

Teri thought it was the longest walk of her life. The conference room was large, with many small tables, and a number of people were already there. The girls chose an unoccupied table in the center and eased into its chairs.

"Are you as nervous as I am?" Teri said.

"Feel my hands." Evie's were clammy.

People continued to come in—the press, fans like themselves, and some who were probably people who worked in the company. Finally, the group appeared, flanked by the CEO and the fan club secretary. Teri gasped when she saw Tim, and not just because he was noticeably looking around the room. When his eyes fell on her, she gave him a big smile.

"Oh, Evie, Tim saw me! I know he did!" Teri whispered.

"He probably saw a lot of people," Evie said, rolling her eyes. "Please don't start this insanity again."

Teri stuck out her tongue.

The CEO introduced the group to the press and gave a short speech, with Teri hearing not a word. Afterwards, the fan club secretary announced the group was going to mingle with the press to answer questions and the fans could ask for autographs during that time.

The girls stared at each other, frozen to their seats, and Evie's eyes got big. "Oh, my god, he's coming over here."

"Who?" said Teri, still eye-locked with Evie. Teri felt a hand on her shoulder like an electric charge, and when she turned she was face to face with Tim Olson. *God, he's handsome!*

"Hello, I'm Tim Olson. Who are you?"

"Yes! I know you are!" *Oh, bummer, bad form.* "I'm, uh, Teri, uh, Teri Darden." *God, I'm babbling.* "This is my friend, ummm…" Teri's cheeks were hot.

"Evie Campbell." Evie gave Teri an amused look as she pulled her autograph book from her purse. "Can we have your autograph?"

"That's what I'm here for." Tim grinned as he signed the page for Evie. When she set out to get the other band members' autographs, Teri handed him a note pad and Tim wrote a little longer, passing her the folded paper he tore off it. "I gave you my phone number. Please don't tell anyone. And please call me." He winked at her and walked away.

Putting the paper in her purse, Teri sat there, totally stunned. Had this really happened? Did Tim Olson actually ask her to call him? Evie came back to the table, where they stayed until the group was ushered out.

On the way home, Evie said, "Teri, I have to admit

I was shocked when Tim walked right over to you. Maybe you weren't completely crazy."

"Thanks for that." Teri gazed at his autograph. *Oh, if I could only tell you everything. I want to, but I don't want to blow this chance with Tim. I don't know how long I'm going to be able to keep this to myself.* She gave a sigh of relief as she waved goodbye to Evie.

The next day, coming home from church, her parents' car pulled up into their driveway and Teri got out. "Are you sure you don't want to go to brunch with us?" her father asked.

Teri shook her head. "I want to do some studying for tomorrow."

Waving as her parents drove off, she unlocked the door and went inside, put her purse on the dining room table, and picked up the phone from its small stand a few feet away. She hadn't been able to call Tim last night, with her parents there, but this was her chance. Teri took the well-worn piece of paper out of her purse, unfolded it, and read for the hundredth time, "To Teri Darden, please call me, Love, Tim Olson." At the bottom was his phone number. After staring at it for a few minutes, she raised the receiver and began to dial.

"Hello?" said a sleepy voice.

"Hello. Is this Tim Olson?" Teri said with a quaver.

"Yes."

"This is Teri Darden." She had a little more confidence.

The voice instantly woke up. "Teri! I was hoping you would call. I would like to see you."

"Where?"

"Do you know where Santa Anita Race Track is?"

"Yes, I learned to drive in the parking lot."

"Could you meet me there in an hour?"

Hesitating a moment, she affirmed, "I'll be there."

"Do you know where the main entrance is?"

"Sure."

"When you go in, take a left on the first aisle and go all the way down to the end. I have a red Corvette. Pull alongside."

"Okay. I'll see you there." *What have I done? I should leave a note for Mom and Dad, but what to tell them?* Teri had hedged before, but never outright lied. Tim was twenty-four years old, six years older than herself. Her dad had freaked when she dated a boy two years older, so what would he say about this? She constructed a carefully worded note. "Dear Mom and Dad, I took a break and went out for a drive. I'll be back later. Love, Teri."

Climbing into her old Ford Fairlane, Teri drove to Santa Anita. There were no races today, so the huge parking lot bustled with student drivers. Turning left from the main entrance, she spotted a red Corvette parked all the way at the end and pulled her old car next to the shiny new one. Tim sat in the car with his long hair tucked up under his cap and dark glasses on. He waved for her to get in beside him.

"Fab car!" she exclaimed, opening the passenger door and sliding in. The leather seat squeaked as the new-car smell filled her nose.

"One of the perks of getting a record contract." Tim gazed at her over his glasses. "I hope you don't mind meeting like this, but since the record contract, it's hard to find any privacy. I don't want you to think I'm some kind of weirdo. I don't give my phone number to every chick I see. But I've seen you before. Say, would you like to go to the A&W down the street?"

Teri glanced at him with a smile of relief. "Sure. Thank you." As they started to the drive-in, Teri continued, "Then I wasn't crazy. You were smiling and waving at me." *Take that, Evie.*

Tim chuckled. "It was kind of fun, watching you look around when I waved to you. I saw you the first night we played at the Scene in Alhambra, and I've noticed you at the clubs we've played, and the band contests." He hopped out of the car and, a few minutes later, came back with two frosty mugs of root beer. As he handed her the mug, he picked up where he'd left off. "I always wanted to meet you, but you were usually gone by the time I had a chance."

"Curfew."

"Oh." He seemed to go through some uneasiness. "How old are you?"

The corners of her mouth curled up. "That's all right, I'm eighteen."

"Well, I told myself if I had the chance, I would introduce myself. So at the press party I decided that was as good a time as any. When can I see you again?"

Teri bit her lip. "I'll be graduating from high school in a couple of weeks. I can see you after that." She took out a slip of paper and a pen. "Here is my phone number." As they chatted, she realized they had a lot in common.

Their root beers finished, he returned the mugs, then drove back to Santa Anita. He got out and stepped to her side of the vehicle, offering to see her back to her car. When she turned to get out, he took her hand and kissed it, and she felt that same electric charge again at his touch. He grinned and waved to her as she ducked into her driver's seat.

****

Tim knew the contract for Virgin Ram was a very generous one. They were given an advance of five hundred thousand each, plus the Corvettes as a welcome-to-the-company gift. In return, they had to produce two albums and four singles within a year.

With the new windfall, Tim and John moved from their small apartment and rented luxury apartments in the Hollywood Hills. John talked his girlfriend, Carol, into moving in with him when she decided to drop out of college for a while, and Tim rented an apartment not far away. He and John helped the other two move near the Strip, where Luke and Roy could hang out.

The Monday following the press conference, Tim showed up at the recording studio in a very good mood. For Mondays, that was a little unusual. He strode over and slapped John on the back.

"She called me yesterday," Tim said with a grin.

John looked up. "You mean the redhead?"

"Yeah. Her name is Teri Darden, and she lives in Alhambra. Cool chick."

"Are you going to ask her out?"

Hesitating a moment, Tim ventured, "Um…not right now. She's a little busy."

"What sort of job does she do?"

"She has senior finals. High school."

John regarded him in shock. "Tim, you're going for jailbait?"

"She's eighteen. That doesn't make her jailbait."

John rubbed his eyes. "I see trouble coming for

you, man."

Setting his jaw, Tim stabbed at the air. "I'm going to go out with her."

Just then the producer called, "Let's do the first take on the title track," and Tim went to his bass and started tuning up.

Chapter 5

At the all-night graduation party, Teri sought out Evie. "I have to talk to you about something or I'll explode." The girls walked outside the gym and the cool night air made them shiver. Teri grabbed Evie's arm. "Remember when we went to the press party for Virgin Ram?"

"Do I ever!"

"Well, when we were there, Tim gave me his phone number."

Evie looked like she had been shot. Catching her breath, she asked, "Why didn't you tell me this before?"

"One, he didn't want me to tell anyone, and two, I didn't want my parents to know."

"Teri, you didn't trust me?" Her expression was one of genuine hurt.

"It wasn't that. The less people who know, the better. But I couldn't keep it to myself any longer. Evie, I want to see him, but I know my dad won't let me go out with someone so much older. What can I do?"

Evie tapped her foot. "You could tell your dad Tim is the same age as you."

Teri shook her head. "That wouldn't work. Both my parents have seen pictures of Virgin Ram. They would recognize Tim."

"How about having him pick you up from my

house?"

"No, your parents would tell mine."

Biting her lip, Evie was quiet for a moment. "Doesn't your sister, Laura, have her own apartment?"

"Yes, in Glendale."

"Maybe you could move in with her for the summer, before you start college. You'll be out of your parents' house, so what could they do to you? And you're eighteen, so you can make your own decisions."

Teri hugged Evie. "I'll call Laura tomorrow. Thanks for the idea!"

"Well, what are friends for? Come on, let's go back to the party. It's cold out here." As if hit by another thought, Evie stopped Teri. "What about David?"

Teri took a breath. "That's what bothers me the most. I have feelings for David, but not the way I feel about Tim. I have to see if this is just a crush. Otherwise, I'll never know if I missed my one true love."

Back in the gym, David and Ken were waiting for them. Grabbing Teri, David steered her onto the dance floor. They moved to the music of a live band through the colorful streamers and balloons in a swirling kaleidoscope.

"Was that a secret powwow going on between you two?" David squeezed Teri tight.

"Well, yes, you might say that."

"Talking about plans after the party?"

"Um...sort of."

Leading her off the dance floor, he headed toward the food table. Then he stopped for a moment and embraced her. "Does that mean I finally get you tonight?" he whispered, stirring her hair with his breath.

Pulling back, she glared. "David, no, and quit asking me."

David grabbed at her hand. "Teri, I thought we had something special. I have loved you since seventh grade, but we didn't go steady because of your father's dumb rule."

Guilt and anger ran through her. "It's not such a dumb rule. David, I've met someone else I want to date."

He gaped at her, then sputtered, "You're kidding!"

Teri's lips tightened. "I'm very attracted to him and I want to see if I'm in love."

"Who?" he said with such venom she was taken aback.

"As a matter of fact, it's none of your business. I never said I was your one and only."

"Fine! Then you can walk home tonight, slut!"

Teri slapped him hard, and after a glance of pure hatred at her, David stomped to his chair, grabbed his jacket, and strode out the door. She stopped for a moment, then ran after him.

"David, wait! I didn't mean to do that. I'm sorry, David!" But he glared and drove off.

"I saw what happened," Evie said, coming out behind Teri and putting her arms around her.

In a few minutes, Teri pulled back with tears in her eyes. "Evie, I didn't mean to hurt David like that, but I'm attracted to Tim, and I don't want to have sex with anyone right now. What could I do?"

"I don't know. Let's see what happens."

Ken came out and glanced around. "What happened?"

Evie chewed on her lip. "Teri and David had a

fight. He left without her. Could we take her home?"

Ken and Evie regarded each other for a moment, and then he took a breath. "I'll get our things."

She bid Ken and Evie a thanks and goodnight when they dropped her off at her dark house. *Good. My parents are in bed. They don't have to know.* She silently opened the door and slipped into her bedroom.

A couple of days later, Teri and her parents sat down to dinner. Taking a deep breath, she started, "Mom, Dad, can I ask you something?"

"Sure, Teri," her mom said. "What is it?"

"I called Laura yesterday and asked if I could move in with her this summer. She said I could, if you agree. Can I?" Keeping her eyes on the plate, she rolled a potato with her fork.

"Why do you want to move out?" her father asked. "You're starting college next fall, so you can take the summer off, if you want to."

She looked directly at him. "I want to get a summer job and earn some money. Laura told me that a bank a block away from her is looking for tellers. She has a two-bedroom apartment and said I could pay half. Please, let me move in with her?"

Her parents studied each other, and her father finally said, "Let us discuss this, and we'll let you know tomorrow."

Those twenty-four hours were the longest day of Teri's life. When the family sat down to dinner again. Teri cleared her throat and asked, "Well, did you discuss if I could move in with Laura?"

Glancing at each other, they smiled. "We'll miss you," her father said.

"Oh, Daddy! Thank you!" She jumped up and gave

them each a hug.

Teri moved into her sister's small two-bedroom apartment the following week. She had no trouble getting the teller's job, and it looked like her scheme was working.

That evening, when Teri called Tim to give him her new phone number, Tim laughingly remarked, "I hoped you would call. I wondered if you forgot me."

"No, I was just finishing school and getting a summer job. I'm living with my sister, Laura, sharing her apartment in Glendale. I'll give you the address."

"Would you like to go out to a favorite club of mine, on the Sunset Strip, Saturday? I'll pick you up at seven."

"Sure, that sounds like fun!"

"Only one thing I have to warn you about. There are members of the press out and about, and it would be wise not to give your real name to them."

"Why?"

"They hound people who are out with celebrities. If you value your privacy, you won't let them know who you are. Okay?"

"I understand. See ya, Saturday at seven." Teri smiled and hung up the phone. Her sister came into the living room.

"Oh, do you have a date on Saturday?"

"Yes, he's picking me up at seven."

"Are you going out with David?"

Teri hesitated. *Should I tell her?* "No, I met someone new."

Laura looked puzzled at her reaction. "Who are you going out with?"

"Will you promise not to tell anyone?"

Laura's eyebrows crinkled. "Sure, why?"

"I'm...going out with Tim Olson of Virgin Ram."

Laura's jaw dropped. "How did you meet him?" Teri told her about the press party and the many times they had noticed each other at the clubs. "Do Mom and Dad know about this?"

"No, and don't you dare tell them. Tim is twenty-four, and I know Dad would forbid me to date him if I still lived at home."

Laura chewed on her lower lip. "So that's why you wanted to move in here. Teri, I feel very uncomfortable about this."

"I feel I'm right about Tim, and I want to show everybody I can take care of myself." With that, Teri walked into her bedroom and sat on the edge of her bed. *Oh, god, I hope Laura doesn't blow this. I've planned this too carefully to let it go now. Laura isn't the confidante she used to be.* She wrung her hands. *I've never done anything like this behind my parents' backs before, but I want Tim so much.* Teri didn't sleep well.

Saturday found Teri dressing in a leather-fringed top and a purple mini skirt with a gold chain. Putting on a hairband to hold back her long hair, she admired herself in the mirror. "Not bad." At a knock on the apartment door, she called, "I'll get it," and ran to answer it. Teri gripped the knob hard to keep her hand from shaking as she opened it.

Tim was in what he referred to as his "ordinary people clothes," looking very handsome in a blue paisley shirt and beige corduroy pants. His hair was tucked up under his cap, and he had his dark glasses on.

"Come in for a minute. I'm almost ready."

Taking off his glasses, he walked into the room.

Oh, those fab green eyes!

Laura came in, and Teri nodded toward Tim, saying, "Laura, I'd like you to meet Tim Olson. Tim, this is my sister, Laura Darden."

Tim held out his hand. "Pleased to meet you. I see good looks run in the family."

She took the offered hand, but for a few moments couldn't speak. "P-pleased to meet you too." She smiled and blushed.

Teri slipped her shoes on. "We'd better go."

Laura asked, "When will you be home?"

Tim grasped Teri's arm. "I'll try to get her home before midnight."

"Well, see ya tomorrow, sis." Teri waved as she closed the door.

After a beautiful ride over the tree-and-flower-coated hills into glittering Hollywood, they went into a popular little club on the Strip. A multitude of psychedelic lights waved colors on the walls, and a strobe light on the ceiling made slow motion of the dancers. The floor was crowded as they wound their way to a little table near the far wall, where Tim's band mate, Luke Knoll, sat with his date, whom he introduced as Cindy. Introductions complete, Tim and Teri sat at the table also.

"Hey, Tim! Why don't we order drinks around?" Luke shouted over the music.

Teri yelled at Tim, "Just order me a Coke."

Luke nudged him. "She doesn't drink booze? Is she too young?" He gaped at Tim with mocked shock. "Are you robbing the cradle?" Luke's date, Cindy, sneered at Teri.

While glaring at Luke, Tim asked Teri if she

wanted to dance. She nodded, and they moved through the crowd to the dance floor, but before they made it, Tim was stopped by a graying middle-aged woman, looking out of place with her dark mink and diamond jewelry.

"Darling, I'm Rita Powers of the *Hollywood Reporter*," she called over the music. "When is your album going to be out?"

"We're working on it. Can't give you a date yet." He tried to go on, but she gripped his arm.

"Are there any films in your future?"

"You'll have to ask our manager."

Turning her eyes on Teri, the woman stared down her nose. "And who might you be, my dear?" she purred.

Teri half-smiled. "Iris Rainbow."

Grabbing Teri's hand and saying, "Excuse me," to the pushy newswoman, Tim pulled Teri onto the brightly lit floor, laughing out loud in her ear. "Iris Rainbow? Couldn't you come up with anything better than that?"

Teri gave a sly grin. "I'll bet she never finds me," she hollered back. Swinging into "Twist and Shout," they did the best they could in the crowded hall. With the Doors' "Hello, I Love You," Teri was thrilled when Tim held her tight. She found herself comparing him to her former boyfriend. David never left her tingling just at a touch. They danced through several numbers, then, breathless, went around the dance floor to the table, finding Luke heavily involved with Cindy.

"I don't think they want company," Teri said, glancing at Tim.

As he eased behind her, Tim put his arms around

her waist. "Let's go to my apartment," Tim said in her ear.

"I don't know if I should." *This is moving fast.*

"Then let's go and get something to drink. Cokes?"

One bar stool stood empty, so Tim directed her to it and ended up leaning around her, ordering two Cokes. When they received their order, Tim said in Teri's ear. "I just thought we could go to a place where we could talk and get to know each other without shouting."

Her Coke was going down fast, because she was thirsty, but she didn't want to make a decision yet. *Do I really want this?* She leaned back on Tim and he kissed her. In a blurry spin, she made her decision. *Yes, I do.*

He held out his hand. "Shall we go, then?"

Biting her lip, she followed him. At his place, he led her to an entrance from the garage and into the apartment. Going down the stairs into the huge living room, Teri saw a breathtaking panoramic view of the lights of Los Angeles. The apartment was tastefully furnished with an overstuffed couch facing the window, and a lovely plant-lined patio.

"It's beautiful here," Teri said as she sat on the couch.

"Would you like some wine?"

Hesitating a moment, she realized she wasn't in a public place now. Wine was something she had been allowed at home on special occasions since she was sixteen. "Yes, I'd love some."

Tim took out a record album from the rack by the stereo. "Do you like Glenn Miller?"

"Yes, I do. I really love all kinds of music."

Tim grinned at her. "You're one of the very few girls who even know who Glenn Miller is."

"My parents have a lot of his music, and other big bands, too."

Putting the record on the turntable, he bowed. "I'm impressed."

He went into the kitchen and brought out two glasses of wine. "Here's to us." He toasted, raising his glass.

Teri followed suit and took a sip. The wine had a warming effect on her, and she relaxed.

"Shall we dance?" Tim stood up and held her tight. They swayed to "Moonlight Serenade" and before long, as they swayed, he was kissing her. Every nerve awakened as his mouth moved down her neck to her shoulder before he guided her to the couch, where they sat with his arm around her. Giving a little shudder, she looked at him tentatively. Was it the music or the wine? She had never felt this way with David. Teri snuggled into his touch and he kissed her neck again. His fingers lightly settled on her left breast, and he gazed at her as if to ask permission. She put her hand on his, and then, underneath her leather top, her nipple hardened. A thrill shot through her.

"May I?" Tim touched the buttons on her leather top. Teri nodded, hoping she wouldn't lose control. Unbuttoning her top, she undid the front closure on her bra. Both nipples became erect when it opened. "Oh, Teri, you're beautiful." Teri lay on her back across his lap and smiled nervously while he continued to kiss her until she thought about launching through the ceiling. *Remember, keep a clear head.* But she found herself wanting more.

Tim caressed down her stomach and she felt her body quiver. "I can't stand it," Teri cried out and reached for him.

He took a deep breath. "Do you want me to stop?" She moved his hand under her skirt and onto the warm wetness of her panties. Tim moaned and shifted uncomfortably while he started rubbing her, then stopped. "You're still a virgin, aren't you?" Tim asked between gasps.

"Yes, but why did you stop?"

"I want you to be sure about this before we go any further." Tim cupped her face and kissed her on the forehead. "I don't think I could stop myself if we go on, and I want this to be your choice."

Surprise overcame her. "Thank you."

"And if you have any doubts on how I feel about you…" Tim took her hand and put it on his crotch, where she could feel a hard erection. "I really want you, baby."

Teri felt her face burn as she pulled away. "I'm not ready to go all the way, yet." Flustered, she glanced at the clock on top of the upright piano. It showed a little past eleven. "I should be getting back. Thank you for not forcing me."

Tim stroked her hair. "My mother raised a gentleman."

Teri patted his cheek. "Your mother would be proud." She got her clothes back together, and they left.

Laura was sitting at the table when Teri came out of the bedroom the next morning. "How was your date last night?" she asked, as Teri poured herself a cup of coffee.

"Magic." Teri sat and helped herself to the doughnuts.

"Teri, I'm a little worried about you. Remember,

you're a child of the suburbs, and the Hollywood crowd lives on a faster track than we do. I just don't want you to get hurt."

"Sis, thanks for your concern, but I can take care of myself. I'm not a child anymore."

Laura shook her head and picked up the newspaper.

****

The following Monday, Luke wandered over to Tim during a break. Tim was working out a tricky part on the bass for a song. Luke dragged a chair next to Tim and plopped down.

"Hey, Tim, that Teri is a hot chick. I noticed you two left early." He winked.

Tim studied him with amusement. "The way you were working Cindy, I'm surprised you noticed anything."

"Did you score with her, man?" he persisted.

Tim leaned his arm on the neck of the bass, looking at Luke thoughtfully. This was a game they'd played since high school, seeing how many girls they could lay, and Luke was way ahead. "How did you do with Cindy?"

"Nailed her. How about you?"

Tim's male ego wanted to lie, say he'd had sex with Teri, but there was something in the competition that wasn't there before. He didn't want to talk about Teri like that. There was a difference in the way he felt. "Luke, let's just say I had a fabulous evening and let it go at that."

Luke snorted. "Didn't score. Tough luck, Tim." He sauntered away with a self-satisfied grin. Tim glowed with the memory of Teri and went back to work.

Chapter 6

After they had dated steadily for a few weeks, Tim called Teri about a music festival the group was invited to. "It's an outdoor festival, up the coast, and I wondered if you would like to come with me."

"Sure! It sounds exciting!"

"It's a weekend festival. We'll be there from Friday evening until Sunday morning."

"Where will we be staying?"

"In a trailer the promoter is providing."

"Hmmm..." Teri was silent for a moment, wrestling with her moral self. But there was a strong pull toward Tim, and she gritted her teeth. "Yes, I'll go with you." Quickly, before she could change her mind.

"Fab. I'll pick you up at your apartment after work on Friday."

"I'll be ready." Teri hung up.

Friday, Teri was putting on her long blue peasant dress when Laura knocked on the door. "Teri, do you really think you should be going away for the weekend with Tim?"

"Sis, this discussion is getting old. Why can't you accept that I'm eighteen now and can make my own decisions?"

"Is this one of your decisions, too?" Laura picked up the packet of birth control pills on Teri's bed.

Teri grabbed them. "Would you please mind your

own business and quit snooping through my things!" She stormed out of the apartment as Tim pulled up. Tossing her bags behind the seats, she slid in beside him and slammed the door a little harder than she meant to.

Tim had a puzzled look. "What's wrong, Teri?"

Pounding her fist on her thigh, she sighed. "I'm sorry, Tim. I just had a fight with my sister."

He nodded. "About going with me this weekend, right?"

Teri set her jaw. "I don't care what she said. I'm an adult and I can do what I want." She gazed at Tim. "And I want to be with you."

He kissed her. "Then let's get going."

As they drove up the coast, they listened to the radio and Teri's mind wandered, thinking about their last few weeks together; they had learned many things about each other and found they had much in common. One was a crazy sense of humor and a love of practical jokes. The weekend before, Tim had taken her to a Japanese restaurant, knowing Teri had never eaten that type of food before. All the way, Tim kept raving about a dish that was out of this world and he ordered it for her but got something else for himself, which Teri didn't think about at the time. After the soup and salad, the waiter brought the main dishes to the table, and on her plate was a grayish mass of something. Hesitantly, she moved it and gasped. It was an octopus tentacle, and she jumped away from the table. She glanced over and Tim was wiping tears of laughter. "Do you want a doggy bag for that?" he managed to choke out.

"You watch your back, Tim Olson," she had said. Teri smiled as she watched the scenery go by. *I know what I can do to get him good.*

Tim pulled into a beautiful park by the beach, the venue for the weekend festival. Its green expanse of lawn and trees was covered by colorful tents and canopied stages, and the park sloped to a wide beach. As he drove into the participant's parking lot, John and Luke waved to a spot near their equipment van. Tim and Teri got out of the car and noticed Roy was driving in as well. John went to direct him.

"Hello, Teri!" Luke said as she walked around the car. Nodding, Teri acknowledged him and was a little uncomfortable with the way he looked at her, as if she were naked.

"What's going on?" Tim closed the car door.

"There's a conference for us at the press tent in five minutes. We were hoping you and Roy would show up."

What a perfect setup to get back at Tim. Teri walked to the press tent with Luke and Tim, writing, 'I'm not wearing any underwear' on a piece of paper that she folded and handed to Tim. "It's something for you to read when you're up on the stage." The corners of her lips twitched as she gave him the paper. Not being able to go into the tent because she wasn't a member of the press, she stood by the entrance to get a view of the proceedings. Tim stood at a mike, unfolded the paper, and read it. Groaning, he glared at her, shifting uncomfortably as she grinned, giving him a comic salute.

Roy and John came into the tent, and Roy slapped Tim on the back, saying, "Hey, Tim, I'm happy to see you too, old man." Looking miserable, Tim groaned again, a visible lump in his jeans.

A couple of newswomen in the front row looked at each other and chuckled, while a blush spread over Tim's face. Teri couldn't watch anymore without laughing. *Am I going to be in trouble!* She went to a nearby picnic table and settled to wait.

After the interview, Tim roared out of the tent, shaking his finger in Teri's face. "I'm going to get you for that!"

Teri slipped her hand into her purse, pulled out a packet of pills, and waved them under his nose. "I certainly hope so." She gave Tim a wide grin and wrinkled her nose.

Gazing at her, he gently eased his body between her knees and gave her a good long kiss before saying, "We still need to get our things out of the car and put them in my place." Each performer had his own trailer with a bedroom, bath, and kitchen. Once their bags were stowed, Tim and Teri followed the greasy scent of cooking to a small white tent serving as a food center, with a table in use there as a counter. Turning to Teri, Tim asked, "Two burgers and chips with Coke?" Teri nodded, and the young black man on the other side of the table delivered their order. They found seats at one of the weathered picnic tables surrounding the tent.

As they were eating, Luke came up behind Teri and put his hands on her shoulders. "Hey, Teri," he said in her ear but loud enough for Tim to hear, "why are you staying with this loser when I'm available?"

Tim whacked him on the head with the flat of his hand. "Get out of here, you leech! Go find your own girl." Tim smiled at Teri. "I've got a claim on this one."

Luke stuck out his lower lip in a fake pout. "You could share." He walked off, grinning. "See you later, kids."

The sun was going down when Tim and Teri headed to the communal tent for a party with all the musicians. Smelling a peculiar sweet odor in the air, she wrinkled her nose. *What is that?* She didn't ask the question out loud, though, and soon forgot as she looked around at the people assembled in the tent. She had to pinch herself. There were members of the Byrds, Jefferson Airplane, and Iron Butterfly, and over on the other side she saw Jimi Hendrix, Janis Joplin, and a couple of the Beach Boys with the Mamas and Papas. British groups were represented by the Who and the Kinks. *It's a rock lover's fantasy, and I'm right in the middle of it!*

They strolled to an open bar in the center, where a young man was bartending. When he offered them a drink, Teri declined, but Tim got a can of beer. A girl in hiphugger bellbottoms and a tie-dyed T-shirt came over and eyed Tim. "Aren't you Tim Olson of Virgin Ram? I really dig your music. By the way, my name is Mindy. I'm a backup singer with Stutz Bearcat out of San Francisco."

"Hello, Mindy. I'm glad you dig our music, but I'm afraid I never heard of your group."

"Oh, we got together a few months ago, and this is our first big gig."

Tim moved on to someone else as Mindy turned to Teri. "And who are you?"

"I'm Teri Darden."

"Are you in a band, too?"

"No, I'm here with Tim."

"Oh, you're Tim's screw. Groovy."

Teri gaped at her. Could she have heard right?

"What?"

"You're Tim's screw. That's cool. There are a lot of chicks here like you. I'll talk to you later."

Teri froze like someone had kicked her in the gut. Going to the bar, she poured something from a dark bottle into a plastic cup and, taking a big gulp, she gasped.

Tim, on his way back to her, saw and yelled, "Hey! That's eighty-proof whiskey! Be careful with that!"

Splashing seltzer water in her drink, she took it out of the tent and sat on one of the park benches facing the ocean. She stared at her cup and watched the glowing sunset colors reflected there.

Tim followed and sat beside her. "What happened in there?"

Silent for a moment, she said, "Mindy asked me if I was in a band and I said no, I was here with you. Then she said, 'Oh, you're Tim's screw.' I realized that was all I was and I couldn't defend it. It's a drag to feel I'm little more important than your right hand."

Tim had a bemused expression. "Teri, you're a hell of a lot better than my right hand." She didn't smile, but he continued, "Look, I asked you along this weekend because I enjoy your company and you're fun to be with." He poked her lightly on her ribs. "Are you my girlfriend?" The bemused expression came back. "A close friend?" A bit of the devil crept in. "A very close friend?" She giggled and Tim kissed her. Searching his face, she wondered, *What am I to you? Are you teasing me?* They watched the stars come out over the ocean. The sea breeze played gently with her hair and Teri put her head on his shoulder, wishing this night would never end.

Putting his arm around her, he caressed her breast. She saw a fire behind his green eyes as he studied her. Teri's nipple hardened and she felt the thrill down her body. "Have you really made up your mind about having sex?" he asked.

"Yes, I have." She gazed at him. "I want you to make love to me."

"You do realize that once you cross that line, you can never go back."

"I want you that much. I've been thinking about this for days and I'm ready to cross that line." Teri didn't flinch an inch.

"Come on." Taking her hand, he escorted her to their small trailer.

They went into the dark and Tim turned on a lamp. Shuddering with sweet anticipation, Teri watched as Tim turned down the bed. He embraced her and she felt an electric charge as their tongues met in a kiss. As she slipped her sandals off, he moved the shoulders of her peasant dress down, and it slid over her arms to the floor. Tim gave a small gasp as her breasts came into view and he realized she was nude all the way down. "You really aren't wearing any underwear."

He moved closer to her and heat spread across her face. He undid his belt and pulled out his shirttails while she worked on the buttons. Caressing the taut skin of his chest, she moved the shirt back and down his arms as they embraced and kissed again. Removing his shoes and socks, he turned to her. "Well, are you ready to go on?"

Her face burned. "I'm ready." Teri summoned her courage and moved her hands to the zipper on his pants. In a moment, she had them and his briefs down. Teri breathed, "Oh, Tim!" She moved her hand toward his erection, then hesitated. He gently took her hand, putting it on his shaft, and moaned as she moved her hand up. She felt a tightening in her belly as they held each other and their breathing quickened. She was reeling with the sensation of his naked body next to hers.

Tim moved her to the bed, kissing down her neck and gently stroking her nipples. Teri moaned, floating off into a world of feelings while he continued to kiss and caress her until he moved down. She was vibrating with an intense tingling when he rose above her. "This is it. Are you still sure?"

She almost shouted, "I'm sure!" and then she felt her body resist him as he bore down. When he suddenly thrust in, she felt the delicious pain and pleasure of being opened for the first time.

"I hope I didn't hurt you too bad," he breathlessly said, starting to move. With a quick shake of her head, Teri surrendered to the spasms she couldn't control, and she kept calling out to him. He shuddered and moaned, and then his body contracted. When he relaxed, he kissed and held her.

She was in bliss until she felt a stinging. "Oh, ouch, that hurts!"

Tim slowly pulled out while Teri put her hand between her legs and there was blood. "I think I'd better clean up." Getting out of bed, she went into the bathroom and took a shower. When she came out of the bathroom, Tim patted the bed and they spent the night in each other's arms.

The next morning, the sun rose on a beautiful day. The small window was open and an ocean breeze brought the salty aroma up the park, mingling with the grass and flowers. Everything was so fresh, and Teri awoke with her head on Tim's shoulder. As he was lying on his back, she gently rubbed her hand down the dark hair of his chest and stomach. "Mmm, Teri." He woke with a smile and rolled over to put his arm around her. Embracing him, she felt him hardening and they shared their bodies in the golden morning light. Teri was sore but didn't care. After the loving, she snuggled in his arms again. *This was even more than I thought it would be. I hope this will make him love me.*

Two hours later, Teri sat on the grass, listening to Virgin Ram rehearse. *Oh, man, they sound great!* Mindy showed up and sat next to her.

Regarding her, Mindy said, "Teri, I'm sorry I bummed you out last night. I didn't mean anything by what I said."

Teri nodded. "That's all right, I'm cool."

Taking out what looked like a hand-rolled cigarette, Mindy lit up, but that wasn't tobacco. *So that was the sweet smell in the tent last night.* After a drag on it, Mindy offered it to Teri. "Here, take a pull on this weed. It will mellow you out."

Teri had never taken illegal drugs before, but she'd heard weed wasn't so bad. Accepting the offered joint, she took a drag and started choking as Mindy watched and giggled. Teri waited for anything to happen as she inhaled the pot. *I wonder what all the shouting is about over smoking this stuff.* "Thanks. Mindy, why aren't you rehearsing with your band?"

Mindy laughed. "Our drummer, Mike, drank like a fish last night and now he's barfing up his socks. So we have to wait for him to put his head together." She glanced at Teri. "Since I have some time, would you like for me to braid some daisies in your hair?"

"Sure."

Putting the joint out, Mindy picked some daisies nearby while Teri pulled her brush out of her purse. Her new friend did an expert job of French braiding Teri's long hair and working in the flowers. She stood up and admired her work. "That looks great. You really have beautiful hair. I'm jealous!" She held out her thinner, straight blonde hair.

A guy in a fringed leather jacket walked toward them. His dark hair was long and curly and he was waving at them. "Hey, Mindy! We're ready to rehearse!"

"I'll be right there, Joe!" she called back. Mindy clasped Teri's hands in hers. "See you around, sister."

"Break a leg, Mindy!" Teri waved as Mindy walked away.

Taking five a few minutes later, Tim came over to sit beside her. "Your hair looks good, Teri."

"Thanks. Mindy came to apologize for last night, and she did it for me."

Gazing deep into her eyes, he brushed a stray curl from her forehead. "Speaking of last night, sex with you was fabulous." He kissed her, and Teri felt her body tingle.

"Wonderful. Mmm, wonderful."

"I have to go back." He caressed her face before he rose and returned to the stage.

Saturday passed with a carnival atmosphere. The balloons added their colors to those of the flying banners while Teri strolled to the different stages, listening to the famous, the not-so-famous, and the as-yet-unknown. The crowd was so big she couldn't get close to some stages. When he wasn't playing, Tim wandered around with her, enjoying the many music styles. That night, when the crowds thinned out, some of the bands got together in a huge jam session that lasted late into the night. Teri settled under a tree near the stage to listen, fell asleep, and was only vaguely aware when Tim spread a blanket over her and curled up beside her.

When she woke the next morning, still under the tree, lacy shadows fluttered over her. Rubbing her eyes, she saw Tim's Corvette parked a hundred feet away, with him and the rest of the group helping the roadies load the equipment. Suddenly, Teri felt something on her legs and, glancing down, saw there were several ants crawling on her. She shuddered and headed toward the trailer. Once inside, She removed her dress, and put a towel around herself as she looked around for her suitcase. *Tim must have packed all my things in the car.* She shook the dress out the open door and put it on the bed. After a quick shower, she stepped out and heard a loud whistle and glanced out of the bathroom, only to see Tim waving her dress at her as he ran out.

"I got you back!" And he took off, running into the park.

"Come back here with my clothes!" Teri screamed, hastily wrapping the towel back around her. It barely covered her body, but with no thought for that she took out after him. She found him on one of the park benches, a naughty little boy look on his face. "Give me back my clothes!"

"Say pretty please."

"Tim Olson, you son of a bitch, where are my

clothes?" Teri hissed.

"Oh, ouch! That didn't sound like pretty please."

Making a low growl in her throat, she said between clenched teeth, "Pretty please."

Tim held up her dress. "Come on. Say it like you mean it."

"Tim Olson, you bastard!" she exploded with the towel flapping up and down while she stamped her foot.

"Oh, and Teri, I really wouldn't jump around like that if I were you."

Roaring at him, she grabbed her clothes and ran back to the trailer with a round of applause from a crowd that had gathered.

Later, Teri sat on a picnic bench, loosening her hair and brushing out the braid. Tim came over with a couple of Styrofoam cups of coffee and some doughnuts. As he set them down, she glared at him. "You embarrassed me."

"Hey," he said, putting up his hands. "You don't think I was embarrassed when you turned me on in front of the press corps?"

Teri tried unsuccessfully not to smile. "Yeah, I guess I had that coming." They finished their breakfast, enjoying the sea breeze and the warm sunshine.

"Come on, we'd better start back." And they got into the Corvette and headed to Los Angeles.

A few hours later, Tim pulled up at Teri's apartment and cupped her face in his hands, giving her a long kiss. "I really enjoyed being with you this weekend."

"Thank you for asking me along." Teri gave him a wide grin.

"I'll call you," he said as she exited the car, waving

as he pulled away.

Teri was so high in the clouds, her feet never touched the ground as she danced to the apartment. When she opened the door, there were her parents, waiting with Laura.

There was a cold hard look on her father's face that she had never seen before. "Teri, where have you been this weekend?" he said between clenched teeth.

"I—I went up the coast to a music festival."

"Who went with you?"

"A guy I met a while ago. Why?"

"Why did you lie to us, Teri?" her mother broke in.

"I didn't lie to you."

Glaring, her father asked, "Then why didn't you tell us about Tim?"

She suddenly turned on Laura. "You rat! I told you—"

"Answer me!" her father thundered.

"Okay, Dad, I'll tell you why I didn't say anything about Tim. Because if you found out he was twenty-four, you wouldn't let me go out with him."

"You're damn right! He's too old for you."

"Daddy, I'm eighteen. I can decide who I go out with."

Her mother regarded her sadly. "Teri, is it true you're on the pill?"

"Yes, Mom." Turning to her father, she asked, "Doesn't that show I'm responsible?"

He pounded his fist on the coffee table and everything bounced. "No, that shows you're a whore. Now you either come home with us or get out of your sister's apartment."

Trembling, she stood there, stung by her father's

rage. Laura sat on the couch with a troubled face, not looking at Teri. Teri turned on her heel, striding to her bedroom. Glancing back, she hissed, "Fine! I'm leaving this apartment, and I'm not going home!" Slamming the door, she began to pack.

Teri's emotions were on a roller coaster. From the high of a few minutes ago, she was now hurt, angry, and confused. The world she'd set up was unraveling before her eyes. Stifling a sob, she opened her suitcase. She would never let her father see her cry. Opening the tote bag she'd brought back from the festival, she pulled out a tissue-wrapped package Mindy had given her. Inside the tissue were three fresh joints.

She put her clothes in two large suitcases and her personal things in the tote and had just taken them off the bed when there was a knock. Teri quickly put the tissue into a pocket of her suitcase as the door opened and her mother said, "Teri, please think about what you're doing."

"Mom, I can't live with Dad if that's what he thinks of me."

She crossed the apartment and her father called after her, "Don't expect me to fund your college education!"

"Don't expect me to go to college!" Giving her mother a hug, she transported the suitcases to her car, put them in the trunk, and opened the driver's door. Looking back at the apartment, she heaved a big sigh.

Sitting in the car a few minutes, she wondered where to go and decided on the YWCA on the main street in Glendale. There she parked her car and went inside. A pleasant-looking woman at the desk smiled and said, "May I help you?"

"Do you have a room I could rent?"

"Sure. That will be five dollars a night."

Teri gave her the money and received a key to room thirty-six. After going up a flight of stairs, she unlocked the door to one room with a bed, sofa, and a table. A small kitchenette completed it, with a bath down the hall. Setting the suitcases down, she shuddered. *How can my father do this to me?* She cried for a while, sitting on the edge of the bed.

Finally, pulling herself together, she set her jaw. *I've got to go on and quit feeling sorry for myself. I've got a job and money. I can take care of things.* She marched out and had dinner at a restaurant across the street. While there, she noticed a book of matches and put it in her purse.

On her way back to the Y, she picked up a few things at the supermarket, then put them away in the small kitchen. Settling in, she tried to read the newspaper, but started trembling. *I've got to talk to someone.* Drumming her fingers on her knee, she opened her purse, shaking out some change. Teri found a pay phone in the hallway and tried to call Evie, but there was no answer. Tapping the receiver on her forehead, she sighed. *There is only one other person I can call.* She dialed Tim's number, and he answered the ring.

"Tim, this is Teri." Suddenly, her voice broke and tears started rolling down her face.

"Teri, what's wrong?"

"My father threw me out of my sister's apartment," she said between sobs.

Tim was silent for a moment. "Because of me, right?"

She told him what had happened. "Tim, I don't know what to do." She started crying again.

"How about moving in with me?"

"What?"

"A lot of people I know are living together now. It's not that big a deal anymore."

Feeling a little like a child learning to swim and being asked to jump into the deep water for the first time, she still knew she would like to be with him. She struggled again with her moral self for a few moments, hemming and hawing. *What can I do?*

"Well? What's your answer?"

"Okay—yes. I guess that will be all right."

"Good. I'll come pick you up."

"No, I have my car. I can pack up tomorrow and drive over after work."

"Do you remember how to get here?"

"No."

Tim gave her the address and directions. "And I have a two-car garage. I'll watch for you and open the garage when I see you coming."

"I'll be there after work, around five o'clock."

"I'll make sure I'm home then." He hung up.

Teri hung up and automatically checked for change in the pay phone. Then she went into her room and closed the door and locked it. Digging into the deepest pocket of her suitcase, she drew out the small tissue-wrapped package. Teri looked around and noticed an ashtray on the small table. She pulled the book of matches from her purse and lowered herself into the chair. *What have I done?*

She opened the tissue, took out one of the three joints, and lit it with a match, breathing in the sweet smoke and then letting it go slowly out of her mouth. Teri sighed and watched the sunset as she thought about how her life had changed. This was not the same Teri that had left for the music festival. *My father doesn't understand true love.* The thought startled her a bit. *Do I really love Tim? What is love?*

Teri thought about her family. *My mother was upset at what I did, but my dad seems to hate me. And why did Laura tell? We were able to share confidences before and I could trust her. Was she jealous?* These thoughts swirled in her head like the smoke flowing from the joint. *And what about Tim? Will he turn out to be like Luke? Can I trust him or is he using me until he gets bored?* Sighing, she put out the joint and walked to the window to close the curtain. *Well, I guess I'll see what tomorrow brings.*

****

The next day, at the recording session, Luke greeted Tim at the door of the lunch room at their midday break.

"Hey, Tim, you finally nailed Teri, didn't you? How was she?"

"How about that flower child I saw you with Saturday?"

Luke grinned widely. "Man, that chick could give head like nobody's business. But you didn't answer my question. If you nailed her, can I have her next?"

"No. And Luke, I'm not playing that game with you. Not when it comes to Teri. She's moving in with me this evening."

"You're kidding. You went and bought an old lady?" Luke shook his head. "This competition isn't going to be as much fun."

Tim patted him on the back. "I'm out of the game for a while, Studley. Teri's worth it."

"When you're through with her, let me know. She must be great in bed."

Tim poked a finger at Luke's nose. "Stay away from Teri!" He was feeling very protective of her. "This is one girl you're not getting away from me." He pushed past a startled Luke.

Chapter 7

Teri pulled into the apartment complex, scanning the numbers above the garage doors. When she found Tim's, the garage door was already going up. Driving her Ford in, she parked it next to the Corvette, and Tim helped carry her luggage. Taking the last two bags, he set them inside the door, then turned and gave her a long kiss.

"You're home now," he said with a smile.

"Uh—um, I have to go unpack." She still reeled from the kiss.

"There'll be plenty of time for that." He swept her off her feet and carried her inside. "I'll take you on a tour of our apartment." He passed the steps going to the living room. "You've seen that." Across from them was a dining tier with a wooden railing overlooking the living room, and up a step to the right was the kitchen, with a window above the dining room. Continuing through the kitchen to a hall that connected with the stairs to the other side, he breezed past a guest bathroom that was stylishly gray, with a sink and toilet to match. He carried Teri down the hall to a huge bedroom with a full blue-tiled bath. "This is our bathroom," Tim said as he turned on the light. "And this," he said, dropping her on a big, royal blue, king-sized bed, "is our bed." Plopping down beside her, he gave her a deep kiss. "Welcome home, baby." There was a beautiful fire in his eyes, and she put her hand on the hard bulge in his pants.

"Now teach me how to pleasure you," she cooed. A slow smile spread over his face.

The next morning, Teri awoke to the smell of coffee. She stirred in bed and opened her eyes. *Where am I? Oh, yes, I'm with Tim now.* She got up and, after freshening up in the bathroom, she shrugged on her robe and padded to the kitchen.

Tim grinned and kissed her. "Morning, sunshine."

She melted into his kiss, then glanced around the room. "Let me make some breakfast for us." Teri opened the fridge. There was plenty of beer and Coca-Cola, but a quarter carton of milk, one egg, and a half stick of margarine was all she found useful. She crossed her arms and tapped her toe.

Tim coughed. "I guess I forgot to get more groceries yesterday." He went to the cupboard and pulled out a box of corn flakes. "There should be enough milk for two bowls." He dug out some chocolate donuts. "There. Breakfast!"

With a sigh, Teri determined, "I'll take care of the food situation today."

After Tim left for the recording studio, Teri went to work changing her life. Calling the bank, she asked to transfer to their Hollywood branch and made arrangements to see Mrs. Costello the next morning. That gave her a chance to settle in. She was still in awe of Tim's spacious apartment. It was as big as her family home. Teri knew she was supposed to start college in a couple of weeks, but that didn't fit her life right now. Instead of thinking about it, she busied herself restocking and making the kitchen her own.

That evening, she searched through the sparsely equipped cupboards. "Tim, we need more pots, pans, and utensils if you expect me to cook for you."

"Make a list of what you need, and we can pick things up tomorrow night."

The next day, Teri called her mother to tell her she was all right.

"Where are you, Teri?"

"I moved in with Tim in his apartment and I've transferred to the Hollywood branch of the bank I work for."

"Why are you doing this? You know it's wrong."

"Mother, I also know I wouldn't be able to see Tim otherwise. Daddy would forbid it."

"It's really not like you to be so defiant. What's happened to you?"

"I love him, Mom. It's as simple as that."

She heard her mother sigh. "Take care of yourself, Teri."

"I will. Bye, Mom." Hanging up, she was torn apart. She loved her family, but had such a strong pull toward Tim. *I don't know what else I can do.*

Later that week, Luke and Roy stopped over with their girlfriends. Sue Thomas was a young actress, the latest of Luke's many women, and Linda Denton, who had been dating Roy for a year, was in a folk-rock band on the Strip called Just Folk. They all sat around talking and Teri got to know these new friends.

"There's something I'm curious about," Teri said to the guys. "How did you come up with the name Virgin Ram?"

Roy smiled. "Two of us were born under the sign of Aries and two under the sign of Virgo."

Giving Teri a leer, Luke said, "Yeah, I wanted to call us Ram Virgin, but the others thought it was a bad idea."

John and his live-in love, Carol, came to visit a few days later. Carol was the only girlfriend besides Teri who wasn't in show business. Tim made the introductions. "You know John," he said with a sweep of his hand. "This is Carol Wehring, whom he never stops talking about. Carol, this is Teri Darden."

"Who Tim never stops talking about," John added with a wry grin.

Both girls put out their hands. "Pleased to meet you," they said at the same time, then laughed. Teri tried the hostess skills she'd learned from observing her mother, sending them to the living room and then bringing down drinks and snacks.

Before long, Teri sat studying the pretty blonde. "What do you do? I heard you're not in show business."

Carol's eyes sparkled. "I was in college a couple of years, studying to be a nurse. But then I moved in with John and decided to put off the studies. I work as a receptionist in a medical clinic."

"Did your parents get upset over that?"

"Yes, but I didn't think we were ready for marriage. I want to go back to college in a year or two."

Teri nodded. "I've been thinking the same thing."

By the end of the evening, Carol and Teri were close friends.

Teri didn't forget her best friend, Evie, and they often had long phone conversations. On a bank holiday, she invited Evie to see the apartment. There were several parking places across from the garage, available for guests, and Teri gave her the address and directions.

Watching for Evie's car from the bedroom window, she saw the Buick drive into one of the spaces and she ran out to greet Evie. After the two friends had hugged and exchanged exclamations, Teri took Evie by the hand and led her into the apartment.

"Oh, Teri, this is beautiful!" Evie's eyes were wide.

"Go down and sit on the couch, and I'll bring us something to drink." Teri soon came back with a couple of bottles of Coke. "What's happening in Alhambra?" She put two coasters on the glass coffee table.

"Well, I heard from my mother that your father is kicking himself around the block. He blames himself for driving you into Tim's arms and now you're living in sin."

Teri winced. As she absentmindedly ran her finger down the frosty side of the bottle, Teri mused, "I don't really think of it that way, Evie. Something inside me had to be with him. I've never felt that way before and I can't explain it. I can't be without him."

"You never felt that way with David?" Evie glanced at her with an unreadable look.

Teri grimaced at the mention of his name. "Not like this. I liked David, and I suppose I even loved him, in a way, but this feeling for Tim is so different. I do feel guilty about what I did to David on graduation night. I could have been a little kinder."

"Ken says David is still hurt and angry, especially when we heard you moved in with Tim." Evie stared steadily at her. "Are you sure that Tim feels the same way about you?"

"I hope so. I mean, he's never said he loves me, but he seems happy to have me here. Tim does many things for me. He's very thoughtful…" Her voice trailed off. "Evie, I'm so confused. I want it to be worth all the pain and hurt I caused. I wish I could give you an answer to your questions, but I can't."

Evie shook her head sadly. "Are you going to start college?"

She felt a pang, because she'd always wanted to become a teacher. "No, I thought I would put it off. My life is in such a whirl right now, I know I couldn't put my mind to school work."

"I was hoping we could share a dorm room, but I guess we won't. I'm going to miss you."

"We'll stay in touch. I need you." They held on to each other, and Teri knew that this was a person she could always trust.

The girls went on to other topics during the sunny afternoon. Soon it was almost five o'clock and Evie had to leave. As the girls were heading for the door, they heard the garage open and they met Tim coming up the stairs with a pizza box.

He grinned and kissed Teri. "Hi, babe! I thought I'd bring dinner home tonight." Noticing Evie standing behind her, he put out his hand. "Evie, it's good to see you again."

She took a breath. "You remembered me?"

"Sure, you were with Teri at the press party. And besides, she always talks about you and Ken. Both of you are welcome here anytime."

Evie nodded. "Thank you, Tim." She put her arms around Teri. "See ya. Take care of yourself." She glanced at Tim. "Bye, Tim."

Both waved as Evie got into her car, and she waved back. Tim kissed Teri again as they went inside.

Putting the box in the dining room, he helped Teri clear the empty bottles off the coffee table. "What would you like to drink?" she called back as she went into the kitchen.

"Beer will be fine," he said as he opened the box.

Teri went to the fridge and pulled out a bottle of beer. Instinctively, she reached for a bottle of Coke, then stopped. *I like beer. Well, why not?*

Teri smelled the warm pepperoni-and-cheese aroma as she carried in the two bottles of beer and a couple of paper plates. "How did the recording session go? You're home earlier than usual." Lifting a gooey wedge of pizza, she put it on her plate.

"The production panel blew a tube and they didn't have a spare one. It should be repaired by tomorrow morning." Tim chewed slowly. "I got a call from my mother today, and she invited me this Sunday for dinner."

"Oh? And?" Teri looked expectantly at him.

"And you're invited, too."

"She knows about me? How does she feel about us living together?"

"She said she doesn't agree with it, but she doesn't hold it against you, either. She wants to meet you."

Teri took a drink. "Tell me about your family."

"Well, my mother and father are Eileen and Dan Olson. My father owns a service station in Encino. I'm the oldest and have a brother and sister, Michael and Colleen. Just a normal, run-of-the-mill, working-class family." He paused a moment. "A lot like yours."

"Evie told me my father blames himself for driving me into your arms and thinks now we're living in sin. I feel guilty about it, because everything I was taught tells me I'm morally wrong, but I've never been happier than since I moved in. How do you feel?"

He seemed to gather his thoughts. "Teri, I have to be honest with you. In my late teens and early twenties, I fooled around with a lot of girls. I really didn't have an emotional connection with any one girl. You could even say I used them, but since you've been here, I haven't wanted anyone else...although I'm not ready to get married yet."

Thinking about her conversation with Evie, she ventured, "Tim, I think I'm falling in love with you."

Taking a deep breath and glancing down, he responded, "I'm not sure I know what love is, but I know I'm happy having you with me."

Teri would take that for now, but it bothered her that he couldn't say he loved her. She tugged at a piece of pepperoni, pulling it from its cheesy prison. Popping it in his mouth, she kissed his cheek. "I'm here for as long as you want me."

Tim blew a greasy kiss her way. "Oh, by the way, I have some fresh joints for this evening while we watch TV."

Clearing the leftovers from the table, she put them in the fridge, then went to the couch in the living room and snuggled next to Tim. Lighting up in front of the blue glow of the TV set, they settled in for the evening.

****

Sunday afternoon, the pair pulled up at Tim's parents' house, a modest two-story with white siding and green shutters in a quiet neighborhood. Teri sighed and wrung her hands as Tim turned off the motor.

"Come on, Teri." Tim grinned. "My parents haven't been known to shoot anyone yet."

Teri opened the car door. "Not funny, Tim."

They walked the white concrete path to the front. As they arrived at the two steps, the door opened and they were greeted by an attractive lady with emerald green eyes and dark brown hair lightly streaked with gray.

Well, I see who he looks like.

The lady stepped out of the house and hugged Tim. "Hi, honey, it's good to see you."

Turning, Tim took Teri's arm. "Mom, I want you to meet Teri Darden. Teri, this is my mother, Eileen Olson."

Teri rubbed her palm on her skirt before she offered it. "Pleased to meet you, Mrs. Olson." She smiled as pleasantly as she could.

Mrs. Olson smiled back and took the offered hand. "Come in, you two." As they went into a small hallway next to a living room, a tall well-built man with thinning blond hair and blue eyes rose from an easy chair. "I'm going into the kitchen to work on dinner," Mrs. Olson called as she disappeared through a door.

"Dad!" Tim led Teri over. "This is Teri Darden. Teri, this is my father, Dan Olson."

"Hello, Mr. Olson." Teri offered her hand again.

Mr. Olson studied her critically before he took it. "Hello, Teri." Shuffling his feet a little bit, he and Tim glanced at each other, then at Teri.

Teri sidled to the door of the kitchen. "Um—I think I'll see if your mother needs some help." She quickly exited the room.

Mrs. Olson stood by the sink, rinsing lettuce, and Teri swallowed her nervousness. "Uh, Mrs. Olson, can I help you with anything?"

She eyed Teri over her shoulder. "You can cut up the cantaloupe into wedges for me."

Going to the kitchen table where the melon, a knife, and a paper plate waited, Teri looked around. "What would you like me to put the wedges on?"

Setting down a bowl, Tim's mother directed Teri, "Put them in here. I'm going to put the cantaloupe on the lettuce to serve." Teri started her task. "Where are you from?"

"I'm from Alhambra." Teri didn't look up from her job.

"Do your parents know where you are?"

"They know I'm living with Tim, if that's what you mean." *Oh, god, am I going to fight both sides? First my parents, now his. Will we ever get any peace?*

"How do they feel about that?"

Glancing up, she found Mrs. Olson watching her. "Not good. They don't agree with what we're doing."

"Then why did you decide to move in with Tim?"

Teri chewed on her lower lip. "My dad didn't want me to be with Tim because he was so much older. But I love your son, Mrs. Olson."

"Does he return your love?"

Teri's frustration pounded in her heart. "He's never said so, but he's very kind and thoughtful to me. He told me he didn't know if he was in love or not."

"Teri, you seem like a wise and sensitive girl. I think Tim is caught up in sudden riches and fame, and I don't know if he's thinking clearly. I don't agree with this living arrangement, and there's nothing I can do to stop it, but please think about what I've said."

Teri lowered her eyes. "I will, Mrs. Olson." Finished cutting the soft orange wedges, Teri put the paper plate with the rind into the garbage can.

"Help me take the food in." A delicious-smelling pot roast, with roasted vegetables and gravy, was transferred to a platter. On the side, in addition to the cantaloupe wedges, were piping hot rolls and butter. Everything looked wonderful as Teri set the dishes on the table.

The four of them sat and Teri glanced at Tim, who looked a little flushed, but he smiled at her. They started eating in silence and Teri tried to break the tension. "Tim told me he has a brother and sister."

"Mike has been working as an intern at UCLA, and Colleen is on vacation with some of her friends," Mr. Olson said, not looking up.

"Oh. I'd like to meet them sometime." Teri tried to mask how uncomfortable she felt.

"By the way, Tim," Mrs. Olson said, glancing at him, "Dana called yesterday asking about you." Tim paled visibly. "I told her you were coming to dinner tonight with your girlfriend."

"Dana?" Teri stared at Tim. *Do I have a rival?*

"Old girlfriend." Tim squirmed a little. A smattering of short conversation went around the table for the rest of the meal. After Teri helped carry the dishes to the kitchen, Tim said, "We should be going."

Teri hesitated. "Maybe I should help your mother with the dishes."

Mrs. Olson shook her head. "No, that's all right. Dan can help me. Thank you for your help." Unexpectedly, she hugged Teri. "I do like you."

"I like you, too. Thank you for a wonderful dinner."

Mrs. Olson nodded. "You're welcome." She

hugged her son next. "I love you, Tim."

"Love you, too, Mom." He turned to Teri. "Come on, let's go."

Mr. Olson walked them to the front door and said to Teri, "I'm sorry about the tension at dinner, but I'm not comfortable with this living arrangement. You seem to be a lovely girl. I hope you understand."

"I do. Thank you, Mr. Olson."

As he slapped Tim on the back, he said, "Good luck, son."

"Bye, Dad." They went to the car, where Tim opened the door for her. After they'd traveled a few blocks, he took a deep breath. "This bothers my dad especially because you're the same age as my sister. He asked how I would feel if Colleen was living with her boyfriend."

"Is that what you and your dad talked about?"

Glancing at her with an "ouch" expression, he answered, "To put it mildly. I got the 'where did you leave your brain' talk. He agrees with your father that we are living in sin."

"Have you changed your mind about us living together?"

"Oh, Teri, no. I can't stand the thought of us not being together. Please stay with me." He snuck another glance.

"I can't seem to refuse you anything."

Almost back to the apartment, Tim looked into the rearview mirror. "That's odd."

"What's wrong?"

"I might be mistaken, but I think the same car has been behind us all the way."

Feeling a flare of concern, she watched as they

pulled into the driveway and saw the car go slowly by. It was too dark to make out any details, then Tim shook his head. "Must be mistaken about that. Come on, babe, let's go in."

Going down the steps into the living room, Tim turned on the TV to *The Ed Sullivan Show*. "Who's Dana?" Teri asked, snuggling up beside him.

Putting his arm around her, he lifted her chin. "She was a girl I dated in high school and for a little while after. We had a very nasty breakup."

"I thought you said you never had a connection with any one girl."

"I'm not proud of how I toyed with her. I never really loved her, but I liked her and strung her along. She wanted to get married, but I blew her off, and that's when we had a fight. In a lot of ways, Dana is very spoiled. If she doesn't get her way, she loses her temper."

"Did you lose yours?"

"I'm afraid I made it worse by acting like it was up to her to wait for me to make up my mind about marriage."

"Oh." Still feeling troubled about Dana, Teri settled down and didn't say any more.

The next morning, Teri was still uneasy about that car. Tim was leaving for the studio as she got ready for work. "Be careful, Tim, in case that was a stalker last night." She kissed him goodbye.

"Don't worry, babe. I don't think that was anything. See you tonight." He left the bedroom and she listened for the Corvette engine to start, going to the window and watching him pull out. As the car entered the street, she looked to see if there was anyone following. Not seeing any other cars, she breathed a sigh of relief. Tim must have been right, there was nothing to worry about.

Teri finished getting ready for work and locked up the apartment. As she drove past the first cross street, a white car turned in behind her. Traveling the mile and a half to the bank, she noticed the car followed hers the whole time. As Teri turned into the parking lot, the tailing car went past the bank. *Teri, you're getting paranoid. Stop imagining things.*

Later, Teri returned from lunch and was back at her teller's window. An attractive brunette came up to her. "Hello. I just opened a new account and would like to put some money in."

Teri took out a money receipt. "Do you have your new account number?" She showed Teri one of her temporary checks and Teri copied the number. "Your name?"

"Danielle Stanley. And I have a hundred dollars in cash to deposit."

Writing it up, Teri counted the cash. "Here's your receipt. Thank you for opening an account with us."

"You're welcome." Flashing a smile, she walked toward the door.

When Teri drove back to the apartment that evening, she watched to see if any cars followed her, but she saw nothing suspicious. Tim reported that he wasn't tailed either, and the incident was quickly forgotten.

Soon, Virgin Ram released their first two singles from the album they were working on. Both songs hit the top ten Billboard charts within a week and the group were appearing on local and national television.

At work, Teri had a new employee to train. Her boss, Carmen Costello, introduced her to Barb Adams. "Let Barb watch you with the customers today, and help her out the rest of the week."

"Sure." Teri turned to smile at the black-haired, brown-eyed woman. "If you have any questions, be sure to ask me after the customers leave, all right?"

"I understand."

As the days went by, Teri got to know her co-worker. Barb was a big Virgin Ram fan and had a huge crush on Luke Knoll. Struggling over whether or not to tell that she knew the band, Teri decided to keep her mouth shut. She didn't want a fuss made over it. Anyway, she didn't know Barb well enough to give up that information and trust Barb would keep it to herself.

That was the case, until one evening when Teri hurried into the bank after leaving for her car. Barb was clearing up and getting her things together when Teri picked up the phone. "Tim, I went out to the car and turned the key. Nothing happened. Do you think your dad would help me out?"

"No sense dragging him down here. I can do that."

"You know how to work on cars?"

Tim laughed. "I worked at my dad's service station all through high school. I have tools and car parts in my trunk just in case. Look, I can get away from the studio because we're basically finished for today, so I'll be over in a few minutes."

Teri hung up and found Barb watching her. "Did you get help for the car?"

"Yes, my boyfriend is going to be here in a few minutes."

"Teri, I'll stay with you until he comes."

"You don't have to do that, Barb. You can go home. Thanks anyway."

Barb finished clearing off her teller's desk and retrieved her purse from the locked drawer. By then, Teri saw the red Corvette pull up next to her Ford. Tim raised the hood on her car and Teri was heading out when Barb grabbed her arm. "That looks like Tim Olson of Virgin Ram." A rasp was in her voice.

"It is."

Barb's mouth flew open. "Why didn't you tell me he was your boyfriend?"

"I don't broadcast it, for various reasons. Would you like to meet him?"

A strange expression crossed Barb's face. "Oh, no, I can't—I mean, I'm too shy." Grabbing her purse, Barb ran to her car, not looking in Tim's direction, and tore out of the parking lot.

How odd. Teri crossed to her car, and Tim glanced up. "Hey, babe, try to start it." He motioned to the driver's door. Sliding in, she turned the ignition key and it fired right up. Climbing out, she went to where Tim stood watching the engine run.

"What was wrong with it?"

Tim held up an old piece of wire. "Starter wire broke apart. I replaced it."

Rubbing a dirty smudge off his face, she kissed him. "My hero. Let's go home."

That evening, Tim played the upright piano while Teri cleaned the dinner dishes. "Teri, come in here when you're finished. I've got a surprise for you."

"What is it?" She sat beside him on the bench.

"Listen to this." And he started to play a melody and sing:

I didn't realize when I saw you that day, Beloved.
That you would steal my heart away, Beloved.
I swear I never knew
Any girl quite like you.
And I know you'll always stay, Beloved.
It will always be that way, Beloved.
I didn't know what I had found, Beloved.
But you turned my head around, Beloved.
I looked into your eyes,
And found to my surprise,
My heart was forever bound, Beloved.
And you'll never let me down, Beloved.
I will never make you blue, Beloved.
'Cause forever I'll be true, Beloved.
Say that you'll set a date,
Please don't make me wait,
I will love only you, Beloved.
Can't wait to say 'I do,' Beloved.

Teri gazed at him with awe. "Tim, that's beautiful. Did you just write that?"

"I've been working on it for a few days. It's a song that you inspired, baby."

There were tears in Teri's eyes. *Tell me straight out, do you really love me or are you toying with me? Say it. Say the words I want to hear. Do you really want to spend your life with me? Say it, damn it.* But Tim only cupped her face and kissed her. Her doubt grew like an undiagnosed cancer.

The next morning at work, Barb kept watching Teri. At noon in the lunch room, she plopped in a chair beside her. "Do you know all the members of the band?" Her eyes opened wide. "What are they like?"

"They're like anybody else, really. And yes, I've met them all."

"What's Luke really like?"

A little overbearing and full of himself. But why burst Barb's bubble? "He's quite outgoing, with a unique personality," she finally answered.

"Are you going to see him soon?"

"As a matter of fact, I'm going with Tim to a TV studio Saturday to watch them tape a piece for American Bandstand. Then everyone is coming to our apartment for a party."

Barb bounced. "Oh, Teri, can you do something for me? Could you give Luke a note? I could send it to his fan club, but I'll never know if he saw it, and this way I know he will."

Teri thought for a moment. *Well, why not?* "Okay, Barb, but give it to me by Friday."

Grinning widely, Barb shook Teri's hand. "Thank you. I owe you one."

Saturday morning, Teri got ready to go to the TV studio. "Tim, when are we leaving?" Standing in the bathroom in front of the mirror, she had just finished her makeup when Tim came to the door.

"You look beautiful in that green mini dress." He leered comically.

"Thank you, but that's not what I asked you."

A twinkle sparked in his eye. "We'll leave when the limo gets here."

Teri's mouth dropped open. "Limo? Really?"

"Cool, huh? They're picking up John and Carol first, then us. Roy and Luke are coming in another one. Linda and Sue decided not to go, since they could be recognized. You and Carol can fade into the background with the other people and not be bothered. The two of you can stay in the green room with us, then go to the theater to watch the performance."

Hearing the doorbell, Tim went to answer it. Teri came from the bathroom when Tim waved her over. "Let's go. He's here." Checking her purse, she made sure the sealed letter from Barb was there. They locked up and climbed in the long, sleek, black limo. John and Carol greeted the two from the soft plush leather seat facing them.

Carol and Teri stared awestruck at each other. "A limo, wow!" they said together, then laughed. Carol was stunning in a pretty white eyelet minidress and a white mod cap to hold her hair back.

It was twenty minutes to the TV studio. The limo went through the gates to the rear of the building and the girls were escorted to the green room, while the guys were taken to the dressing rooms. Platters of different types of food and drink were on a large table. "Help yourself to anything," the stage manager said.

Carol shook her head. "Teri, we could gain a ton in here."

A half hour later, the fellows showed up in their band outfits, flanking Dick Clark, and the girls had trouble keeping their cool. John remarked as he walked in, "These are the girls we were telling you about. Will there be any problem getting them into the studio?"

"I don't see any problem. I'll alert the crew." Their host turned to Teri and Carol. "I'm Dick Clark, and you are?"

"Carol Wehring..." "Teri Darden," they said breathlessly. He shook their hands and then excused himself and left.

In a haze, Teri almost forgot her mission, pulling out the sealed envelope from her purse. "Luke, can I see you a moment?"

He gave her a sidelong leer. "Yes, my dear, what can I do for you? A date, maybe?"

"Be serious. My co-worker at the bank wanted me to give you this note, so I said I would." Luke went to the couch to read it. The stage manager called the band a few minutes later. Teri kissed Tim for luck as he passed by.

"Catch you later, Teri," Luke threw over his shoulder.

What was that for?

Carol laughed. "I think I'd better warn you about those two." They headed to the audience seating. "You've walked into a noted rivalry."

"What do you mean?" Teri slid into one of the seats next to the wall, and Carol sat beside her.

"In high school, those two fancied themselves the studs of Encino. Luke was the one girls most often latched on to, but Tim had a following, as well. Many times, Luke had an ego problem if Tim happened to get a girl Luke had never dated, and he would be relentless until he got her away from Tim. I'm afraid you're a challenge."

Teri chuckled. "I never was attracted to Luke. He's too overbearing."

Carol laughed. "Good. That's going to drive him crazy." They turned their attention to the stage as Virgin Ram was introduced. They watched the rest of the show except for the last ten minutes, when they had to get back to the green room because the limos were leaving before the show was over, to cut down on problems with fans.

The four of them were quiet as the limo headed back. Tim put his arm around Teri and she put her head on his shoulder. *Is this really me? I've never lived a life like this. I've read and dreamed about it, never thinking I would be in the middle of it so quickly. I don't know if I'm the old Teri anymore.* Sighing, she gazed at Tim and he smiled. *I'm happy as long as I'm with him.*

Carol was dropped off at Tim's apartment to help set up for the party. Tim made sure the bar was stocked while the girls created the snacks.

The party started about seven o'clock, with twenty-some people there: band members, roadies, and girlfriends. The booze, pot, and food flowed freely. Teri couldn't remember ever having this much fun before. She was positively giddy.

Luke followed Teri around all evening, annoying her. Sue, his girlfriend, didn't look happy, and Teri saw Tim scowling a number of times. Four hours into the party and, after many joints and drinks, Teri was tired and dizzy. Noticing that the snacks needed to be replenished, she wandered in a gray fog to the kitchen, leaning against the sink in an effort to steady herself. She heard a faltering tread behind her, and someone thumped into the drainboard. Whirling to see who it was, she gasped. Luke was making an attempt to grab her dress and had his pants unzipped with a large erection coming through.

"Oh, Teri, I want you." Lunging, he tore her dress.

"Luke, no! Stay away from me!" she screamed and was knocked to the floor with Luke on top.

Tim dashed in a second later. "What's going on in here?" Grabbing the smaller man by the back of his collar, he hauled him up until Luke's feet barely touched the floor. Luke tried and failed to grab his jeans and briefs, which were now past his knees and his erection a distant memory.

"Wait a minute, Tim. You don't understand." Luke radiated panic.

Tim shook him by the collar. "You're on top of Teri with her dress torn and your dick hanging out. What am I not understanding?" By now, most of the guests who could move were congregated at the door.

Stalking in, Sue slapped Luke across the face while Tim still held him. "Roy, could you take me home?" Her voice quivered with repressed rage.

"Sure, come on," Roy said. She followed, and Teri heard people exiting the apartment. The ones who were mobile must have managed the ones who were too out of it to walk. The party was over.

Tim threw Luke out of the kitchen. "Get out of my apartment!" he yelled going out the door after Luke. Teri heard a scuffle, and the apartment door slammed again. Curled up in a ball by the kitchen cabinets, she sobbed. Tim returned and picked her up, carrying her to bed, holding her close until they fell asleep.

Tim made Teri stay in bed the next day while he cleaned up the apartment, although both were suffering extreme hangovers. Midafternoon, she came out of the bedroom, showered and dressed in jeans and a pullover sweater. On the couch in the living room, Tim appeared tired and pale, but he managed a smile. "How are you feeling?"

"Like hell. How are you?"

"Same."

Snuggling up on the couch, she kissed him. "Thank

you for cleaning up the apartment."

"Just don't look in the kitchen sink. I couldn't stomach doing dishes." He caressed her cheek. "Teri, John and Carol are coming over this evening. They drove Luke home, and he showed them a letter you gave him yesterday and said it was an explanation of what happened. John sounded upset on the phone. Seems like there's a misunderstanding on Luke's part."

"Tim, I don't even want to think about it. Or him."

The rest of the afternoon, Teri drank white soda and ate crackers to settle her stomach. John and Carol came over as the sun was setting. Coming to the couch, Carol sat next to Teri. "How are you doing?"

"I'm feeling better," Teri replied as Tim and John plopped into the two overstuffed chairs on either side of the couch. John looked angry.

"Teri," John began, "we took Luke home last night, and he showed us a letter you gave him yesterday." Handing her an envelope. "Is this it?"

Taking the envelope, Teri scanned it. On the front was "Luke Knoll" in Barb's handwriting. "This is the envelope, but I didn't know what was in it."

He seemed surprised. "Where did you get it?"

"From a woman I work with who is a big Luke Knoll fan. Why?"

John's mouth tightened. "Read it."

She did, with a gasp. It read:

Dear Luke,

My life with Tim is getting dull. I'm really attracted to you. Let's find a place where we can be alone.

Love, Terry

Clamping a hand over her mouth, Teri ran into the

guest bathroom, where she was sick. Carol and Tim were at the door when she came out and walked her to the couch.

Teri cradled her face in her hands. "I'm sorry. That was a shock to me. I didn't know Barb would do that."

"She didn't." Tim compared the note with the envelope. "At least, not by herself. If you look at the way 'Luke' is written on the envelope and in the letter, they're different. And that isn't the way Teri spells her name. I think someone played a horrible joke on you."

John softened. "I'm sorry, Teri. I thought you might have written this for some reason, but Carol said that wasn't like you and it must have been a prank. I told Carol this morning and I'm going to tell you, too, something we were told by our agent. When you get to be well known, people who are jealous may try to take advantage of you or hurt you in some way. Don't trust anyone. I think that ought to extend to you and Carol as well. Going with us to special outings, you two will be recognized. Be very careful who you talk to."

Teri sighed. "I guess I had to learn the hard way. Thank you for the advice."

"By the way, don't be too hard on Luke. He was drunk and high and thought you were willing. He may be a jerk, but he's not a criminal."

She frowned. "Just tell him I'm not interested and to stay away from me."

Monday morning, Teri decided to face Barb and find out why she had played that trick on her. Reaching the bank, she was surprised Barb was nowhere to be found. Peeking in on her boss, Teri asked, "Mrs. Costello, where is Barb today?"

"Didn't she tell you? Her husband was transferred

to Hawaii. Her last day was Friday."

Teri gasped in shock. "I didn't know she was married. Looks like there was a lot I didn't know about her."

Carmen Costello looked at her steadily. "Is there something you want to tell me?"

"No, I guess it doesn't matter now. Thank you, Mrs. Costello." Teri went to her teller's station and had time to think as she counted out the money in her drawer. *Seems to me, all she told me was a lie, but what did I do to her to make her play that awful trick? Was it jealousy?* She thought back to what John had said. *I guess I can't trust people anymore. If that's the price I have to pay to be with Tim, it's going to be a hard one.*

The next week, Tim came home with a fistful of envelopes. "Babe, we're getting invitations to charity parties. It's swank stuff and we have to dress formal. I want you to go with me."

Putting her magazine down, Teri frowned. "But I don't have anything fancy to wear, and what I make at work is too little for a gown."

He sat next to her on the couch, hugging her. "That's the beauty of making all this bread. I'll give it to you. All you have to do is go and get it made."

"But—"

He kissed her. "No buts. I insist."

She sighed. *This may be fun.*

Carol and Teri decided to go to one of the exclusive shops on Rodeo Drive, glancing at each other as they walked in. No clothes were on racks like they were used to and, in fact, it looked like a small lunch room with a table of food. An impeccably dressed woman came out from the back and glared at them.

"What do you want?" she asked coldly.

Carol hesitated a moment. "We want gowns for a party."

"There's a Sears on Olympic. I suggest you go there," she sneered.

"It's a celebrity function," Teri countered.

"Oh, are you two celebrities?" She dripped with sarcasm.

"No, but we're going with some," Carol said with venom. "Are you going to help us or not?"

"Who, of any note, would be seen with you?"

"John Simon and Tim Olson of Virgin Ram," Carol's blue eyes started to flash.

The woman laughed at them.

"We can call them up and have them talk to you," Teri said.

The woman wiped her face with a handkerchief. "Anyone could tell me anything over the phone. Get out of my shop before I call the police." Teri angrily slammed the door as they left.

Sitting in Carol's red Dodge, they looked at each other. "Well, what do we do now? Who in this snob crowd is going to believe us?" Teri drummed her fingers on the armrest.

Carol slowly smiled. "I think we can use two big guns. What would Snobby Bitch say if we brought our two celebrities in with us?"

"Probably that they were a figment of her imagination." Teri snorted.

Teri talked over their problem with Tim that evening. "Carol and I were wondering if all the formal wear shops on Rodeo were like that. Maybe we should just go to a department store to get our dresses."

Tim was silent for a minute. "I think this is where we can start throwing our weight around. This could be fun. I always wanted to cut down some of those snobs. I'm going to talk to our agent tomorrow and see if he can help."

The girls, through the agent, received appointments at one of the dressmakers. They arrived a couple of days later at a small shop a short distance from the one they had visited earlier.

A fashionably dressed young woman at a desk turned to greet them as they came into the shop. "Hello! You must be Carol Wehring and Teri Darden."

Nodding at the friendly greeting, they said, "Yes."

"Come with me." She led them to a room with large mirrors, several modern chairs, and a couch. "Wait here. I'll get Miss Lamont."

The girls glanced at each other. "What a difference," Teri said, and Carol nodded.

An attractive older woman with gray eyes and salt-and-pepper hair came in, checking a list, and studied them. "Let's see, you're going to a charity event with John Simon and Tim Olson. You'll need something trendy and hip." Miss Lamont walked around them, looking them up and down. Teri shuffled her feet. "I'll need your measurements. Nancy! Vicky! Come in here with your tapes!"

The girls were measured in every conceivable way, and Teri wondered why her arm had to be measured straight out, down at her side, and with the elbow bent. Miss Lamont made sketches as her assistants brought out several kinds of fabric, holding it up to the girls' faces. Teri expected Miss Lamont to ask her which one she wanted, but before she could say anything, Miss

Lamont barked, "I want the dark emerald silk for Miss Darden and the deep azure blue velvet for Miss Wehring." The assistants disappeared as fast as they had appeared.

"May I say something?" Teri ventured.

"No. Now I want the two of you to come back next week, same time, for a fitting. We can talk about shoes, hair, and jewelry at that time."

The girls seemed to have stepped out of the eye of a hurricane as they left the shop and stared at each other. "I wonder why she wouldn't let us say anything. Didn't she want our thoughts?" Teri remarked, leaning on a concrete wall.

"I know I tried several times. Come on," Carol said with a wave of her hand. "We're supposed to meet the guys for lunch at the fish-and-chips place across the street."

In the lunch room, they saw Tim and John in a back booth with a busty brunette waitress hovering over them. She eyed Teri and Carol, giving them a sardonic smile. "These must be the ones you were waiting for." The girls slid into the squeaky booth seat beside their fellows. The waitress picked up the menus and left. Carol and Teri studied each other, then the guys.

"We've already ordered for all of us," John said before they asked.

"What did you order for us?" Carol said sharply.

"The regular fish and chips, why?"

"I guess we're tired of being told what we want."

"Didn't it go well at Miss Lamont's shop?" Tim asked.

"It was a difference in attitude," Teri answered. "We didn't say a word. She was totally in charge. We have to come back next week for a fitting. I think we both wanted some say in how the dresses are going to be made."

"We're having our tuxes made by the tailors there," John put in. "They do everything for the outfits. I think we're even having custom-made underwear." All four of them laughed.

Their order arrived and, putting the food down, the busty brunette made an extra bend when she served the fish and chips to the guys. Teri was sure they could see down her low-cut uniform, because the movement brought her bust within inches of Teri's nose and she had a fleeting thought of stabbing the boob with her fork. As the waitress straightened up, she banged Teri's head with her elbow. "Oh, did I hurt you?"

"No." Teri grabbed her fork with both hands to restrain herself from misusing it.

They started to eat as soon as the waitress left. "We have a plan to get revenge for you two at Madalane's, by the way. That's the Snobby Bitch you went to first, right?" John said between bites.

Carol nodded. "Yes, her shop is down the block."

"Good. All of us will go in, but you let us do the talking."

Three times during lunch they were bothered by patrons asking for autographs. The waitress "accidentally" splashed water on Carol when picking up the dishes.

"Do you mind if I leave her a tip?" Teri asked as they were getting ready to go. The three of them looked at her curiously while she took six quarters out of her purse and picked up one of the thin plastic placemats. Putting the quarters in her water glass, Teri made sure it was full to the brim. She put the plastic mat over the top, and flipped the glass over, then carefully slid the mat out from under the glass, and it adhered to the table. "There, she gets wet, no matter how she gets the tip out."

Tim laughed. "You are devious, babe. How did you think that one up?"

Teri had a slight pang because that was something David used to do to rude waitresses. "It's just something my friends and I used to do."

After they paid for lunch, they went down the street to Madalane's, and the girls went in first. The Snobby Bitch was sitting at the desk and looked up, sneering, "What are you two doing back?" Then the fellows walked in and a look of disbelief quickly crossed her face. "Oh, you do know them."

"Yes, and we don't like the way our girlfriends were treated in this shop," John said evenly.

"Well, I didn't know. I suppose I could come up with something…"

"Forget it," Tim said. "You had your chance and you blew it. You won't be getting any more business from the Stern Agency."

"I'm sorry, please..." Staring at them tight-lipped, she watched them go out the door. They gave a victory cheer as they split to go to their respective cars.

When the girls went to their fitting the following week, Miss Lamont brought out shoes, purses, jewelry, everything they could possibly need. Teri tried to make suggestions on what she wanted, but she was shushed by Miss Lamont. *I feel like a life-sized Barbie doll.*

Miss Lamont tried the necklace on Teri, a beautiful emerald one. "Yes, that will go perfectly."

Teri stared at it in the mirror. "My god, is that real?"

Miss Lamont smiled. "Of course, dear."

"But that must cost a fortune!"

"It does. It's from our collection. You'll only be renting it."

Teri became lightheaded. *I'm going to hang on to this. I can't afford to lose it!*

On the day of the event, Carol and Teri had their hair done at the salon next door, then picked up their dresses. When they left, Carol dropped off Teri with a cheery, "See you later."

At six o'clock that evening, Teri gazed with awe at her reflection in the full-length bathroom mirror. Her dress, of dark emerald green silk, went past her knees in an uneven hemline, with a white silk panel draped over one shoulder and stitched carefully down the side of a deep vee neckline. As she turned in front of the mirror, the silk dress flowed with her. Her high heels were silver, to match her silver clutch purse, and the beautifully matched emerald necklace, bracelet, and earrings set off her red hair, which was done up in a cascade of curls held with a silver band. *Hello, Cinderella. I don't think I could possibly have come up with anything like this. Miss Lamont really knows what she's doing. Although, I'm afraid of getting it dirty. I'm sure it cost Tim a tidy sum. So this is what it's like to be wealthy. It doesn't seem as if they ever make their own decisions.*

"Come on, the limo should be here any minute," Tim called from the bedroom. At the sight of Teri, he blew a long, low whistle. "Baby, you're gorgeous!"

She gasped when she saw him in a tux with a bow

tie that matched the color of her dress. Teri had never seen him so handsome, and she sighed, "You're gorgeous, too." Hearing the doorbell, he offered his arm, and she strolled out with her Prince Charming.

****

Later that week, Carol suggested Teri come with her to her yoga and transcendental meditation study. Teri was hooked, and after that she and Carol frequently got together after work at one or the other's apartment, learning meditation and the Indian chakras, or centers of power in the body, and how to make them work.

One afternoon, the girls were on the patio at Tim's apartment with a Ravi Shankar album on the stereo. The sitar music helped them to relax, along with the incense burning at the four corners of their mats. They had decided to try the nude meditation, to allow universal power to flow in and out without the encumbrance of clothes. When Tim and John came in earlier than usual, they found the girls sitting in the lotus position on pillows. The guys were speechless.

Opening her eyes, Carol intoned, "We are savoring the universe without the limitation of clothing. Why don't you come out with us?"

"What are we supposed to do?" John asked.

Carol shaded her eyes. "Get a pillow, shed your clothes, sit in a cross-legged position, and get in touch with your inner self."

The guys glanced at each other, shrugging. Doing as they were told, they settled down across from the girls. Closing her eyes again, Teri went back into her meditation. She felt a light tap on her shoulder and saw Carol, who tried not to laugh. She gestured toward the guys who were cross-legged on the pillows, both with full erections. Teri whispered, "Well, it looks like they got in touch with their inner selves." The girls burst out laughing and, with the sound of sitar music in the background, the two couples made universal love.

****

Company parties at the apartment turned Teri into an excellent hostess for record executives and radio station owners they wanted to promote Virgin Ram records. Teri loved to cook, so she and Carol made the hors d'oeuvres or else, if the party was being thrown on short notice, Teri called the caterers. At one of these parties, a recording executive slipped her a small vial of white powder. "Try snorting some of this, my dear, it's prime stuff."

Teri took a deep breath. "That's so expensive! I can't accept that!"

"Look at it as a gift for the hostess." Dropping it in her hand, he moved on. She'd never tried any drugs besides pot, but Teri took the vial, hiding it with her things in a drawer. She and Tim could try it later.

She brought out the vial the next evening. "Tim, do you know how to snort this?" Teri gave it to him.

He frowned. "Where did you get this?"

"From one of the recording executives. He said it was a gift to the hostess."

Tim shrugged. "I tried it once. Go get your hand mirror and one of my razor blades."

Puzzled by the odd request, she went to get the items. When she came back, Tim rolled a dollar bill into a tube. Taking the mirror and razor, he divided the cocaine on the mirror into two lines.

He handed her the rolled bill. "Now put this in your

nose like a straw and hold your other nostril closed. Then breathe in one line of coke."

Teri did, and while Tim was snorting the other line, Teri experienced a tingling in all her nerve endings like an intense orgasm, then settled into her own little world of sensations. What she loved about this drug was the way it made her feel. She remembered talking to Tim and dancing around the apartment, and then everything was hazy. Gazing at the clock, she noticed six hours had gone by. It was three o'clock in the morning and Tim was still beside her, with a glassy-eyed stare. *Wonderful feeling, but pot and liquor seems to be more fun. Coke isn't something you can do with friends.* She found her way to bed, but Tim never joined her.

****

One Saturday morning, Tim called Teri from the recording studio. "We're hosting a party this evening for about thirty-five people. The band has big news to announce."

"What time should I have things ready?"

"Around seven."

"What's the big news?"

"It's a surprise." And with that, Tim hung up.

Checking the clock, she sighed. *I have to get everything ready by seven.* It was ten o'clock now. Then the phone rang again. It was Carol.

"I just got a call from John about the party. I'll be over in a half hour to help you."

"Thanks." Teri hung up, sighed, and called the caterers, thinking she couldn't possibly finish cooking in that amount of time. Nevertheless, the girls had everything set up by six-thirty, when people started to arrive. Managers, producers, roadies, and everyone connected with the band—all were invited. Tim and the band showed up at seven.

He came in, shaking a champagne bottle. "Attention, everyone! I have an announcement to make. Virgin Ram's album, *Taking On*, has made it to number one on the Billboard charts, along with a number one single from the album! Not only that, we have charted in eleven countries!" Everyone cheered the news. "There's more," Tim continued. "We're going on a one-year world concert tour. We leave Friday for the *Ed Sullivan Show* this Sunday to kick off the tour!" He popped the cork to more cheers.

At this, Teri's yell stuck in her throat and she became subdued. *A year! Tim will be gone a year?* Carol sat beside her.

"What do you think this means?" Carol asked. "Do you think they can take us, too?"

"I don't know. I guess that would be up to the record company. I don't hear about that happening, though."

"I know I should be happy for John, but all I feel is emptiness. I feel guilty for that." She sighed and went to find John.

Coming over, Tim gave her a kiss. "Aren't you happy, babe?"

Teri forced a half-hearted smile. "Congratulations."

Tim moved on to someone else, and Teri sank into the bottle of booze in front of her. Luke eyed her, but she glared at him. Fortunately, he kept his distance.

Next thing Teri knew, the sun was streaming through the window. Groaning, she buried her head in the couch, then felt a hand on her arm. Carol held a pill and a glass of water. "Here, take this. It will make the hangover go away."

"What is it?"

"Mother's little helper."

After a few minutes, Teri lifted her head, taking in everything around her, and groaned again. Food and mess everywhere. Suddenly, she clamped her mouth and ran to the bathroom. On her return, Carol sat in the kitchen, waiting for her.

"Feeling better?" Carol asked. Nodding, Teri pointed to the mess. Carol laughed. "Don't worry about that. I called a cleaning crew that's used to Hollywood parties."

When the crew arrived, the girls moved to the patio and Teri found her voice. "Where did everybody go, or are they still under that pile?"

Carol shook her head. "They took it on the road somewhere. I elected to stay here since you had passed out."

"What day is this?"

"It's Sunday."

"That means it's five more days before they leave." Carol had tears in her eyes as she nodded. Holding each other, they cried.

By Monday, Tim was reasonably sober as they cuddled up. Teri gazed intently at him. "Do you think I can go along with you?"

Tim hesitated a little too long. "Uh…I don't think so."

"So what should I do?"

"Stay here, of course."

"It will be awfully lonely without you. A year! That seems like forever."

"You could go back to your parents."

Teri seethed. "How dare you suggest that! I haven't spoken with my dad since the blow-up. I think he hates me. Maybe I'll ask Carol if she wants to share an apartment."

Tim looked at her with a surprising amount of sadness. "I'm going to miss you." Holding her tight, he buried his face in her hair. She gave up her anger at his tender touch.

Tuesday evening, the two couples had a final dinner at John's apartment. The guys were happy and excited about the coming tour, and the girls were quieter than usual.

"Will you two be able to come home any time during that year?" Carol asked.

John shook his head. "I can ask, but I don't think so."

Teri chewed her lower lip. "Carol and I talked about getting an apartment."

Tim sighed. "Why? You don't have to move. I can't speak for John, but I'm sure he feels the same way."

"Sure do." John nodded.

"We'll be alone in these big apartments without you, and everything will remind us of you. It's better if we live together while you're gone," Teri said earnestly.

"Suit yourselves, but the apartments are there if you want them."

"Unless we have one of the groupies move in." Tim winked at Teri, but she didn't smile.

The next day, Carol and Teri took a morning off and sought an apartment, finding a small one-bedroom they could afford, just off the Strip. It was strange for

Teri in the new apartment, knowing it would fit in one corner of the ones they'd been living in. But with both of them working, the smaller one would be easier to take care of.

The girls went to the Farmer's Market for lunch. Carol parked in the big lot, then strolled the cool corridor between the butcher shop and grocery into the market, looking at all the colorful, cheap kitsch items on display. They took a turn to the right and followed their noses to the pizza vendor, where they each purchased a slice of fresh hot pizza and a Coke, then sat at one of the outdoor tables.

The girls had just started to eat when they heard, "Carol. Carol Wehring, is that you?"

Turning to the speaker, a curious expression crossed Carol's face. "Dana, hello. I haven't seen you in some time."

"May I sit down?" She indicated the empty chair.

"Okay. Dana, this is my friend, Teri Darden. Teri, this is Dana Stanley."

Dana studied Teri closely. "I've seen you before. Don't you work at the First National Hollywood branch?"

Teri nodded. "Yes, I do."

"I've also seen your picture in the paper, at events with Tim Olson."

Carol intervened quickly. "Teri, Dana is Tim's ex-girlfriend."

Suddenly uncomfortable, Teri said, "Oh."

"Don't worry, Teri, it was over long ago. Tim seems to think only of himself and his pleasure." Dana still stared.

"I've found him to be very thoughtful." Teri felt

very defensive.

Dana looked her in the eye. "Has he ever told you he loves you?" Teri shook her head. "When he does, you'll find him gone. That's what happened to us. He told me he loved me, and then I never saw him again."

Teri felt a rock in the pit of her stomach and Carol said quickly, "He could have changed."

Dana shook her head. "He's done that so many times. He gets tired of a girl, then moves on to the next conquest. I've known both Tim and John longer than you. They're both cut from the same cloth, just you wait and see. This fame will bring them so many girls, they will forget all about you." She got up to leave. "It was good to see you again, Carol. Nice to meet you, Teri."

Both girls were stunned as they watched Dana walk away. Teri turned to Carol. "Oh, Carol, do you think what she said is true?" Tears started to form in her eyes.

Carol bit her lip. "Teri, I started going with John when I was a sophomore in high school and he was a senior. I know Tim called Dana his girlfriend, but he went out with many other girls. If he didn't have a date for an event, he called her. I do remember they were constantly fighting. I never liked Dana, but I felt sorry for her, the way Tim treated her."

"Do you think he's gotten tired of me? Think about all the girls that are going to be throwing themselves at the guys. Could he find a girl he likes better?"

"Teri, I've thought about that myself. I'm waiting for John to ask me to marry him. We've been together for six years now, and he says he loves me, but he's never gone any farther than that. Now, with the fame, maybe he's looking for something better."

Teri put her hand on Carol's. "Maybe something big will happen before they leave."

Carol cast her eyes down. "I hope so."

Thursday evening, Teri fixed a special dinner and dressed in one of her off-the-shoulder gowns, with her hair in an upsweep, hoping maybe, just maybe, Tim would ask her to marry him. Around eight, she heard the Corvette pull into the garage. Putting a Glenn Miller record on the stereo, she lit the candles on the dinner table as Tim came in.

"Wow, I feel like I've walked onto a movie set." Pulling her chair out for her, he sat across from her. He looked at the wine glasses. "Sparkling wine?"

Teri shook her head. "Sparkling grape juice. I don't want liquor or drugs to spoil things tonight."

After dinner, they danced to the music and, at the end of the record, Teri removed two clips from her hair, letting it fall in red cascades. Unclasping the brooch from one shoulder, she let the gown fall. She had nothing on underneath. Tenderly taking her in his arms, Tim carried her to the bedroom, where he set her on the edge of the bed and sat beside her. He lifted her chin and kissed her, their tongues caressing hungrily while his fingers slid down her neck to her breast and her nipple tightened.

As she unbuttoned his shirt, she gazed into his eyes. "Let's have a night to remember." She rubbed his chest.

Tim stood up, unbuckling his belt and unsnapping his pants, then kicked off his shoes and removed his socks. She rose, holding him in an embrace before she pulled out his shirt and finished unbuttoning it.

Removing it, she kissed down his chest to his stomach, and Tim moaned with pleasure. When she removed his pants and briefs, he enfolded her in a passionate kiss, and she felt him getting hard. She pulled him down with her on the bed and caressed him. Tim moaned again. "Oh, baby," he said, running his fingers through her long hair.

Tim kissed her again, guiding her shoulders gently and easing her onto her back. Opening her legs, he worked her with his tongue and fingers until she shattered in ecstasy.

Teri changed position with him, pushing him on his back and straddling him, then lowered herself onto him. She moved up and down in her own rhythm until she came again.

Pulling off, she drew him on top. "Please make long, slow love to me." He entered her and, for a while, they were one. For the first time, they had an orgasm together and lay there in each other's arms, enjoying the closeness.

As they settled down to sleep, he wiped her cheeks. "Why are there tears?"

"I just realized how much I'm going to miss you." Teri snuggled up in the crook of his arm.

"I'm going to miss you too, baby." Tim drew her to him and kissed her damp cheeks.

The next morning, Teri put away the last of the dinner dishes while Tim packed. When he brought out the suitcases, setting them just outside the door, Teri sighed. "When is the limo coming?"

"Soon. Teri, you know you can live here while I'm gone."

"I'm sorry, but I can't bear to live here for a year

without you. Too many things would remind me how lonely I'll be. Carol and I are moving into a small apartment off the Strip. She couldn't stand living in John's apartment alone either."

Just then, there was a knock at the door and a handsome chauffeur stood there. "Mr. Olson?" he asked, and Tim nodded. "Your limo is here."

Pointing to the suitcases outside the door, Tim directed, "You can load these in the trunk. I'll be there in a few minutes." The chauffeur nodded as Tim closed the door.

The couple locked in an embrace, tears streaming down their faces. Finally finding his voice, he cupped her chin. "I'll look for you when I get back, I promise." She could only nod. "Teri, I love you." He kissed her, and then he was gone.

Teri sobbed at the door as she watched the limo pull out of sight. Why did he pick now to tell her he loved her? He'd never said that before. She thought of what Dana had told them and knew it had all happened like she said. Closing the door, Teri went to the couch, where she cried for a long time.

****

Tim watched Teri as the limo pulled out. *God, it hurts to leave her. Now, I start my new adventure.* He blew his nose in his handkerchief and stared out the window. *This is what I've been waiting for most of my life. All those chicks throwing themselves at me.* He felt strangely torn. *I've got Teri on a string, I won't lose her. She doesn't have to know what happens. Being a rock star means one big party, doesn't it?* Tim chewed on his thumbnail. *I'm going to miss her.* The thought of her gave him a hard-on. *Get a grip. But losing Dana*

111

was never like this. Teri will wait for me.

Watching the landscape fly by, Tim knew he wouldn't see the familiar mountains and seashore of home for a long time. He wouldn't see Teri for a long time, either. *If I work it right, I can have Teri and enjoy other women, too. One more time, I'll open the competition with Luke for the tour, then come back to her for good. I told her I loved her, didn't I?* Settling back in his seat, he smiled.

When Tim arrived at the airport, he met with the other three band members at the charter plane after giving his suitcases to the attendant. The whole entourage of manager, roadies, band members, and equipment was going on the same plane. The cabin was very plush, and Tim slid into an overstuffed seat while their manager passed out a several-page itinerary. Mel, a fiftyish man with salt-and-pepper hair and dark brown eyes, then proceeded with his speech.

"Well, boys, you're all on your way to the big time. You can study the itinerary at your leisure, but basically, you'll start in Canada and Alaska, through Hawaii, and on to Australia and New Zealand. We'll take Japan and Hong Kong and some of the islands in that area, but we will skirt the war zone in Southeast Asia. Then we'll hit South Africa, and next the Middle East and Europe. Finally, we will hit the major cities in South America and work our way up for the United States tour. My public relations department will feed progress reports to the media to keep your name in front of the public during that time. Any questions?"

"Do we get any time off?" John asked.

"We have in your contract that you get one week off every two months."

"Can we go home during that week?" Roy questioned.

Mel shook his head. "The expense of flying you back and forth is too great. You'll have to stay in the area where you are at the time. I'm sorry, I know it's hard to be away from your family and friends for a year, but if you really want fame, you have to make this sacrifice. Anything else?"

"Can our family and friends come visit us?" John asked.

"Sure, but at their own expense. The company won't pay for it."

"How about the second album we need to fulfill the contract?" was Tim's question.

"You boys have enough tracks ready to fill another album. If the tour goes well, the way I expect, I can probably get another sweet deal for you. That's why this tour is so important. Is that all?"

The guys looked at the stacks of paper in their hands and nodded. Mel clapped John on his shoulder. "Break a leg, boys. I know Virgin Ram will be a great success." With that, he went back to his seat.

John sighed. "Well, this is what we've been working for. It's hard to believe we've made it this far. Although it was hard leaving Carol this morning."

Roy nodded. "I know what you mean, man. That's why Linda and I got engaged last night."

A chorus of "What?" "Congratulations!" and "You crazy son-of-a-bitch!" rang through the cabin.

"We set the date for two weeks after we come back from the tour. She and my family are going to arrange everything."

John shook his head. "I should have asked Carol,

but I plan to call her as much as I can. How about you and Teri, Tim? Are you going to keep in touch?"

An evil carnal side took over Tim's brain. "I have her so mesmerized now, she'll wait the year for me. I told her I loved her and would look her up when I get back. I plan this tour to be my last fling, so Luke, the competition is on again. Teri doesn't have to know what goes on."

John gaped. "Aren't you taking Teri for granted?"

"You should have seen her last night. She won't leave me, no matter what."

Luke grinned. "Okay, man, scorecards start in New York. I know I'll win all around the world."

"You're on, sucker."

John and Roy looked at each other, rolling their eyes.

A couple of hours later, they arrived in New York and were whisked to a hotel in Manhattan. The next day, they arrived at the theater to rehearse for the Sunday night show. They set up and started their first song, "Taking On." At the satisfying conclusion of the music, clapping was heard in the wings.

"Excellent performance, boys! It's good to see an American band taking the world by storm." The host himself appeared on the stage with a few men behind him.

Mel went over and introduced the band members. Tim found he couldn't speak above a whisper as he greeted Mr. Sullivan.

Ed turned to a man who was introduced as the director. "Gene, I want them to play two spots on the show."

"Yes, sir!" He hurriedly wrote on his clipboard, as

the entourage left the stage.

Sunday evening, in the green room, they waited for the stage manager to call. Tim had a bad case of the opening night jitters, knowing something would screw up. Finally, the man called them to the stage. They went to their instruments, ready to play.

"And now on our stage," they heard Ed Sullivan say, "is a group of youngsters from Southern California…"

There were screams from the audience and they glanced at each other, giving the thumbs up.

"…that have been making waves on the music charts. Give a welcome to Virgin Ram!"

The curtains parted and Tim's jitters went away. The cheers and screams from the audience seemed to energize him. *God, we're playing to millions of people sitting in front of their TVs.* The thought gave him goose bumps. How many years had he dreamed of being on the *Ed Sullivan Show,* and now he was. It was everything he had thought it would be. Launching into the back-up vocal on "Taking On," he had a new energy. *We're going to wow the country tonight!* Ed invited the band to the edge of the stage after their second spot to congratulate them. *We're stars now!* Tim basked in that thought.

Chapter 8

Sunday evening found Teri and Carol in their apartment, waiting to watch the boys on TV. Carol picked at a thread on the arm of her overstuffed chair. "Teri, Linda called this morning. Roy proposed to her Thursday night and they're getting married when he gets back. She said to tell you." Sighing, she studied her hand.

"I take it John didn't." Teri glanced up from the couch where she had been reading the newspaper. "Tim didn't either. Seems like Dana was right."

Checking the clock on the bookshelf, Carol rose and turned on the small portable TV. "It's time for the show."

They stared numbly at the screen and at the first performance of Virgin Ram, Carol said, "They sound great, don't they?"

Teri eyed her. "You can't cry anymore either, right?" Carol nodded.

When the last appearance on the show was finished, Carol waved at the screen. "Goodbye, John."

Teri followed. "Goodbye, Tim." Turning off the set, they sat in the dark. "Do you think they'll call?"

"They haven't yet. They're probably out celebrating tonight. I really don't think we're going to hear from them." Carol turned the lamp on. "How about you and I move the hell out of LA? There's quite a scene happening in San Francisco, and I think we could use a change."

"Where should we go?"

"Let's go to Golden Gate Park and see what happens."

Teri jumped up. "We can start making plans in the morning."

Two weeks later, with the continued pain of Tim and John not calling, they headed up the coast, unsure where this adventure was going to take them. They had quit their jobs, sold Carol's car, and pooled their cash. Arriving in San Francisco, Teri pulled into a parking lot at Golden Gate Park and they got out of the car to stroll to where the flower children were gathered.

It looked like an international gathering of peace, with everyone decked out in colorful clothes, reminding Teri of the music festival. Some people listened to musicians singing folk songs and joined in on the chorus. Artists worked on crafts of all kinds—leather, beading, jewelry, and more. Here and there small groups were scattered, talking, eating, and, yes, there was a sweet smell of pot. Teri found herself being drawn into the subculture. *I need someone who's happy right now. These people seem to be content.*

Someone called her name and Teri turned and saw Mindy, the girl she had met at the music festival. "Mindy, hello! It's great to see you again. This is my friend, Carol. Carol, this is Mindy, the girl I told you about."

Mindy nodded a hello to Carol. "What are you two doing up here in 'Frisco?"

Teri looked down. "We needed a change of scenery."

"Yeah, I heard about Virgin Ram going on a year-long world tour. Bummer." She turned to Carol. "Were you going with one of them, too?"

Carol sighed. "I was with John Simon."

"I feel for the both of you."

"Are you still with Stutz Bearcat?" Teri asked.

"No. We broke up after two of the band members got busted by the narcs. Say, do you have a crash pad?" They shook their heads. "Then come meet my friends, and you can stay with us. We're using an old building in the Haight-Ashbury district. There's plenty of room."

Carol glanced at Teri with a shrug. "Why not?"

"Good. Come on." Mindy took them by their hands and introduced them one by one to a very strange and mismatched group of people. Redman, the self-proclaimed leader of the pack, was a good-looking American Indian with long braids. His old lady was a small Asian girl called Seagull. Also in the group was a black couple: Trace, who wore the black beret of the Black Panthers, and his lady, Cassie, who was very pregnant. While they talked to everyone, Trace glared. Mindy's former bandmate Joe was with her, and Dash, a former Stanford student, was in hiding as a draft dodger. There was a boy Mindy didn't know, but he said his name was Chris. He was a runaway whom Seagull had found and invited to join them.

"Praise the Great Spirit! We now have an even match!" Redman intoned.

"What does that mean?" asked Mindy.

"That means we now have a cosmic balance of male and female."

Teri wasn't sure what they were getting into, but she figured she would go along with it for now. At least it was a free place to stay. Later that afternoon, Teri followed Redman's old pickup back to a building near Haight-Ashbury. They turned into a small parking lot in back.

Redman led them back around the building to the front door to enter the old commercial building. Sheets covered the store windows. Teri hadn't seen anything like this in her life. Mattresses were scattered along against the walls, with a small kitchen set up in one corner and a full bathroom in the back. Redman explained, "It's like the lodges built by my forefathers, where all family members live together. We must pair off to keep the cosmic balance."

With a slight pang of jealousy, Teri watched handsome Dash approach Carol. "Will you join me?" She'd noticed him eying Carol earlier, and admired his sandy hair and blue eyes.

Carol glanced questioningly at Teri, then shrugged. "All right."

Brown-eyed Chris was the only one left. He seemed lost and scared and very young, and Teri's heart went out to him. *I guess I feel like a runaway myself.* Looking at Teri, he blushed to the roots of his light brown hair.

Redman stood in the center, clapping his hands. "It's time for the evening council. For our new family members, you must bring one of the blankets from the stack and spread it out to sit around the center." He pointed to a bookshelf by the far wall.

Teri watched and followed what everyone else did. Spreading their blankets on the floor around Redman, they sat cross-legged. Redman filled what looked like an Indian peace pipe. "We welcome our new members, who the Great Spirit has sent us to live in brotherhood and peace. Please rise, Chris, Carol, and Teri." As they did, Redman lit the pipe and took a draw on it, and Teri smelled the familiar sweet odor. "When you take the pipe, you'll be part of our family and will live with us in harmony and peace." There was a slight snort from Trace.

Teri took a draw from the pipe when it was her turn, blurring a bit, because it was stronger than she was used to. She went into a blissful high.

Redman indicated the three new members. "Can any of you cook?"

Teri nodded in her dazed state. "I can."

Pointing to the mattress nearest the kitchen, he said, "Then that place is yours."

After the council meeting, everyone paired off to their areas and Chris looked nervous about lying beside her with the sounds of lovemaking coming from around the room.

"It's all right, Chris. We don't have to do anything but sleep," Teri whispered and, seemingly relieved, he stretched out.

As the days went by, Teri got used to the strange arrangements. Even Trace said a couple of words to her instead of glaring, and Carol and Dash became a couple. No one was the wiser that Teri and Chris were still simply sleeping through the night.

Mindy reintroduced her to coke. Teri was hesitant at first, but all these drugs were giving her a feeling of wellbeing and made her happy again. Without them, she felt the pain of Tim walking away and never getting in touch. Carol was doing the same, she noticed, and they talked a couple of days later. "Do you think the guys ever tried to call us? What if they did and we weren't there?" Carol asked, crying.

Comforting her, Teri sighed. "I try not to think about that. They didn't call in those two weeks we were getting ready to come here, and that was the last straw for me. You'd think they would have found a minute, if they really cared. Carol, we were there for them through all the victories on their way to the big time. After the *Ed Sullivan Show*, it really hurt that they didn't call. I can't listen to their music anymore without cringing."

Carol nodded. "When I talked to Linda, she said Roy had given her a schedule of where they were staying and when. I didn't get one from John."

Teri's stomach knotted. "I didn't get one either. Let's face it, they just don't care about us." Teri pulled a couple of uppers out of her pocket and handed one to Carol. "Here, I think we need this."

A week later, Teri found Chris sitting on the flower planter in front. "Chris, can I talk to you?" He nodded, and she continued, "Why did you run away from home?"

He looked at her sadly. "My parents got a divorce and the man my mother married kept slapping me around until I couldn't take it anymore. So I left home."

"You didn't graduate from school, did you?" He shook his head. "Chris, listen to me. Don't ruin your life like this. Go back home and finish school, then leave them forever, if you have to."

"Are you a runaway, too?"

"In a way, but I did finish school first."

"And you ended up here, anyway."

Smart kid, he got me. "Other things messed me up.

Don't use me as an example. Just think about going back."

A few days later, Teri was lying down on the mattress to go to sleep when Chris came over and sat beside her. "Teri, I've been thinking about what you said. I think I'll go home."

"Good for you, Chris. I know you made a wise decision." Teri smiled, giving him a kiss on the cheek.

"Before I go, there's something I want to do to you...er...for you, uh, me. Oh, hell!" Taking her hand, he put it on his crotch and she felt his erection.

Teri laughed, then lifted the covers. "Come on in."

The next morning, everyone gave Chris a big sendoff. "May the Great Spirit go with you, my brother!" Redman said as Chris boarded the bus. Waving to all, Chris blew a kiss to Teri as the bus left, and she returned the kiss as Redman stated, "We have to find you a new partner. It's not good to be alone."

"No hurry. I'll just take care of the rest of you."

Teri was taking particular care of Cassie, who was due any day. Cassie wasn't as cold to white people as Trace was. The only one he trusted was Redman. Carol, with some training as a nurse, told Cassie to let her know when the baby was on the way. It decided to make an entrance a couple of days later.

In the middle of the night, Teri heard Cassie get up and, with a low moan, go to Carol. Then she heard Carol tell Dash to go to a pay phone and call an ambulance.

"Teri," Carol called, "bring some clean towels over here, just in case the ambulance doesn't get here in time."

Teri bounced up, grabbing several towels and

wetting one down. Everyone gathered around Cassie, while Teri put the cool towel on her forehead.

"Thank you, Teri," Cassie said through clenched teeth, then she gave a cry of pain. "I think the baby is coming!" Carol moved her gently into position. Just then, the ambulance pulled up and Dash brought them inside. The emergency crew took charge of the rest of the birth, and soon Teri heard a lusty cry.

"It's a boy!" Carol called, and everyone cheered.

Trace slowly came to Carol and stood uncomfortably in front of her as the crew bundled mother and baby out. "You know, for a cracker girl, you're okay." Trace gave her a short nod.

When he left, Carol leaned on Teri, putting her arms around her. Carol was shaking. "Teri, do you have a downer? I've run out, and I need one badly."

Teri was sweating rivers. "Sure, I think we both need one."

****

When the bellboy had been tipped, Tim settled on the big couch in their hotel in Calgary, Manitoba. He and John shared a suite with Roy and Luke next door. Exhausted from a grueling schedule, they savored some free time before the concert. Canada for them was mostly hotel rooms, the way they were hustled around.

"Since we have some free time, I'm going to call Carol," John said, breaking in on Tim's thoughts. "I feel bad I haven't called her yet."

"We've been busy these last couple of weeks. I don't think we've had time to sleep or eat."

Pulling out his phone book, John put in a call and, after a few moments, hung up with a funny look. "Tim, the girls' phone has been disconnected."

"Maybe they moved someplace else. Why don't you check information?"

John called information for Los Angeles. "There's no number under either Carol's or Teri's name."

"Call Linda and see if she knows anything." Tim suggested, an uneasy feeling in the pit of his stomach.

John made the call to Linda, then turned to Tim. "Linda saw Teri and Carol a couple of days after the *Ed Sullivan Show*, and they were depressed. They had decided to go to San Francisco for a change of scenery, and she doesn't know if they came back."

"Who would know if they were back? And where are they?"

"I'm going to call Carol's family, in case she moved home. I know they dislike me, though." After the call, he regarded Tim with a look of concern. "Carol's mother said that they haven't heard from the girls since they left for San Francisco."

Tim felt a stab of foreboding, but he shook it off. "Probably wanted to get away for a while." But to him, that didn't sound convincing. "Why don't you try again in a week or so?"

John nodded and stepped out onto their balcony, shutting the door behind him.

Tim settled back on the couch. *Maybe it wasn't such a good idea to shut Teri out for a while. Where could she be, and what's happening with her? Should I call her, or her family?* He steeled himself. *She's a big girl now. She can take care of herself.* But the rock didn't go out of his stomach.

Chapter 9

A few weeks later, on a beautiful warm day, everyone decided to go to Golden Gate Park. Teri could have sworn there were people who never left the gardens; it always looked like the same crowd as before. She was absorbing the sun, lost in her thoughts, when Carol and Dash came over.

"You look like you need company," Carol said.

"Don't mind me, you two. I was enjoying the sun and the breeze."

They sat next to her, and then Mindy and Joe showed up with a small paper bag. Mindy whispered, "Have you ever dropped acid?" The girls shook their heads, and Mindy opened the bag. "Here, take a ride on a sugar cube." Everyone shrugged and each took one.

Not feeling any effects at first, Teri stared at the sky, seeing flowers blooming among the clouds. *Oh, this is beautiful!* Teri glanced down and saw colorful clouds moving along the ground—and then she saw Tim walking toward her. With a cry of joy, she reached out her hand to him and it passed right through his body. *Oh, god, he's dead!* Horror filled her as Tim turned into her father, glaring with hatred, saying, "You're a whore!" She screamed, and then all dissolved into weird shapes and colors. When she finally came to, everything was bathed in a strange half-light. *We must have been here all night.* She spotted Carol, who was shaking and her lips were blue.

Teri shook her. "Carol, wake up!" There was no response and she slapped Carol's face. "Carol, please wake up!" Still nothing, and Teri screamed, "Somebody, please call an ambulance!"

Mindy jumped up, staggering away to find a pay phone, while Teri and Dash tried to revive Carol. When the ambulance arrived on the grounds, the crew loaded Carol inside, and one of the crew asked Teri, "Did she take anything?"

Over the man's shoulder, she saw Dash making motions to say no. "I don't know." Teri stood. "Can I go with you?"

"Are you a relative?"

"Yes, I'm her sister."

"Get in."

Teri tossed her keys to Dash. "Here, take my car. I'll meet you at the hospital."

All the way, Teri prayed, "Please, god, don't let Carol die." At San Francisco General a few minutes later, one of the crew told Teri to wait inside the emergency room. Dash arrived five minutes later.

"Have you heard anything yet?" he asked.

"No. They just took her in."

A half hour went by before a grim-faced doctor came out to them. "Are you the one who came with the girl in the ambulance?"

"Yes. How is she?" Teri gripped the arms of her chair.

"You're not really her sister, are you? I have some questions. First, what is her last name?"

"Wehring."

"How can I get in touch with her family?"

"Her parents are Jim and Grace Wehring. They live in Encino, near Los Angeles."

"Thank you. We'll call them."

"Wait! You didn't tell us how she is." Teri squeezed Dash's hand. He sat silent, as if he already knew.

"I can't discuss particulars of her case with you since you're not a family member, but I will tell you she didn't make it." He walked away as Teri and Dash hugged each other, crying.

Pulling back a minute later, Dash grabbed her shoulders. "Teri, we better get out of here fast. When the doctor discovers it was LSD that killed her, they'll call the cops on us."

They ran out of the hospital to Teri's car, and Dash turned to her as she drove out. "This makes my decision to leave a little easier."

"Leave? Where are you going?"

"The government is cracking down on draft dodgers. I told Carol I was going to take the underground to Canada to avoid the Feds."

"Can I drop you off someplace?"

"There's a little building down the street from Fisherman's Wharf. It's one of the underground stations. Could you take me there?"

Teri nodded numbly. "Sure."

As they pulled up in front of his destination, Dash gazed at her intently. "Teri, are you going to be all right? You look white as a ghost."

Teri said tonelessly, "Yes, I'll be fine. Just go."

Dash kissed her cheek. "Goodbye, Teri."

Teri nodded and waved as he disappeared into the building, and then she drove up the bluff to an overlook by the bay. Teri turned off the engine and got out. No one was there, and she had a bench facing the cliff all to herself. Drawing her legs up, she wrapped her arms around her knees and rocked gently back and forth, her face buried, sobbing.

Now what? You've wound around this maze of your own making until you hit a dead end. Your father hates you, you've probably lost Tim forever, and now Carol's dead. What are you going to do? What can I do? Should I call my mother? I don't want her to see me like this. Evie? I got so close with Carol that I neglected my best friend. I'm too ashamed to call her.

Teri rose and went to the edge of the wall, watching the waves crash on the rocks below. She heard a voice behind her. "Hey, gal, you look like you need something."

Turning, she saw a strange-looking figure coming up. "I'm all right. Just leave me alone."

He was very thin, emphasized by his worn jeans and a black turtleneck. Black bushy hair made him look like a dark mushroom. "I'm Willie, the local dealer, and I've seen you in the park. We know all the users. Who are you?"

Maybe this is the way to make me forget. "I'm T...Iris Rainbow. What have you got and how much is it?"

Willie smiled. "Now you're talking my language."

Things became confusing for Teri after that. She took her car to a used car lot and got cash for it, then drifted to the seedier side of San Francisco, with Willie helping her numb her pain. All she really knew was that she went through a lot of money buying drugs and she experienced a strange parade of places she woke up in, not knowing where she was.

She came to in an alley, lying with her face on the rough bricks. Her sandaled feet felt wet, and she eased up to see a drunk passed out a few feet away, with the stream of urine from him reaching her. Jumping up, she vomited into a dumpster, then leaned her head against the cold metal. The smell of rotten garbage and human waste was overpowering. *I've got to get out of here.*

Staggering out of the alley, she made her way to an old gasoline station and locked the door on the dank and moldy ladies' restroom. Squinting at the stained mirror above the sink, she could hardly recognize the reflection. Her hair was dark and dirty, and she looked like a skeleton of her former self, with deep dark circles around her eyes. As she tried to clean up with the greasy soap she found on the sink, Teri thought back to a few months earlier, when she'd seen Cinderella looking back at her. *See what you've done to me, Tim Olson?*

She removed a slim wallet from her jeans pocket. *Damn, I'm out of money. Maybe Willie will give me a break.* Wiping the dirt off her brown pullover sweater, she started down the street toward Fisherman's Wharf. In one of the side streets, she saw Willie leaning against an old brownstone building. "Willie, I need a favor. I'm out of money, but I need an upper to find a job."

"Sorry, Iris, I'm not into charity work. That's not my bag. I need bread."

"You can't spare just one? I'll pay you back, I swear."

A young man with shoulder-length brown hair came from the opposite direction. "Hey, Willie, what's happening?" He gazed at Teri. "Who's this?"

"I'm Iris Rainbow. Do you have any money I can borrow? I'll pay you back as soon as I get a job." Teri was surprised to hear that come out of her mouth, but she knew the shakes would start if she didn't get something soon.

"Hello, Iris. I'm Skye, and I'm an artist. Have you ever worked as a model?"

"Yes," Teri lied.

"Good. You can come with me. Willie, give her what she wants, and give me my usual. I'll pay for it."

Willie counted out five uppers for Teri and gave Skye a bag of coke. Skye waved Teri forward. "Come with me."

Heading up the hill to the ancient Victorian row houses that had somehow survived the earthquake, he turned his gaze on her. "Hey, Iris, where you from?"

"No questions." Teri popped one of the uppers into her mouth. *I don't want to talk about myself. I want to forget.*

"Okay, I'm cool. Do you need a place to crash?"

Teri looked down. "I've been sleeping on the street."

"If you want to join our group, you can. We don't have much, but it beats the hell out of sleeping outside."

"Thanks, I will."

Arriving at a shabby row house, they went up the weathered front steps, where the paint was peeling off the old wood but the door glowed bright orange and red. Skye opened it and waved Teri in. "Welcome, Iris."

An old parlor spread out on her right, with fluorescent posters in black light on the walls and a doorway cluttered with strings of beads. A television droned in the background, and everywhere was a smell of incense.

Skye drew up next to her. "Everyone, this is Iris."

Waving his hand to a small, bright-eyed black girl, he said, "This is Star." He pointed to a long-haired, blond young man with thick glasses, seated at a desk, reading. "This is Egghead. On the couch is Raja." He indicated a dark, heavyset man with a beard. "And in the corner, in the lotus, is Moon." Teri saw a tall, thin girl with short, blunt-cut, blonde hair. Everyone acknowledged Teri, then went back to what they were doing.

Motioning for Teri to follow him, he said, "Might as well get started on my painting, since it's still early in the day. My studio's back here." Walking behind him, she came to a small enclosed porch off the kitchen. "Can I get you something to eat first?"

Teri seemed almost normal after the upper. "What do you have?"

"There's a couple of pieces of cold pizza in the fridge," he said on inspection.

Sitting at a small table covered by a stained red gingham tablecloth, she munched gratefully on the pizza.

"Would you like to take a shower before we get started?"

"That sounds good."

"Don't bother getting dressed again. I paint nudes."

Teri enjoyed the warm shower in the old-fashioned footed bathtub with the curtain all around it. *I swear I feel almost human.* Returning with the towel around her, she reached the enclosed porch. "How do you want me to pose?" she asked him as he got his paints ready.

"Over there." He pointed to an old Victorian parlor couch with worn purple velvet material and a few black throw pillows, all in front of a draped yellow sheet. She dropped the towel and he gave a whistle. "Great body!"

Arranging her into a reclining position on the couch, he warned, "Don't move."

Teri slipped into a reverie as she relaxed her body into the position. *Well, Teri, what now? Are you going to spend your life drifting from one place to another? You were going to be a teacher before you got sidetracked. You gave up everything for Tim. Was it worth it? I don't know. He said he loved me, but did he really mean it? What about my family? I was very close to them until I took up with Tim. Can I ever go home again? What about Evie? I used to tell her everything, but she wouldn't understand me now. Is that me or the drugs talking?*

On her break, she took a small portion of valium. *I don't want to think anymore.* Blessed calmness flowed through her the rest of the afternoon.

As the daylight started to wane, Teri found aches in her body from holding still. "How are you doing?" she ventured.

"Getting tired? We can do this tomorrow." He rose from the chair.

Pulling the towel around her, she went with Skye into the kitchen. At the table, with Tarot cards spread out before her, was a heavyset girl in a colorful red print muumuu. She brushed her long black hair out of her eyes as they came in. "Hello, Skye, who's that?"

"This is my new model, Iris. Iris, this is Gypsy, our fortuneteller."

"Greetings, Iris. Would you like your fortune told?"

Teri picked the Death card off the table. "This seems to be all that's ahead of me."

Skye and Gypsy glanced at each other, and Skye

shrugged.

In the evening, there was no dinner, just snacks of junk food, booze, and drugs. The group was unlike Redman's, where the ideal of brotherhood was embraced. Skye's friends were an odd assortment of eccentrics who got money from the artwork Skye sold and the fortunes Gypsy told in a small tent near Fisherman's Wharf. Egghead gave them a lecture every evening on the workings of the universe. Moon shed her clothes and did Yoga exercises in the nude. Star gave blow jobs to Raja, who was addicted to television, and to Egghead as he read. Gypsy always worked the Tarot cards in the late evening.

Teri was preparing to go to sleep when she found out Skye's peculiarity. She reclined on an air mattress in the back room with Star and Moon on others nearby. Teri discovered that the girls were lesbian lovers, and they tried to include Teri in their lovemaking, but she wasn't ready for that. Skye came into the room naked and lay beside her. "I have to take your sexual energy reading every night so I can paint your soul."

Almost catatonic, she spread for him. He used her, then left, with no more emotion than a casual hello. But at this point, Teri didn't care what happened to her.

This strange existence went on for days, weeks, months, Teri didn't even know or care how much time had passed. She posed for Skye during the day, then sat without speaking or seeing for the rest of the evening, even when Skye used her. She couldn't call it making love, because there was nothing there. All she cared about was numbing the pain.

One evening, a television program drilled into her brain as she took a drag on a joint. It was a report on

Virgin Ram reaching Europe on their grand tour, and Teri was startled to hear a screamed "No!" accompanied by shattering glass. Glancing around, she realized the scream had come out of her mouth while swinging the chair into the television. Skye and Raja quickly subdued her by forcing a downer into her throat.

When she came to from her drug stupor, Teri didn't know how long she had been out. A knock at the door had Skye opening it, to Willie, the drug supplier.

"Hey, Willie, can you get rid of her? She's gone psycho. I need another model."

"Yeah. I'm going to Griffith Park in LA to pick up some stuff. I'll dump her there."

"Good. Here's the bonus we agreed on." Skye took out a wad of cash and gave it to Willie.

"Skye, can you put her in my bus?" Teri felt herself being picked up like a sack of potatoes and carried out to the back of a VW Microbus, losing consciousness as she was unloaded in the back.

****

Coming back from a date that had lasted all night, Tim whistled softly as he rode the elevator to their suite in the hotel in Munich, West Germany, thinking about pretty Heidi Weiss. The band was on their bi-monthly week off.

Tim strolled into the hotel room, grinning, and John sat on the bed by the phone.

Looking at Tim with amusement, John smirked. "Well, your date with Heidi must have gone all right."

"Man, German girls know things American girls haven't dreamed of. What have you been doing?"

"I'm having the switchboard operator put in a call

to Carol's parents. I haven't been able to try a call in months, and I'd like to know what's going on."

"If you're interested, Luke, Roy, and I are going to the local beer garden tonight. Would you like to join us?"

"I just might."

"Good. I'm going to take a shower." Tim went into the bathroom and closed the door. He was glad they were booked at an American-style hotel. There wasn't a shower to be found anywhere else. After finishing, he came out carrying his dirty clothes and put on some clean ones. As he put the dirty ones in their laundry bag, he noticed John on the bed with the phone receiver and a stunned look.

"John, what's wrong?"

John glanced at Tim and drew a slow breath. "Carol's dead." As he hung up the phone, he struck his forehead with his fist. "If only I wasn't on this damn tour."

Tim's blood drained from his face. "What happened?"

John stared into space. "Carol's mother said it was several weeks ago. They got a call from a hospital in San Francisco. Carol took LSD and had an allergic reaction to the drug. It put her into cardiac arrest." Turning his attention to Tim. "A girl with Teri's description went with her to the hospital. Teri must have been the one to call the ambulance."

Tim gave an inward sigh of relief. At least Teri was all right. "I don't know what to say. I'm so sorry, man."

As the shock started to wear off, tears formed in John's eyes. "I loved her so much. I should have been there." Hitting his forehead again, he broke into sobs.

135

Tim sat on his bed across from John until John gained control. "John, is there anything I can do for you?"

John blew his nose in a handkerchief. "No. Go with the others to the beer garden and let me be alone tonight."

Tim clapped him on the shoulder. "The hell I will! Look, bud, I'm not leaving you alone tonight, no matter what you say."

"I'm going to be pretty lousy company."

"Not any worse than some others I've had."

Managing a weak smile, John rasped, "Thanks, Tim."

Tim called the others to let them know and settled in with his friend who needed him.

Chapter 10

Coming to on a concrete step, Teri tried to focus her eyes in the morning sun's glare. She sweated and shook so badly it felt like an earthquake. Squinting at the building as it reflected the sunlight, she felt the warmth. *That looks like the Griffith Park Observatory. But that's crazy. I'm in San Francisco, aren't I?* The sound of a car flowed into her brain and seemed to stop nearby. Teri eased up to see what was happening, and a wave of nausea hit. She gagged and retched, but nothing came up. As the wave passed, Teri realized the car was a police cruiser. An officer got out of the car and ran up to her, talking on his hand radio.

"Get an ambulance to the east steps of the observatory, and hurry!"

Attempting to rise, she felt a sharp pain through her gut, and then blood started running down her legs.

"Lie down, miss! I've got help coming!" He appeared a little younger than her father. "What's your name?" he asked taking out his notepad.

"Iris Rainbow."

"No, no. Your real name, please."

"Teri—Teri Darden."

"Where's your family?"

"They live…in Alhambra. My father's name is… Ted Darden." The blackness came over her again.

When Teri woke, she was shaking and sweating,

but now in a hospital bed. A nurse hurried out of the room and a stern-faced, gray-haired man came in.

"Miss Darden, you're going through drug withdrawal. What drug did you take?"

"I don't know."

"You had a miscarriage, as well."

Teri started to cry. "I didn't know I was pregnant."

The doctor shook his head. "Well, the good news is you don't have a venereal disease. You'll have to stay in the hospital a couple of weeks until the drugs are out of your system."

"Doctor, what month is this?"

"You don't know?"

Teri shook her head.

"It's August." He looked her in the eye. "1968."

My god, I've been gone for over a year. The doctor patted her shoulder.

"I want you to see a psychologist friend of mine. You're going to need some therapy and, by the way, there's someone here to see you." The doctor disappeared out the door. When it opened again, in walked her father.

"Daddy!" Teri cried out. "Oh, Daddy, I'm so sorry! I want to go home. Please, let me go home." She sobbed into her hands.

Her father sat on the edge of the bed, holding her like he used to when she was a little girl, rocking her gently. "I'll take you home, sweetheart. I'll take you home." That was the first time she'd ever seen her father cry.

A light tapping sounded at the door and her mother came in. Her father quickly got out his handkerchief and stood up while her mother went to Teri's side.

"Teri?" she said softly.

"Mom, I'm sorry I did so many stupid things. Help me through this."

"Teri, I love you very much. I prayed that you were still alive so I could tell you..." She broke down and wrapped her arms tight around her daughter.

The next couple of weeks in the hospital were the closest thing to hell that Teri ever experienced. She felt turned inside out, being sick when she was awake and having deliriums on and off. She begged for any drug to stop this and for some reason, in her madness, she saw David. His appearance gave her a warm glow.

The day after Teri was finally allowed to go home, she sat on the couch, wondering what to do with her life. As she finished the lunch her mother had brought her, she heard the doorbell and her mother answering it.

"Teri, it's for you."

"I don't want to see anyone."

"It's Evie. Come on, you can't shut yourself away forever. Please, talk to her."

"Okay, Mom. I'll see her."

Her mother went out as Evie came in. "Oh, Teri, I'm so sorry," Evie said as the two girls embraced. "I lost track of you after you left L.A."

"I lost track of myself, but I really don't want to talk about it. What have you been doing this past year?"

Evie held up her left hand and there sparkled a wedding ring.

"Evie, you're married! Congratulations! To Ken?"

Evie nodded. "I got married this spring. I wish you could have been there."

"I really messed up. I let everyone down, including myself. I feel so stupid." Teri held Evie's hands. "I should have been there for you instead of off on my own selfish pursuits."

"What's past is past. Why don't you start from here and let everything else go?"

"I wish I could. Living with Tim was a dream come true. When he left to go on tour, it felt like everything inside of me died."

"What did he say to you when he left?"

"He said he would look for me when he got back, and"—Teri's eyes filled with tears—"that he loved me."

"Have you heard from him since then?"

"No, and I don't know if it's my fault or his."

"If he did try, he probably couldn't find you. I know none of us could."

"I think I ruined everything." Then Teri started to cry, and the two friends hugged each other again before Evie pulled back.

"Teri, let me do some checking for you. I might be able to get some answers. I'll be back tomorrow."

"Before you go, have you heard anything about David? When I was having deliriums, I thought I saw him in the hospital room."

"That wasn't delirium. He was there with you several times. When Ken told him you were found, he ran over as soon as he could. He held your hand through some of your worst days."

Teri felt ashamed when she thought of David caring so much.

"Thank you for coming by, and thanks for everything." Teri hugged Evie again and watched her friend leave.

The next day, Teri kept drifting in and out of

wanting to know what Evie might have found and at the same time dreading it. About midafternoon, Evie came over with a fan magazine in her hand and, from the look on her face, Teri knew it wasn't good.

"Teri, I went to the fan club secretary this morning to see what she knew. She gave me this newspaper clipping and fan magazine to show you."

Teri scanned the entertainment gossip column dated a couple of months back, and part of it was circled. "Virgin Ram's Tim Olson has been seen around Geneva with an attractive blonde on his arm. It seems to be the same girl, Heidi Weiss, that he dated in West Germany when the band was there. I wonder what happened to the redhead he used to be seen with in Hollywood, the one known to the press only as Iris Rainbow." Teri started shaking. "Oh, Evie, what have I done?"

Putting her arm around Teri, Evie picked up another. "There's more." She handed her the magazine, where a page was marked. Teri saw a picture of Tim and Heidi with a headline of "Engaged?" over it. "I'm so sorry," Evie soothed as Teri began to cry. *Oh, god, I wish my mother hadn't banned booze from the house, because I need a drink now.*

After a few minutes, Teri took a tissue and blew her nose. "It's over, I know it is. He's found someone else, and there isn't anything I can do."

Evie pulled back. "I have to go now. Are you going to be all right?"

Teri nodded. "Yes, I guess I just had to face up to it. Thank you for everything." The two friends hugged, and then Evie left.

In a few minutes, her mother came in and sat

beside her. "I take it Evie didn't have good news to tell you."

Teri glanced at her mother. "Mom, I really loved him, and I thought he loved me, too. Why did this have to happen?"

"Teri, I'm not going to pretend that I have all the answers. Things seem to happen for a reason, and we have to find our own way in life. Take this as a lesson and move on." She kissed her on the forehead. "I love you, Teri. If you need me, just call."

"Thanks, Mom."

Her mother started to leave the room, then turned. "Oh, Teri. I invited Laura over to dinner tonight. She wants to see you. I hope you can forgive her. She's been very concerned about you."

Teri felt a flush of shame. "I hope she can forgive me."

When Laura arrived, she brought her fiancé with her, a man with beautiful brown eyes. She introduced him as Kyle Thompson. "Pleased to meet you." He shook Teri's hand.

And then the sisters flew into each other's arms. "Laura, I'm so sorry. You were right to tell Mom and Dad."

Laura cried. "Teri, I don't ever want to be split from you again."

At dinner, Laura turned to Teri. "Kyle and I are getting married in three months. Will you be my maid of honor? I was hoping you would turn up so I could ask you."

Teri gave them both a sad smile. "I missed my best friend Evie's wedding. I'm not going to miss my sister's. You bet I'll be there."

The doorbell rang as the family finished dinner. Her father went to answer it while Teri picked up dishes to take into the kitchen. Her father appeared at the dining room door. "Teri, it's for you."

"Who is it?" she asked as her father took the plates, going past her.

Shrugging, Teri went to the door. A man stood there in a neat suit and tie. A good-looking man with short sandy-colored hair and blue eyes. Tears blurred her vision. "Oh, David…" Her cheeks burned.

"Teri, I need to talk to you. May I come in?" David moved toward the screen door.

"No, I'll come out. Let's go sit in the back yard." Teri called into the kitchen, "I'll be out back."

Opening the gate to the yard, she and David went inside. Sitting on the wooden picnic table bench on the patio, both were awkwardly silent before Teri spoke.

"David, I'm really sorry for what I did to you at the graduation party. I hurt you, and it's been bothering me ever since."

David gazed at her steadily. "Teri, at that point, I figured it was over between us and I should move on. And believe me, I tried. When I started college the following fall, I dated like crazy, but I couldn't stop thinking about you. When you moved in with Tim, I hated you, but I realize now I was jealous of him." He studied his hands. "When I heard you were missing, I didn't know where to search for you."

Teri put her hand on his. "David, I'm so ashamed of what I did to you and everyone else. Please, please forgive me." Her voice cracked, tears ran down her face, and David put his arms around her.

"Yes, I forgive you. I love you." He rubbed her

shoulders. "Remember what you said to me one time? That no matter who you dated, you would always come back to me. Come back to me, Teri. Marry me."

Dumfounded, she said nothing. *I wasn't expecting a proposal right now. I don't think David knows me anymore.* She caught her breath. "But, David, I'm damaged goods. I had a miscarriage, and I don't know what the effect of all those drugs has been. Now I'm in therapy for who knows how long. You deserve better than me."

"I don't care about that. We can adopt kids if we have to. Look, I'm getting into computer programming, the next big thing on the horizon. I'll be getting in on the ground floor, and we could be living comfortably. Please, say you will."

Teri thought about Tim. She didn't know if he wanted her anymore. David was a comfortable love, like old shoes, but there still wasn't the passion that she had with Tim. *Start being practical. See what disasters happen when I follow my heart. But I wish I could talk to him one more time. I'll give Tim one more chance.* She grasped David's hand. "I want to think about this. So much has happened to me, I need some time to clear my mind. Please understand."

"You can have all the time you want." David put his arms around her and they sat that way for a few minutes, then went inside the house.

When Laura, Kyle, and David left, Teri sat with her parents. "Mom, Dad, David proposed to me this evening."

Glancing at each other, then back at Teri, her mother asked, "What did you tell him?"

"I want to think about it. I'm going to give Tim one

more chance."

"What? Why? Look what he did to you!" her father exclaimed.

"What happened to me was more my fault than Tim's, although he was taking drugs, as well. I need to know if he still wants me. I do love him."

"What about David?"

"I love him too. If I don't have Tim's love, I'll say yes to David."

"How are you going to find out? Do you know where he is?" her mother questioned.

"Linda Denton, who's engaged to Roy Gardner, has a schedule and the hotel numbers of where they are. I want to talk to her about letting me call Tim."

"No!" said her father. "I'm not letting you back into that crowd again!"

"Linda isn't like that, Dad. She and Roy weren't into drugs. Can I invite her over here?"

Her father backed down. "I guess you have to know. Okay, but promise you won't go back into using."

"Believe me, I don't want to go through that again." Although her brain was screaming for anything right now. *Is he still using drugs? Can I live with that? It's hard enough trying to silence that devil in my head without being around it again. Maybe I've changed.*

The next day, she made a call to Linda.

"Teri, you're back! We were so worried about you after hearing Carol died. Where have you been?"

"I took a wrong turn into drugs and nearly killed myself. I'm back at my parents' house in Alhambra. Could you do me a favor?"

"What do you need?"

"Could you come over to my house with the schedule so I can make a long distance call to Tim?"

"He didn't give you one of these?"

"No. I want to know if he still wants me."

"I'll be over tomorrow morning."

"Thanks, Linda." Teri gave her the address and directions.

When Linda arrived the following morning, the two girls embraced, just before Teri's mother walked into the room.

"Mom, this is Linda Denton."

Linda put her hand out. "Hello, Mrs. Darden."

"Aren't you with the group Just Folk? I've seen you on TV."

"Yes, I am."

Teri turned to her mother. "Can I use the phone for an overseas call?"

"Of course you can." She excused herself.

Teri led Linda into the dining room, setting the phone on the table. Linda checked the time and date against the schedule, and they found the group was in Glasgow, Scotland. Teri talked to the overseas operator, who said she would call when there was a connection.

"From what Roy told me, these numbers are for special operators in the hotels who screen calls for the VIPs. We can't get through the main switchboard. I'm surprised Tim didn't give you one of these."

"That's why I'm checking to see if he still wants me. I seem to have been cut off."

After a few minutes, the phone rang and the overseas operator connected Teri with the hotel screener.

"Yes, Miss Darden, may I help you?"

"Could you connect me to Tim Olson's room?"

"I'm sorry, he said he didn't want to be disturbed tonight. Is this a family emergency?"

Teri sighed. "No, it isn't. Thank you anyway."

Linda watched her. "What happened?"

"He didn't want to be disturbed tonight. I'll bet it's that German girl I saw with him in the press picture."

"You don't know that."

"Please, Linda, I know Tim. Thanks for your help. I guess I can let him go." Teri banged her fist on the table.

"I hate to see it end like this. You know, I really envied you and Carol."

"Why?"

"You seemed so close. Tim was a lot like Luke before you came along, but he settled down. John and Tim always hung out together, and Roy and Luke were more friends. Luke never had a girlfriend for long, so I never had the friendship that you and Carol did. That's why I loved the parties so much. I got to see you two." She checked her watch. "I'd better go. Keep in touch, Teri."

"I will."

They hugged, and Linda left, while Teri sat staring at the phone number written on the pad. *I think I'll try the call when it's morning over there.*

At eleven in the evening, Teri sat in the dining room with the phone after her parents went to bed. Turning the ringer down, she put in an overseas call to Glasgow. When the phone gave a ring, she picked it up quickly.

"Miss Darden, can I help you?" said the hotel operator.

"Can you put me through to Tim Olson's room?"

"Yes, I just gave him a wake-up call. One moment."

The phone rang, and Teri held her breath.

"Hello?" said a female voice.

"Is Tim Olson there?"

"Mmm, yes. Hey, lover, it's for you."

But Teri didn't wait to hear his voice. She put the receiver back on its cradle and proceeded to make confetti out of the phone number. Throwing the paper in the trash, she wanted to scream, and she slammed the back door harder than she meant to, and took one of the patio chairs and flung it into one of the trees. The light came on by the back door, and she saw the outline of her father as he came out. Teri sat on the picnic bench, bursting into frustrated tears while he sat beside her.

"Hey, sweetheart, what happened?"

"I tried to call Tim again and got through this time, but a woman answered the phone. I can't do this anymore. I can't trust him," she said between sobs. "I'm going to marry David."

Her father held her until she quieted down. "It's all for the best, Teri. Come on, let's go inside. We can deal with this tomorrow."

Teri was on the phone the next day. "Hello, Mrs. Kelsey. Could you tell David I'd like to see him tonight after dinner? This is Teri…Thanks." Coming into the kitchen where her mother was working, Teri sat on a chair. "Mom, I left a message for David to come over tonight after dinner."

"Laura is coming over, too. We are going over the items for her reception. Are you going to give him an answer?"

"I'm going to marry him."

"Your dad told me what happened last night. I'm glad you decided to let Tim go. He was bad for you."

"Mom, Tim wasn't all bad. When I was living with him, he was very thoughtful. I know he didn't cheat on me then."

"But he started you on all those drugs."

"The drugs were mostly my doing. Mindy introduced me to pot, and a record executive gave me a vial of coke. Tim drank a lot, but he didn't do many drugs. I got heavily involved when I was in San Francisco later. I wish I could have said goodbye to him. It seems that part of my life is incomplete."

Putting an arm around Teri, her mother nodded. "I know it's hard, but it's for the best that you move on." She hesitated for a moment. "I don't think you should keep in touch with Linda now."

"Why? I told you she isn't into drugs."

"That would put you in close proximity to Tim and might be too much of a temptation. I know how you feel about him. Now that you say you want to marry David, you have to think of him."

Teri slumped. "Of course, you're right. I'll talk to Linda one more time."

She called Linda, explaining the problem.

"Teri, your mother is right. I wanted you to come to our wedding, but Tim is going to be one of the groomsmen."

"Linda, I wish you and Roy all the best in the world."

"The same for you and David. I'm going to miss you."

"Bye, Linda." Hanging up the phone, she shut the

door to her old life.

That evening when David arrived, Teri stepped out on the front walk. "David, I'll take you up on your offer. I love you, too."

"Oh, Teri, I love you so much." He took her in his arms and they kissed. They stood holding each other for a few minutes, then went inside to break the news. There were hugs all around as Teri and David sat at the dining table with her mother, father, and sister.

Her father eyed them with his mouth in a tight line. "David, of course I'm happy that you want Teri to be your wife, but do you understand what she's been through?"

David glanced at Teri. "I know she's been through a lot. I don't know if I would fully understand what happened to her, but I'll support and take care of her."

He turned to his daughter. "Teri, do you really love David enough to marry him? Are you willing to completely forget Tim and devote your life to David?"

Teri was silent, then looked at her father. "Dad, I loved Tim, but when he left, we didn't stay faithful. I'm as much to blame as Tim is." She laid a hand on David's. "I've loved David since seventh grade, and he is standing by me, even after I treated him so rotten. I'll stand by him now for as long as he wants me."

David grasped her hand as she asked, "Does that answer your questions?"

Her father smiled. "Yes, it does. I give you my blessing."

"Now," Her mother said, looking up from the reception paperwork she was going over with Laura, "since that's out of the way, when would you like to set the date?"

Thinking for a minute, Teri ventured, "How about this coming New Year's Eve?"

"What? That isn't fair!" Laura piped up.

"Teri, Laura's wedding is in November. We wouldn't have time to plan another one so soon."

"Mom, I don't want a big wedding like Laura's. Most people know what happened to me, and I don't want them to be pointing and gossiping the whole time. I want a small wedding with just the two immediate families. I want to dump this past year. This is the way it should have been before I got so messed up."

"How can I plan even a small wedding when I'm right in the middle of planning Laura's?"

Teri thought fast, getting a dawn of an idea. "You don't have to. David and I can be married at one of those chapels in Las Vegas."

The other four regarded her with interest.

"Mom, Dad, we can invite the immediate families for a trip to Las Vegas. It would be like a vacation for all of us. Well, what do you say?"

Her father started to laugh. "It sounds like we've got our old Teri back. This scheme sounds like a good one. What do you think, May?"

"It sounds like fun. I love Vegas. David?"

"More than I expected." He clasped Teri's shoulder, gazing deep in her eyes. "I love you, Sweet Stuff."

"I love you too, Tiger."

With her family present, he moderated the kiss he gave her to seal the moment.

After David and Laura left, Teri's dad took her aside. "Teri, are you going to go to college like you originally planned?"

"Dad, I'm not ready to handle that kind of stress. My psychologist said I could easily backslide into drugs right now. I still crave drugs, especially when I'm under pressure. I'll see in a few months if I can handle it."

"I'll give you all the support you need."

"Thanks, Dad." Kissing his cheek, she headed off to bed.

A couple of weeks before Laura's wedding, Teri and David found a small apartment near USC, where David was a freshman. Teri got a job at one of the banks nearby; she could commute to work from Alhambra until she moved in with David after the first of the year, and David would live there until then.

One evening, David came back from classes and found Teri decorating the living room.

"It looks nice." He examined the still lifes she'd hung on the wall. "I'm glad you came over today. There's something I haven't done yet."

Teri grinned. "Oh, and what's that?"

David opened his desk drawer, took out a small box, and removed something from it. "Hold out your left hand and close your eyes."

She did as she was told, felt something slip on her ring finger, and saw a lovely engagement ring. It was gold with a small diamond in the center. "Oh, David, it's lovely."

He gazed deep in her eyes. "So are you." Kissing him passionately, Teri found herself wanting him to make love. "Teri, will you…?"

"Yes, David." He picked her up and carried her to the bedroom.

Undressing each other, Teri wondered why she had resisted David all those years. He was a tender and caring lover, but the fireworks weren't there that she'd experienced with Tim. It was still satisfying, though, and they spent the rest of the evening making love.

Laura's wedding was beautiful, but Teri was happy she didn't have to plan a ceremony and reception for hers. She was grateful that David came with her, and they sat with her parents after the dinner. Leaning toward David, she remarked, "This won't be over soon enough for me."

Tight-lipped, he nodded. "I've noticed how people are avoiding you. And ones like those across the room." He gave a slight motion toward several who were staring and whispering.

She sighed. "I'm glad we'll have a wedding with just the family. I may not have the ceremony I've always dreamed of, but I don't care." She squeezed his hand.

He kissed it. "With my sister's wedding next spring, I don't think my mom minds a trip to Vegas. I'm glad Ken and Evie want to stand up with us."

The more Teri thought about being married to David, the more she looked forward to it. Maybe she'd gotten past Tim.

The day before New Year's Eve, the two families assembled at the Sands Hotel, where they'd made reservations for two nights well in advance. Teri and Evie shared a room that night, with the honeymoon suite reserved for Teri and David the next night.

Teri stood in her bridal dress next to David, with their family all around them. The judge came to the part of the ceremony when he asked if anyone objected to these two people getting married. Suddenly, from the back of the room, Teri heard, "I object!" Turning, she saw Tim at the door of the chapel. Teri gasped and started running toward him, but Tim disappeared. "Tim, no!" she screamed.

"Teri! Teri, are you all right?" Evie shook her awake.

Teri was startled to find herself in the hotel room with Evie standing over her. "I—I'm all right. Just a bad dream. I guess I'm nervous about tomorrow."

Evie stared at her a little strangely. "Teri, you were calling out to Tim."

Teri sat up, twisting the corner of the sheet, and told Evie what she had dreamed.

"You're still not over him, are you?"

"It bothers me that we never said goodbye. I wish it could've ended so I would go on without all these doubts. Deep in my heart, I still love Tim, but I can't trust him. I know David is a better match."

Taking her hand, Evie said, "I know it's hard on you, but I think you made the right choice. I'm going back to bed."

The next day, Teri got ready in the dressing room at the chapel. Gazing into the full-length mirror at her white lace minidress with its empire waist, she remembered wearing beautiful dresses like this not so long ago, feeling like a princess. Teri shook her head. *Tim can't be a part of my thoughts anymore. I'm wearing this for David.* Nevertheless, a tinge of sadness pricked her for the love gone.

Evie came in carrying her veil and a handful of other things. "Sit down at the vanity and I'll fix your hair."

With Teri seated in front of the lighted mirror, Evie started brushing Teri's hair. "Evie, I remember when we used to do this when we were thirteen. What crazy styles we gave each other."

Evie nodded. "We've been through a lot, haven't we?" She pinned the short shoulder-length veil to Teri's hair, standing back to admire her work. Teri rose as her mother came in with Teri's small bouquet of flowers.

Her mother hugged Teri. "You look beautiful. I'm so proud of how far you've come. You look like you did before—"

Teri picked it up. "Before I got involved with drugs. I won't let it get me again."

"I do wish you would have picked out a more traditional dress."

"Mom, this is a very small wedding and we are going to the casinos tonight. It'll be fine."

"Come on, they're ready for you."

The small chapel held Teri's and David's families, and as Teri walked to her dad, who waited by the door, her mother went in to sit in front as the music played "Here Comes the Bride." Then Evie led the way as Teri's dad offered his arm to his daughter, tears misting his eyes.

Teri saw David. *Yes, I love him very much. I want to marry him. He's the only one who cares about me. What a wonderful way to start 1969!*

The wedding went off without any problems and everyone seemed to have a good time. At the objection part of the ceremony, Teri found herself holding her breath. She swore this was the last she would ever think of Tim.

****

In January of 1969, after the Virgin Ram concert in San Francisco, an alarm went off in the hotel room of

Tim Olson and John Simon.

John sleepily looked at the clock. It was ten in the morning. "Who the hell set the alarm? We don't have to leave until two this afternoon. We didn't get to bed until four."

Tim was already dressed. "I did. Go back to sleep, I've got an errand to run."

Mumbling something, John rolled over.

The day before, Tim had thought about being only a few days from home and Teri. He was tired of the many women he'd dated during the tour. He didn't remember many of their names or faces, and all he could think about, the last few weeks, was getting back to Teri. After he'd sung "Beloved" at the previous evening's concert, he knew he loved her. *I made her that promise to find her, and I will. How many fans are loved by their idol? I'm sure she's waiting for me.*

It was a windy rainy day in 'Frisco, so Tim thought it would be a perfect opportunity for him to sneak out. Tucking his long hair under a cap, he slipped on a long coat. The dark glasses should get him by the groupies downstairs. As he stepped out of the elevator, he hunched down and walked past the fans who crowded the lobby and made it safely outside. He crossed the street to a small jewelry store he'd noticed yesterday. A middle-aged lady with iron-gray hair and brown eyes that sparkled with good humor glanced at him from behind the counter.

"Good morning, sir. Can I help you with something?"

Taking off his dark glasses, Tim read her name tag. "Yes. Mrs. Kent, is it? What do you have in engagement and wedding rings?"

"I have quite a few of them in the case. If you see one you'd like to examine, let me know." She looked at him closely. "You know, you look familiar to me. Have you been in here before?"

Tim shook his head. He saw a beautiful set with a large stone on the engagement ring and a number of small stones around it. The two rings seemed to fit together as if they were one. "I'd like to see those."

Mrs. Kent opened the case and handed him the rings.

Tim examined the set closely. "I'll take this one."

She nodded. "This is a fine choice. What size is the young lady's finger?"

He felt the blood drain from his face. "Size? What sizes do they come in?"

Mrs. Kent laughed. "I can see you've never done this before. Can she come in with you?"

"No. I wanted this to be a surprise and, anyway, she lives in the Los Angeles area." He studied her hands. "They're about the same size as yours. What size do you wear?"

"I wear a seven, which is what this set is." She thought for a moment. "I tell you what. I'll let you have this one. If it doesn't fit her finger, you can have it made into the right size by just about any professional jeweler in the L.A. area."

"I'll take it." Pulling out his wallet, he gave her a credit card. "Put it on this."

While processing the card, she noticed the name. "Tim Olson? Aren't you in the group Virgin Ram?"

Tim acquiesced.

"I thought I recognized you. My daughter is one of your fans. She went to your concert last night. Could I get an autograph for her?" She gave Tim a piece of scratch paper.

He removed a pen from his shirt pocket. "What's your daughter's name?"

"Lisa."

He wrote: To Lisa, thank you for being a fan. Love, Tim Olson.

Mrs. Kent finished the sale and handed him the box as he gave her the autograph. "Thank you so much, Mr. Olson. And congratulations to you and your young lady."

Putting his dark glasses back on, he gave a bow. "And thank you, ma'am." He turned and hurried back.

Arriving at their charter plane at three that afternoon, anxious to get to Los Angeles for their final concert the next night, Tim agreed with Roy and Luke that they were eager to get home. John expressed reservations, though. He was afraid the full impact of Carol not being there would hit hard.

As they slid into their seats, John turned to Tim. "What the hell were you doing up so early this morning?"

"I told you. I had an errand to run." He pulled a small box out of his jacket pocket. "I bought a ring set at the jewelry store across from the hotel. I'm going to ask Teri to marry me."

Luke's jaw dropped. "Well, you old son-of-a-bitch, I was just going to rag you on the number of girls I had over you."

Tim put the box back. "Toward the end of the tour, I kept comparing other women with Teri, and I couldn't get her off my mind. She's the one I want."

An hour later, Tim was in the limo the record

company had hired to take the group members back to their homes. Since they were in their hometown, it didn't make sense to get a hotel room. Tipping the chauffeur after the suitcases had been brought up, Tim unlocked the door.

The apartment was clean, because he'd arranged for a maid service to come in once a month. Tim took a deep breath. It looked the same as when he left. The half-burned candles were still on the dining table and the Glenn Miller record was in its jacket on the stereo cabinet. He almost expected Teri to come out and greet him, but the apartment was silent. *I'll take care of that after the concert.*

Their final concert was completely sold out. Although Tim scanned the crowd before and after to see if Teri was there, he couldn't find her.

Mel waited backstage for them when they were finished taking their bows. "Congratulations, boys, on a job well done." He clapped them on their shoulders. "The record execs are very impressed with what you've accomplished. Now remember, we have a meeting with them in two days, at one sharp, to discuss the tour. Then you boys have a well-deserved three months off before starting the next album."

They all nodded.

John drove Tim back to his apartment—Tim had found the battery in his Corvette was dead.

"Tim, why don't I pick you up Tuesday, and we can go to lunch before the meeting," John said as he pulled to a stop in front of Tim's apartment building.

"Sure, give me a call before you leave."

Waking up the next morning around eleven, Tim decided today was the day he was going to find Teri.

Shuffling through the drawer he kept addresses and phone numbers in, he found the slip of paper she'd given him with her parents' number on it. If anyone knew where she was, they would, although he knew he wasn't popular with them.

Trying the number, a pleasant-sounding woman said, "Hello?"

"Hello. Is this Mrs. Darden?"

"Yes, it is. Who's this?"

"This is Tim Olson. I just got back from the concert tour and was wondering if you could tell me where Teri is."

Mrs. Darden was silent for a moment. "I'm sorry, Tim, it would be better if you didn't see Teri," she said coldly.

Tim's throat started to constrict. "Why?"

"It's really none of your business. I shouldn't be talking to you."

"Wait, Mrs. Darden, don't hang up! I was going to ask Teri to marry me." The anguish in his voice surprised even him.

"Teri is already married. The ceremony was New Year's Eve. She got involved with drugs while she was with you, and when you left, she got worse. We almost lost her. She spent time in the hospital withdrawing from them. You were unavailable when she really needed you, so she married someone who cared."

"Did she marry her boyfriend from high school? Was David his name?"

"Yes, she did."

Tears were starting to form, blurring his vision. "Give her my love and best wishes."

"Don't you dare interfere or try to contact her.

She's gone through enough already. If you love her, let her go."

"I will. Goodbye, Mrs. Darden." And he hung up.

Tim imagined he knew how John felt when he learned Carol was dead. Gazing around the apartment, all he could see reminded him of Teri. Wandering into the bedroom, he opened the closet door and touched the designer gowns he'd purchased for Teri to wear to the charity events. Tim ran his hand down one of the dresses, lifted it, and got a faint whiff of Teri's perfume. With a sob, he saw on the dresser a picture of them with John and Carol. He picked it up and stared at it. He tried to will himself into it and then, in a burst of anger, hurled the picture against the wall, shattering it.

Through the dark emotions surging through him, he heard the phone ring. Like a man in a fog, he answered it. "Hello?" he said with a rasp.

"Tim? This is your mother. I called to say welcome home. What's wrong?"

"Mom, I was going to ask Teri to marry me, but I just found out she's married someone else."

"Son, I have to say I'm not surprised, with the way you treated her."

"Why? I told her I loved her before I left, and I said I would find her when I got back."

His mother was silent for a moment. "Tim, you know your father and I thought she was way too young for you. But in a way, she was more mature. Telling a girl something means nothing if your actions show something else."

"What do you mean? I treated her very well."

"While you were here. I kept a scrapbook of the news releases from your tour, and there are many pictures here of you with a lot of different women. I'm sure Teri saw them, too."

"But they meant nothing to me."

"Did Teri know that? How many times did you contact her? How many letters did you write?"

"Oh, god—" He closed his eyes. *I tried to keep the truth of all those women from her. I should've kept in touch. I thought Teri was firmly in the palm of my hand. Stupid, stupid, stupid!*

"Tim, I love you dearly, but you brought this on yourself. Do you want to come home for a while?"

"No, but thanks, Mom."

"Try to make it over here soon, and we'll talk."

"See you. Bye, Mom." Numbly, he hung up and wandered to the bar to check what was left. Lining up the bottles, he took the first one and poured himself a drink.

****

Somewhere, Tim heard a phone ring, then raised his head from the overstuffed chair. That was a big mistake. His stomach lurching, he rolled for the plastic trash can in the corner and vomited the booze he'd consumed last night, falling to sleep again. Sometime later, he heard the doorbell and knocking. Swearing, he crawled to the door with the trash can in tow.

"Who's there?" Tim managed to spit out.

"It's John. Where have you been, man? I've been trying to call you."

Tim braced against the wall, opening the door.

John made a face. "Oh, shit, what happened to you? You reek!"

Tim's back was against the wall and he slid down the painted surface. "Teri married someone else."

162

John glared at him. "So you went and crawled in a bottle."

Tim hiccoughed. "My mother thinks I'm immature."

John put his fists on his hips. "I wonder whatever gave her that idea?"

Grabbing the trash can, Tim vomited again. "Never drink year-old booze, man. It's pure poison."

"Damn it, Tim, we have a meeting with the record company in three hours. I have to get you sobered up." John took him by his shirt collar and pulled him to his feet. Then he half-dragged Tim into the bathroom, turned on the shower full blast, and shoved him into it, clothes and all. "Man, you owe me big time for this one."

Chapter 11

Married life turned out to be agreeable to Teri. The bank she worked for was only a couple of blocks away, so she always walked to work and let David have the car.

While she was busy at her job one morning, her mother called, asking if she would like to have lunch.

"Sure, Mom, that would be great. There's a coffee shop two doors from the bank. I'll meet you there at noon."

"Wonderful, Teri. See you then."

When she got to the small eatery, it didn't take Teri long to spot her mother sitting at one of the booths, and as she slid in on the seat her mother said, "I took the liberty of ordering chef's salads for both of us."

"Good, that will give us more time to talk."

Biting her lip, her mother glanced at Teri. "I've got something to tell you, but your father didn't think I should."

Teri was concerned. "What is it, Mom?"

She held her daughter's hand. "Teri, Tim called yesterday, looking for you."

Teri squeezed her mother's fingers, but couldn't speak. Her brain was about to explode. *He did keep his promise and try to find me. Was I wrong about how he felt about me? And what about that German girl?* Her practical side took over and she realized she couldn't go back on the promise she'd made to David. It wouldn't be fair to him.

"I told him you were married. He said to give you his love and best wishes. He just got back from the concert tour."

Teri sat for a long minute. "That's right, it's been a year since he left. It seems like a lifetime ago."

"How do you feel about that?"

Teri sighed. "I meant what I said before I married David. This doesn't change anything."

Her mother seemed relieved. "I was hoping you'd say that." Sitting back as their salads came, she gazed pointedly at Teri. "I do understand how you feel. Your father wasn't my first choice."

Teri was shocked. "Mom, what do you mean?"

"When World War Two started, I was engaged to another man. Ted, your father, was his best friend, and both of them enlisted in the Army Air Corps, since they were trained pilots. They ended up at a base in England, flying bombing runs." Tears appeared in her eyes. "Mike, my fiancé, was killed on one of those missions. Ted started writing letters to me every week, and the letters were so comforting I found myself falling in love with him. So we got married when the war was over." She stroked Teri's cheek. "You have it tougher than I did, though."

"Why?"

"Because the love of my life was dead and I never had to think of him or hear about him again. Tim is alive and famous, and you will hear about him for years to come. I don't envy you. And don't tell me you don't love him anymore. I know you do. You have to be strong."

Teri smiled. "I never could lie to you. Thank you for being so understanding."

Finishing their lunch, her mother picked up the check. "Don't worry, it's on me."

"Thanks, Mom, for everything. I have to get back to work." After a quick hug outside the coffee shop, they went their separate ways.

****

Teri and David often visited with Evie and Ken, who had moved into a small house in Burbank. Ken was a physical education teacher and coach at a high school nearby. Evie was expecting their first baby in November. Teri called her in October of 1970 with some news.

"Evie, guess what! I just got a call from the doctor and I'm pregnant! The drugs didn't mess up my system after all."

"Teri, part of me wants to say congratulations. The other part says, just wait a few months, and you'll see how great it is—swollen ankles, backache, and all." Evie laughed. "What did David say?"

"I haven't told him yet. I called my mom, then you."

"Oh, that's going to make him feel special. When's the baby due?"

"The doctor calculated around May twenty-fourth."

"Isn't that about the time of David's graduation from college?"

"Evie, what are the chances it will happen on the same day as the ceremony?"

Evie chuckled. "With your luck, most likely. Teri, I can always count on you to make life interesting."

David, of course, was delighted as well as terrified

at the prospect of becoming a father and being responsible for supporting a family. Teri assured him that with the grades he was getting he should be able to get a good paying job after graduation.

In November, Evie gave birth to Kevin Barnes, a robust eight-pounder. David and Teri became godparents at his christening over Thanksgiving weekend. After seeing Kevin, Teri was even more eager to hold her own baby.

*****

Teri had her arms around Tim, smiling that dazzling smile of hers. He said, "Teri, I love you," and she melted away from his arms.

Opening his eyes, he gazed around his old room, the one he used to share with his brother Michael. It was one of his days off from the studio, and he almost wished he could go back to his high school self, when everything was fun and the future was bright. Tim had moved back home temporarily until he could find a house. After a year of deep depression, he'd left his apartment because too much there reminded him of Teri, so his mother had offered the use of his room. If only Teri would get out of his dreams. Tim checked the clock. Its hands said it was ten-thirty. Groaning, he got up. *I've got to stop drinking so much.* Shuffling downstairs to the kitchen, he was surprised to find his father at the table, reading the paper.

"Dad, I thought you'd be at work today."

He raised an eyebrow. "It's Sunday, Tim. The service station is closed."

"Oh, right." Tim sat at the table. His mother was putting away dishes.

"Can I get you something for breakfast?" she

asked.

"Just coffee, please." She poured him a cup and set it in front of him. Staring at the dark steaming liquid, he was lost in thought.

His father put down the newspaper and looked at Tim. "You know, son, you moved out of your apartment last winter, and now it's April. When are you going to find a house?"

"I haven't had a lot of time, working at the studio."

"I've noticed that on your time off you just mope around the house. You know, after my three children left home, I didn't think it would be my eldest multi-millionaire child who would move back in."

"Sorry, Dad, just going through a hard time."

His father looked stern. "Tim, I know Teri married someone else, but after eight months, it's time to pull yourself together and get on with life. In other words, find a house and get the hell out of here." He picked up the papers and went into the living room.

His mother came over, putting her hand on his shoulder. "You know, your father is right."

"I know, Mom. I'll start looking for a house this week."

The wall phone rang and she answered. "Hello?…Yes, I remember you. What can I do for you?…Tim's right here. Would you like to talk to him?" She handed him the receiver. "It's Dana Stanley." She walked out of the kitchen.

"Dana?" *Why is she calling me? I haven't seen or heard from her since the big fight. I don't know what she would want me for, after Steve asked her to marry him. She's an exciting woman, but hard to get along with.*

"Tim, I won't keep you long. I'm working on the ten-year reunion for our high school, and I was wondering if Virgin Ram could play at the hall we rented. It will be for May of next year."

"Dana, before I answer, I'm sorry I acted like such an asshole last time I saw you. I suppose you're married to Steve now."

She was silent for a moment. "No, I'm not."

"Can I take you out to dinner tomorrow night? I'll ask the execs at the record company if it will be all right to play at the reunion."

"Sure. Where are we going? Should I dress up?"

"Just put on a nice dress. I know a little place, but it isn't real fancy. What's your address?" She gave it to him. "Okay, I'll be there around six."

The next day at Dana's apartment, he rang for her.

"Yes?" she said through the intercom.

"Dana, it's Tim. Are you ready?"

"I'll be right down." A couple of minutes later she appeared, wearing a dusty-rose dress that set off her dark brown hair and eyes.

Tim gazed at her. "Dana, you look beautiful."

"Where are we going?" she asked as they settled into the rich leather seats of his Corvette.

Tim grinned. "It's a surprise."

A few minutes later, he pulled into the parking lot of a little Italian restaurant called Antonio's.

Dana gasped. "Tim! This is where we had our first date!"

Tim hurried around the car and opened her door. Offering his arm, he said, "Shall we?" She took it and strolled in with him, and once inside they sat at a booth as they had so long ago.

After ordering, Tim turned to her. "The reunion committee is starting early. If it's in May, that's over a year."

"They wanted to get everything set up. What did you find out from the record company?"

"They won't let us play for free, unless it's a licensed charity. It'll cost ten grand to have us."

Dana's eyes widened. "Ten grand? We don't have that kind of money in our budget."

"I didn't think so. I told the other guys about it, and we decided to pay for it out of our own pockets. Consider it our donation to the reunion."

Dana's smile lit up the room. "This is going to be the best reunion ever!"

The waiter brought their order to the table, and as they began to eat, Tim said, "It's a good thing you asked me now, because in a couple of weeks we're going out on an eleven-month tour of Europe, Canada, and the United States to promote our new album. We'll be back in time for the reunion, so don't worry." They were silent for a few minutes while Tim weighed a question. "Dana, can I ask you something personal?"

"Okay."

"What happened with you and Steve Marshall?"

Dana picked at her food. "Nothing. I lied. He never asked me to marry him."

"Then why did you tell me he asked you?"

"I was wondering if you still cared for me. It was a test, and when you didn't answer, I got very angry at you."

"I'm sorry, Dana. I fell for another girl, but she married someone else while I was on tour."

Dana smiled strangely and raised her glass of wine.

"Well, here's to a pair of misfits."

Tim clinked glasses. "And long may they wave."

After dinner, Tim drove Dana back to her place. She turned to Tim before she got out. "Would you care to come up to my apartment for a nightcap?"

"All right." Tim walked her up. Her apartment was simple but tasteful.

She watched his reaction. "I do receive a fairly good salary working as a secretary at a law firm. In case you're interested." Her eyes flashed invitingly.

He sat on the couch watching her as she brought over a couple of glasses of wine, and he felt a growing desire. "Dana, I was a fool. You really are beautiful."

She looked at him steadily. "I never stopped loving you, Tim. I still want you."

He gently took hold of both their glasses and set them down on the coffee table. She responded by unbuttoning his shirt and sliding her hands inside it to rub his chest. He moaned at the tightening in his crotch as he gave her a lingering kiss. They undressed each other slowly and, for the first time since he'd found out about Teri, he made love to a woman. For several hours, they enjoyed each other's bodies. Getting dressed, Tim gave her a hug. "I'll see you again."

Her lips quirking in a small smile, she responded, "Just call me."

Within the weeks before Virgin Ram left on tour, Tim managed to find a nice house in the Hollywood Hills and moved out of his parents' home. He brought Dana over to see it. The house was a large rambling ranch on a hillside, with several acres of woodland overlooking the Los Angeles basin. A cream stone wall surrounded it, with iron security gates at the entrance to the driveway. The drive traveled several hundred feet and ended in a circle in front of the house. In the middle of the circle was a fountain splashing in a cream stone pool. The stone steps from the drive led to a large handsome hacienda-style house.

Climbing the steps, he glanced at her. "What do you think of it?"

"Very nice. Will you stay in touch with me while you're on tour?"

"You know I will. I'll give you a list of hotels where we'll be staying." He kissed her, and then they went inside.

****

The tour in Europe had been long and hard. The entourage had settled in a hotel in Rome for a couple of days' rest when the phone rang early in the morning. Tim groped to answer it and looked at the clock. It was seven-thirty.

"Hello?" he said sleepily.

"Tim, it's Dana."

"Dana! It's seven-thirty in the morning here. Why the hell are you calling?"

"You bastard. You got me pregnant."

"What?"

"You heard me. Now what am I supposed to do?"

"Dana, wait a minute. Why didn't you tell me you weren't practicing birth control? I carry rubbers with me. Do you have insurance?"

"Well, I won't anymore when the firm I work for finds out I'm unwed and pregnant. You have to get back here and marry me."

"I can't drop everything and run back to L.A. I'm in Rome and under contract. I won't be able to get back there until the end of April."

"Then what the hell am I supposed to do? The baby's due in March and I'm going to lose my job."

"You should have been taking precautions if you didn't want to get pregnant. Or is this another lie?"

She screamed at him and slammed down the phone. He looked at the receiver for a moment and hung up, shaking his head. Tim glanced over to the other bed, where John had his head resting on his hand, watching him.

Tim pointed to the phone. "Did you hear that?"

John half-smiled. "Maybe you should ask the neighbors the same question."

Tim felt a bit sheepish. "A little loud, huh?"

"Yeah. What are you going to do?"

"There's not much I can do right at the moment. She wants me to come back immediately and marry her."

"That won't go over well with management. What did she say about insurance?"

"She has it through her job, but she'll be fired for being unwed and pregnant."

John sat up and was quiet, while Tim felt like he was on a ledge looking into an abyss below.

Regarding Tim, John ventured, "You know, you can try Luke's solution for the problem. He sends his mistakes down Tijuana way, all expenses paid. She keeps her job and you're off the hook."

"You mean abortion? I'm a little uneasy about that. That's why I've always been very careful with sex. This is the first time it's resulted in a baby. Hell, Teri lived with me all that time and she never got pregnant. Before her, Dana was always on birth control." Tim mused on the information. "I don't really love Dana. Maybe I'll call her and offer that idea."

John got out of bed. "Good. I'm awake now, so I'll go take a shower while you call." He disappeared into the bathroom.

Tim had the operator put in an overseas call to Dana. "Dana?"

"Yes?"

"I'm sorry for blowing up at you before. Will you listen to what I have to say?"

She was silent for a minute. "Okay, Tim, I'll listen."

"I have an idea that will solve the problem for you. I say this because I do care about you. I'll fix you up with a doctor in Tijuana and pay your expenses down there and back. What do you say?"

"Tim, that's so typical of you," she said with an edge to her voice. "You can't face up to a 'problem,' so you try to get rid of it. Well, I'll tell you this, my love. I'm going to have this baby, and you are either going to marry me or I'm going to slap the biggest paternity suit on you that I can. Is that clear enough for you?" She hung up.

Tim sat on the edge of the bed with his elbows on his thighs, hitting his forehead with his fists. *I feel trapped. Damn, Teri, why didn't you wait for me? Why didn't I keep in touch with her while I was on tour? I wouldn't be in this mess. Why was I so stupid?* He heard the door to the bathroom open.

"Gee, looks like that went well."

Tim gritted his teeth. "She not only rejected my offer, but she said if I don't marry her, she's going to hit me with a paternity suit. I swear I'm never going to have sex again."

"If you marry Dana, you probably won't."

"Not funny, John."

"Does it look like I'm laughing? Dana will cut off your balls and nail them in her trophy case. She's got you where she wants you."

"I don't see any way out of this. Maybe she'll be different after we're married. After all, that was what the break-up fight was about. If we get married, she'll be happy. I might even start loving her."

"What are you going to do when she's fired from her job?"

Tim thought for a minute. "I'm going to have her stay at my house and wire her money every couple of weeks. My parents have the keys, so I'll have them set her up."

"Your parents are going to love this."

"I know I'm going to hear about it, but what else can I do?"

While John went down to breakfast, Tim put in a call to his parents. He sighed with relief when his mother answered the phone.

"Mom, I need to talk to you. I've got a problem."

"What is it?"

He took a deep breath before he continued. "Dana called here and told me she's pregnant."

"Tim, I suppose you're going to tell me it's yours. Well, what are you going to do about it?"

"Mom, please. I'm going to ask her to marry me. I need for you and Dad to set her up in my house, because she'll be fired from her job for being unwed and pregnant. I'm going to wire her money every couple of weeks. Will you do this for me?"

"I was afraid this was going to happen, with you being so loose around women. I don't know why you continue—"

"Mother, I'm already beating myself up for this. I'm sorry. I was wrong. I'm trying to do the honorable thing. Will you help me?"

She backed down. "All right. It looks like you're trying to fix it. We'll help you. When are you going to get married?"

"That's one of the problems. I can't get off the tour until April, and the baby's due in March. I think it would be best for all if we just have a quiet ceremony at the courthouse with the immediate families."

"Did you discuss this with Dana?"

"Not yet, but I'll put it to her. Can you help her with the plans?"

"Yes, but I'll need her phone number."

He gave it to her. "Just wait a couple of hours until I can talk to her. Thank you, Mom. I love you."

"Love you too, Tim."

Tim then put in a call to Dana and made her understand he would marry her as soon as he got back from the tour. She told him she would fix up the house for them.

When he got off the phone, he was about to take a shower when the phone rang again. "Hello?" he said as he sat on the bed.

"Tim, what the hell is the matter with you?"

"Dad?"

"Where did you leave your brain this time?"

"Dad, I—"

"Listen to me. I let you do your music when I thought you should be in college. I hoped all we taught you at home would stick. Then you got caught up in that fast lifestyle with the Hollywood crowd, but I still held back. The only time I said anything was when Teri moved in with you. Now, with all the women you're laying, and getting Dana pregnant, you've gone off the deep end."

"Dad, I'm not laying women this time on tour. I've learned my lesson. I asked Dana to marry me, and I'm going to stay faithful to her. I asked Mom to help me get things set up."

"How can I believe you? You've done things I never dreamed I should warn you about. For one thing, you've got to get that drinking under control."

"I can handle the drinking. I'm not out of control and I don't plan to be. Now, will you help me?"

He heard his dad sigh. "Yes, I'll help you. Just grow up, will you? I've got to hang up. I'm paying for this call."

"Yes, Dad. Thanks."

Tim went in to take a shower. As he watched the water go down the drain, he wished the drain monster he'd feared as a child would come and take him.

****

In mid-March, Tim was in St. Louis when he got a call from his mother telling him his son was born. She was in the hospital next to Dana's bed and handed the phone to her.

"Tim, I named him Charles Timothy Olson on the birth certificate. They'll file it after we're married."

Tim grinned in spite of himself. "Give the little guy a kiss for me, and I'll see you in a few weeks."

When Tim got back from the tour, he made a beeline to meet his son. "He's beautiful, Dana," he said

177

as he kissed her and picked up the baby. "We'll get married as soon as we can at the courthouse."

That evening, he took out the ring set he'd purchased in San Francisco. *No, that's Teri's ring.* He put the box away in the back of his chest of drawers and went out to buy another set.

Chapter 12

Early spring found David and Teri fixing up a small area of their bedroom for the baby. David was going with her to birthing classes and found out he could be in the delivery room, coaching Teri with breathing exercises. So everything was ready.

The day of David's graduation arrived and the baby hadn't been born. It was two days past the due date, but Teri's doctor assured her babies have their own timing. But that morning she groaned as she got up. "My back is really killing me!"

David looked concerned. "Do you think we ought to go? I can skip the ceremony. I'll still get my diploma."

"No! You worked hard for this. The ceremony is a memory you'll always treasure. You can't miss it. I'll be all right."

The graduation ceremony started at two o'clock, and Teri sat in the auditorium between her mother and her mother-in-law. Suddenly, she felt her stomach cramp.

"Mom!" she said, gripping her mother's arm. "I just felt a pain in my stomach."

Her mother took a breath and looked at her watch. "Teri, tell me if you get that pain again."

Teri nodded and sat back. A little while later, she felt the cramp again. "Mom, I felt it again."

Her mother looked at her watch. "That was twelve minutes. Teri, do you have the doctor's and hospital's numbers?"

She looked in her purse, pulled out a card, and gave it to her mother.

"Teri, I'm going to go to the lobby and call the doctor, okay?"

"All right."

Her mother came back a few minutes later and put her hand on her husband's shoulder. "Ted, we have to get Teri to the hospital now."

David's mother looked over. "Should I go get David?"

"The doctor thinks she has a few hours yet, but he wants her at the hospital."

Teri turned to David's mother. "Let David go through the ceremony, then bring him to the hospital. Oh, and could you stop at the apartment and pick up my bag?"

David's mom nodded. "We'll all be there later."

Teri's father brought the car to the front of the building, and Teri and her mother slid into the back seat. They were met at the emergency area of the hospital by an orderly with a wheelchair, who took Teri to a labor room. Her mother stayed with her while her father went down to admissions.

When the doctor came and examined Teri, he said, "It looks like you still have a couple of hours to go yet, but it's good you came in." He called Teri's mother in and informed her.

She smiled. "That will give David enough time to come from the graduation ceremony."

"Like I told Teri, babies seem to have their own

time." He turned back to Teri. "I'll see you later."

Teri sighed after the doctor left. "I wish I had my bag with me."

"I'm sure David's mother will remember to stop at the apartment for it. Do you want me to stay until David gets here?"

"Please do."

A nurse came in to take her blood pressure. "Mrs. Kelsey, would you like to watch television for a while? You can turn it on with this remote."

After the nurse left the room, Teri turned on the television, stopping on a news program. "In today's entertainment news, Virgin Ram's Tim Olson has returned from his honeymoon with the mother of his infant son." She dropped the remote to the floor and her mother quickly retrieved it and turned to another channel.

"Teri?" her mother said hesitantly. "You went white, and now you're trembling."

"Mother, why does that bother me so much? I'm here having David's baby and I'm jealous of the woman Tim's married to."

She took her daughter's hand. "Do you remember our conversation at lunch about a year and a half ago? That's what I meant. You have to be strong. You'll hear about him because he's famous, but you'll have to continue with your own life. He's not a part of it anymore."

"Thank you, Mom, for reminding me. I love David and our child. That's all that matters now."

Teri and her mother watched television together until David hurried into the room with her bag. "Am I too late?"

Teri got up and went to him. "No, not yet." She took her bag and gave him a kiss. As she was going back to the bed, she felt a gush of warm water over her legs. "Mom?"

Her mother was already headed for the door. "Your water broke, honey. I'm going to get the nurse."

David was helping her onto the bed when a strong contraction hit. He took her hand. "Pant through it, remember?" Teri felt like the old retriever her family had when she was a child, panting heavily.

The nurse came in, followed by the doctor. "Her mother said her water broke."

As they examined her, another contraction hit, but David had gone out for a moment. Teri made a gurgling noise like she was drowning. "Teri, don't push yet."

She grasped the doctor's arm, her fingers making deep impressions. "I want the baby out now!"

He winced. "Take it easy. Just continue breathing and let me get some feeling back in my hand."

David came back in the room. "How is she?" He was pale and shaken.

"I'm going to get the anesthetist. Keep her panting."

"Come on, Sweet Stuff, you can do this." David took her hand.

A strong pain hit as she yelled, "Shut up, damn it. I don't need a fucking Mr. Sunshine!" David grimly held on as his fingers turned purple.

The anesthetist came in with an IV. "Hello, Mrs. Kelsey. I'm Dr. Stone, and I'm going to give you some of this solution, just in case we have to do a Cesarean. It will keep your vein open if we have to give you a transfusion."

"What?"

"Don't worry. It's only a precaution."

Teri endured as the doctor got ready to stick the needle in her hand. He jabbed, and she felt a sting that was as bad as the contractions. She yelped.

Dr. Stone said, "Your vein collapsed, I'm going to have to try again. Calm yourself down."

Teri gritted her teeth, wanting to grab the doctor's balls and pull them up over his head. He jabbed her again and this time was able to tape the needle to her hand.

"There, that's a good girl."

"Get out!" Teri shouted. "Get out of here!" Dr. Stone left.

David rubbed his hand to get the blood flowing again. "Teri, you're pushing up the blood into the tube. Take a deep breath."

"Shut up, David. Don't patronize me."

Dr. Martin, her doctor, came back into the room. "Hey, don't scream at the help. Let's see if you're ready to go yet." He called the nurse after he examined her. "She's ready to go to delivery. Get the gurney."

They took Teri to the delivery room, and David was detoured to put on hospital coveralls. The nurse got Teri's legs up into the stirrups and strapped her arms down.

"Why are you doing this?"

The nurse gave her a syrupy smile. "We don't want you to injure yourself, dear."

I want to injure you most of all. Soon everyone gathered and she calmed. Her contractions weren't hurting as much.

David pointed to the mirror that was angled so she

could watch. "Look, you can see the baby's head."

Teri was entranced. *There's our child. Hello, little one.*

"Next contraction, push." Dr. Martin broke into her thoughts. It wasn't long before she delivered a beautiful baby girl.

David was in tears. He was given the baby wrapped in a hospital blanket, and he laid her in Teri's arms after the nurse undid the straps. "You still like the name Katie Marie?"

Teri nodded. "That's a wonderful name. Wasn't that your grandmother's name?" At his nod, she kissed both of them. "Hello, little Katie, welcome to the world."

****

That summer, David went to several interviews with companies who were looking for computer specialists. He came bursting into the apartment on a day in August and grabbed Teri, swinging her around.

"Teri, I got a job as a branch assistant manager for a computer corporation. I'll be starting at thirty-two thousand a year!"

Teri's jaw dropped. "Wow! That's wonderful! When do you start?"

"They've given me two weeks to move."

"Move?" Teri's face fell. "Where?"

"Tucson. They're opening a new branch in Arizona. We won't be that far away."

"I guess I was just hoping you'd find something around here." She sighed. "But you can't pass this up, and we'll survive."

While Teri's mother took care of Katie, the young couple traveled to Tucson to buy a house. They found a nice one in a new subdivision outside the city. With the company financing the move, all they had to worry about was the mortgage.

Teri stood on the grass in front of the house, gazing at what would be their home. "It's beautiful here, with the mountains in the background. We can do this."

David put his arm around her. "This is all I dreamed of—you, a family, a good job, and a house. I couldn't be happier."

Right now, Teri was happy, too.

At the going-away party at the Dardens' home, there were tears, hugs, and promises to visit as much as they could, but Teri knew it would never be the same. She was leaving behind the life she had known for twenty-two years.

Evie, Teri, and her mother went into Teri's old bedroom to see what was to be kept and what was to be thrown out. Teri looked sadly at the folder full of Virgin Ram things she'd saved.

"I think all of these things should be thrown out." She sighed.

Her mother shook her head. "I know you want to put everything behind you now, but there may come a time when you would regret not saving any of these things. I'll save them for you."

Teri bit her lip. "If you say so, Mom." She handed the folder to her mother.

Things went well for the young family in Tucson. Next door was a family with a four-year-old child. An hour after they moved in, there was a knock at the door. A woman about Teri's age stood there with a tin of cookies. "Hi, I'm Bobbie Dahlman from next door. Welcome to the neighborhood."

Soon Teri and David were spending a lot of weekends with Don and Bobbie Dahlman. Bobbie became Teri's friend and confidante. David was happy with his job, but it kept him away from home for one or two weeks at a time. A couple of years after they'd moved there, Teri gave birth to Dave Junior, in November of 1973.

****

Tim worked in the control booth at the record company, producing a record for a group, Total Wave, that Virgin Ram had taken under its wing. He found he enjoyed producing music as much as making it. Virgin Ram had started to decline in record sales, and Tim had been upset at first, but touring was a grind. He preferred work in the studio, and being able to concentrate on composing and producing.

About midday, John wandered into the control booth and sat beside Tim as Total Wave finished the take. Tim opened the mike. "That was excellent, guys. Why don't you take an hour for lunch, and then we'll start on the next song."

The group gave a thumbs up to Tim as they set down their instruments. Tim turned to John and slapped him on the shoulder. "Hey, how are you, buddy? I haven't seen you for a couple of weeks."

John grinned. "I've got a favor to ask you."

"Name it."

"I want you to be best man at my wedding next June."

"Congratulations! Sure I will."

John had been dating Sandy Hunt, Mel's pretty secretary, for a year. Tim sobered. "I know it will go better than my marriage."

"Things haven't changed between you and Dana?"

"No. In fact, they've gotten worse. We can't be in the same room without fighting. Charlie is three now, and I hate to think what it's doing to him. John, I've given this marriage over two years, and it's been hell. The times I was away from Dana, on tour, have been the best. I don't know if I can keep up this farce."

John shook his head. "I'm sorry to hear that. Hey, I'm hungry. Let's talk over lunch."

John and Sandy's wedding turned out to be perfect. The wedding and the reception were held at John's Malibu home overlooking the ocean. At the reception, Tim's duties as best man were finished, and he busied himself at the bar. He was sitting at a table in the corner when his dad came over and pulled up a chair. "Aren't you hitting the sauce a little hard, son?"

Tim looked up. "Just trying to ease the pain, Dad. I look at Roy and Linda, who have been married five years and are still happily in love. John and Sandy have that look as they stare into each other's eyes. But here I sit, hating my life with Dana."

"You know you're in a problem of your own making. It's time you suck it up and be a man. That woman is the mother of your son."

"I wish I could talk things out with Dana without fighting all the time. I never really loved her, and I'm afraid of what the fighting is doing to Charlie. I should have married Teri when I had the chance." He sat back in his chair and only then noticed a figure standing just a couple of feet away. Tim gasped. It was Dana, her face like a stone mask. Their eyes locked for a moment before she roared as she turned and raced to the door, grabbing her purse off a table as she went.

Stunned, Tim sat there as his brother Mike came over. "Hey, bro, Dana just ran out and took your car."

Tim slapped his hand to his forehead. "She must have heard everything. Mike, she's probably headed home. Can I get a lift in your car?"

"No problem. Let me get Tina."

Tim and his dad stood up and hugged as his dad said, "I hope you can resolve this. Do what's best."

Tim looked at him through a blur of tears. "I'll do what I can."

He found John and Sandy and gave them his goodbyes with a brief explanation of why he was leaving early. John slapped him on the back. "I understand, Tim. I saw Dana leave. Thank you for standing with me."

"You're my best friend. How could I not?"

Tim hurried out and got into the back of Mike's car. At Tim's driveway, they stopped at the security gate, but it was already open. Mike turned in and they pulled up to the house just as the babysitter was driving away. Before Tim got out of the car, he reached forward and put his hands on Mike's and Tina's shoulders.

"Don't ever let your marriage go sour."

Tina squeezed his hand. "We wish you didn't have to go through this."

Mike glanced at him. "Good luck, big brother." When Tim got out of the car, his brother drove away.

Hearing a banging in the back of the house, Tim went to investigate. Dana was slinging clothes and children's items into the trunk of her car.

"What are you doing?" he demanded.

She glared at him with pure hatred. "I'm leaving

you. And I'm filing for divorce the first chance I get. I'm not staying in this house another minute. I heard what you said to your father. You liked that little whore you left me for better than me. I'm glad I got rid of her when I did."

"What are you saying?" Tim yelled. Then he was dangerously quiet.

A slow sardonic smile crossed her lips. "Do you remember the Barb Adams Teri worked with, who almost got her raped by Luke? That was my younger sister who owed me a favor. It's a good thing you didn't see her when you came over to fix Teri's car at the bank. And the final nail in the coffin you did yourself. I just set it up."

He grabbed her shoulder. "How did you know where Teri worked?"

"I followed her one morning." She shook off his hand.

It suddenly dawned on him. "You were the one who followed us home from my parents' house. But how did you know about Luke almost raping her?"

"You and I have friends in common. The news came on the Encino grapevine, and that really made my day! The next part was all too easy," she added with a sneer.

"What did you do?" Tim hissed through clenched teeth.

"Oh, I ran into Teri and Carol over at Farmer's Market just before you left. I told them you would tell Teri you loved her and then leave her for other women. And you did! You fool, you played right into my hand. I made sure my friend Dolores at the fan club would give the most damning press articles to Teri or any of her friends and family who came looking for them. Revenge is sweet." Dana seemed to be having fun turning the knife in his back.

It dawned on Tim how much this woman had ruined his life, and he'd never felt so much rage before. In the heat of the moment, Tim did something he had never done before: balling his fist, he slugged Dana. She fell, stunned, against the car, a trickle of blood trickling from the corner of her mouth. With something between a scream and a roar, she rocketed into the house and brought out three-year-old Charlie, who was crying.

"What are you doing with my son?" Tim was beside himself.

"Your son? It's going to be a cold day in hell before you see Charlie again. You never wanted Charlie. Remember you were going to have me abort him?" She strapped the terrified child into his seat while Tim stood like a dead man.

As she pulled away, all Tim could hear was Charlie screaming, "Daddy!"

Chapter 13

Hearing about Tim wasn't affecting Teri as it once did. She could even listen to Virgin Ram songs on the radio and enjoy them again. The group was slowly fading in popularity, and by the time her third child, Marcy, was born in July of 1979, she heard the members of the band were going their separate ways. *Finally, I can close that chapter of my life.*

****

Tim beamed in George Carlson's office. George was his divorce lawyer.

"Since Dana remarried, does that mean I won't have to send her seven hundred grand a year in alimony anymore?"

"That's right," George said, as he went through the papers on his desk. "But you still have the hundred grand a year for child support until Charlie reaches eighteen."

"Can we change anything on the sole custody? Can I have joint custody now?"

"The judge said no. You are to continue with the visitation every other weekend at your parents' house. Even though you have no history of violence, Dana really screwed you up with the battery charge. Her face was bruised and you loosened four of her teeth."

Tim nodded sadly. "Yes, I know, and she has spent all of Charlie's nine years making him afraid of me. Six years of only seeing him two weekends a month hasn't helped."

"Sorry, I couldn't get you a better deal, Tim. That judge is a tough one on domestic violence, and Dana really played it up."

Tim stood and shook George's hand. "Thanks for all you did do. I probably would have gone to jail, if Dana'd had everything she wanted."

George nodded. "You're welcome. I'll keep working on the judge for you."

Tim slid into his blue Mercedes and headed to the movie studio, where Luke was starring in a film. Tim was composing the soundtrack and needed to watch the rushes from the last week's shooting, but first, Luke had invited him to lunch.

When Virgin Ram split up the previous year, Tim had become head of the recording company's production staff, John had opened an agency for aspiring young musicians, and Roy and his wife, Linda, had gone into recording country music. Flamboyant Luke's choice had been movie and television acting.

Tim pulled up to the guard's station at the front of the studio. The guard stuck his head out the window with a clipboard in his hand. "Name, please?"

"Tim Olson, working on *Love on the Run.*"

"Yes, Mr. Olson. Go to sound stage fifteen."

Tim drove over to the building and parked, then found Luke's dressing room/trailer and knocked on the door. A voice from inside said, "Who is it?"

"Get off your lazy butt and open this door!"

The door opened and Luke hurried out. "Tim, you old son-of-a-bitch, how are you doing? Let's go to lunch."

They walked over to the commissary and took a tray full of food to a table. "I got some great news this morning," Tim said between bites. "Dana has remarried."

Luke smirked. "Well, it looks like you got that monkey off your back. I wish my ex would take the plunge...or a flying leap."

"At least you didn't have any kids. Dana's still being a pain about Charlie."

"That's too bad..." Luke glanced up and waved. "Sara! Come over here and join us."

A pretty blue-eyed redhead came over to the table with a tray in hand. She joined them and looked at Tim, and then her eyes got large. "Oh, my god, you're Tim Olson!"

Tim laughed. "You have me at a disadvantage. Who are you?"

Luke cut in, "Let me introduce you to my co-star, Sara James. She told me she was a big Virgin Ram fan when she was in high school."

"You look just like the poster I had on my wall. What are you doing now?"

"I'm head of production at the record company, and I compose music. I'm doing the soundtrack to the movie you're working on. I came to see the rushes and talk to the director."

"How come you're not performing anymore?"

Tim gazed at her straight-faced. "I don't look that good with spiked purple hair."

Luke choked and Sara giggled. After lunch the two men went into the theater, spending an hour and a half going over the previous day's filming. Tim discussed the music with the director and took notes.

Outside the theater afterwards, Luke turned to Tim and shook his hand. "It was real good seeing you again. Don't be a stranger."

"I plan to be here at least once a week to go over the music with your director. I'll stop and say hello."

Sara came up behind them and put her hand out to Tim. "It was so nice to meet you."

Tim took her hand and kissed it. "Pleased to meet you, too. I hope to see you again."

She blushed, then a smile spread over her face and she wrinkled up her nose. *She looks like Teri when she does that.* He got into his car and, with a wave of his hand to them both, he drove off.

The following Saturday was Tim's weekend with Charlie. His son would be dropped off at Tim's parents' house and they would both stay over Saturday night there. Because of Tim's drinking and temper, Dana wanted the visitation supervised.

That morning, Tim went into the living room, where nine-year-old Charlie was playing Pong with Tim's dad.

"Gotcha that time, Grandpa!" Charlie exclaimed.

"Hello, Charlie," Tim said with a smile. He sat on the couch by the sunny window.

Charlie sobered. "Hello, Dad."

"Charlie, come over here. I want to talk to you." Charlie obeyed the order as Tim's mother came in from the kitchen and sat on one of the chairs.

"Tell me about your new stepdad," Tim said, putting an arm around his son.

Charlie shrugged. "His name is Martin Baxter, and he's with the sheriff's department. Why?"

"I would like to know. Is he good to you?"

"Yeah. He's a great guy. We do a lot together when he has time off."

A pang of jealousy hit Tim. "You let me know if he ever hurts you, okay?"

An edge came into Charlie's voice. "He never hit my mother like you did."

"Charlie, I was just concerned about you."

"Yeah, right. He also said if you ever hit me, he'll put you away for a long time." He shrugged off Tim's arm and stood up. "Can I go out back, Grandma?"

Tim reached for his son. "Charlie, I would never hurt you. I love you." Charlie turned an icy stare on Tim. *So much like his mother's eyes. This man has Charlie every day of the week and I only get him twice a month. Who has the real influence over him? He seems to have Charlie's love and respect.*

"Grandma, can I go outside?"

She said very low, "Yes, you can."

Charlie darted out. Tim put his face in his hands as the tears started to flow. "I've lost my son."

His father stood. "You know, you brought this all on yourself."

His mother rose and stomped her foot. "Dan, stop it!" She went to Tim and sat beside him, cradling him in her arms.

A few days later, Tim was at the piano in the theater on the studio lot, waiting for the director. He was noodling on the keys, playing "Moonlight Serenade," when he felt someone come up behind him. Turning, he found Sara standing with her hands behind her back.

"Oh, don't stop, Tim, that was lovely."

"Do you like Glenn Miller?"

Ilona Fridl

"Yes, I do. Most guys I know think that's fogey music, but I love it."

Tim's throat tightened. "There is only one other girl I've ever met that loved Big Band like I do."

She gazed at him. "I'm sorry if I brought up a bad memory for you."

Tim played a few chords on the piano, then turned back. "Don't worry about it. That was a long time ago. Say, there's a Big Band retrospective at the music center in a couple of weeks. Would you like to go with me to see it?"

"It sounds like fun." She wrote her phone number and address on a piece of notepaper. "Call me when you get the details." Sara checked her watch. "Oops, my break is almost over. Gotta go." She put her hand on his shoulder, and then she was gone.

The next day, Tim got the information on the retrospective and set up the date with Sara. He was in a reflective mood on his way to her apartment. They were going out to dinner, then to the music center. *Do I like Sara for herself or because she reminds me of Teri? Sara's sweetness, humor, and looks are so much like hers. Maybe this is a way to put Teri behind me and fall in love with someone else. Everyone got on me because Teri was six years younger, and now Sara is fourteen years my junior. Oh, well, who says this can't work?*

All through dinner and at the music center, he studied her. He listened to what she said and watched what she did. While the music was playing at the center, he asked her to dance and she fairly jumped to the dance floor that was set up. He found himself falling in love with Sara for herself. *I'm going to go slow with her.*

After the date, Tim drove Sara back to her apartment. He parked the car on the street.

Sara took a breath. "I really had fun tonight, Tim. Thank you for asking me along."

Tim put his hand on her cheek. "I had fun too. For the first time in a long time."

"Luke told me you went through hell with your ex-wife. I'm sorry, because you seem like a nice guy."

Tim took her hand and kissed it. "Thank you for that."

Sara kissed him. "Goodnight, Tim. Call me again." She smiled and got out of the car. As Sara got to the door, she turned and waved. Tim started the car and pulled away, whistling to himself all the way home.

A few months went by, and Tim and Sara saw each other steadily. Tim knew gossip columnists' tongues were wagging about the thirty-six-year-old former band member and the twenty-two-year-old actress. Luke gloated, saying he knew Tim's type of woman when he saw it.

Tim decided to ask Sara to marry him. He took the ring out of the chest of drawers again and looked at it. No, he still couldn't give Teri's ring to someone else, so back it went. He prepared this date very carefully. Tim made reservations at an exclusive restaurant next to the beach in Malibu. He rented out a private balcony overlooking the ocean.

The dinner was excellent, and then Tim took the wine out of the ice bucket and poured them both a glass. "Here's to us," he said, as they clinked glasses and took a sip. Then Tim stood up and skirted the table. Standing in front of Sara, he took her hand while going down on one knee, and she gasped as he pulled a small box out of his dinner jacket pocket. "Sara, I love you. Will you marry me?"

Tears puddled in her eyes. "Oh, Tim, it's beautiful!" she said as he opened the box. "Oh, yes, yes! I love you too!" Her hands on his face, she kissed him thoroughly before he put the ring on her finger.

"Thank you, Sara," he whispered.

The following weekend was his visitation with Charlie. He decided to introduce his son to Sara. Tim discussed this with his mother, and she thought he ought to call and prepare Charlie for this, instead of springing it on him.

Tim sat, staring at the phone, wanting to call Dana about as much as he'd like to swallow a poisonous puffer fish alive. Finally, he got up the nerve and heard her say hello.

"Dana, this is Tim. Is Charlie there?"

"No, he's not. What do you want?"

"Could you have Charlie call me when he gets home? I need to talk to him about this weekend."

"Why?"

"Just have him call me." Tim hung up.

Charlie was on the line a couple of hours later. Tim told him how he was getting married to Sara and he wanted Charlie to meet her. Fifteen minutes later, Dana called.

"You're getting married again? Why? Did you knock her up too?" she said with acid in her voice.

Tim gritted his teeth. "No. Not that it's any of your business."

"What little backstreet whore did you find this time?"

"Damn it, Dana, Sara is not a backstreet whore.

She's a sweet girl whom I love very much."

"Love? You're incapable of love. You must be in lust and she's the only one that will accommodate you. I know what kind of tramps you attract."

"Yeah, after all, you were my first wife, weren't you?"

She screamed and slammed the phone down. Tim toyed with the thought of ripping her head off. He wondered what Dana would say to Charlie, if anything. It would be just like her to work against him, again.

Saturday, as Tim and Sara walked into Tim's parents' house, Sara was warmly greeted by his mother. They went into the living room, and Charlie was sitting on the arm of the chair next to Tim's dad.

"Charlie, come over here," Tim said. The boy came over and stood in front of Tim. "This is Sara James. She is going to be my wife. I want you to get to know her. Sara, this is my son, Charlie."

Sara put out her hand. "Hello, Charlie. I'm pleased to meet you."

Charlie didn't respond. He looked down at the toe of his shoe.

Tim tried again. "Charlie, say hello to Sara."

Charlie put his hands behind his back and glared at Tim.

"Charlie! That is rude. I want you to apologize to her."

Charlie looked at Tim's dad. "Grandpa, can I go up to my room?"

Tim's dad also looked upset. "Your father is right. You are being very rude to Sara and she deserves an apology."

"Mom said I don't have to be nice to trash."

Before anyone else could move, Tim's dad came up next to Charlie, put a firm hand on his shoulder, and said, close to his face, "You apologize to Miss James right now."

Charlie looked scared. "I'm sorry I was rude." He was subdued but polite for the rest of the visit.

Tim agonized about what poison Dana had told Charlie. How could she do that to a child? He poured out his fears about Charlie to Sara. She was at a loss as to what he should do. "Maybe when he grows up he'll see what his mother did to drive a wedge between you. I hope he seeks you out then."

Tim sighed. "I hope someday he'll understand how much I love him."

They got married in March of 1980, at John and Sandy's house in Malibu. All of their friends and relatives were there, except for Charlie, who refused to attend, to Tim's sorrow. Sara was originally from Omaha, Nebraska, and her parents, three brothers, and one sister all came for the wedding.

It was a couple of months later when Sara found herself pregnant. She was just finishing a movie and asked her agent to put her on hiatus until the baby was born.

Tim, of course, was excited. He and Sara spent many hours fixing up the nursery. He was able to do all the preparations he'd missed with Charlie. Tim waited on Sara hand and foot, and then, a couple of weeks before Christmas, her mother flew out to be with Sara when Tim was at work.

A week before Christmas, Tim went to sleep with his hand on Sara's stomach. He loved to feel the movements of their child in her womb. He woke during the night and felt her stomach go rock hard just as she woke with a groan.

"Oh, god, that hurts," she moaned.

Tim sat straight up. "Was that a contraction?"

"I think so. Will you call the doctor?"

"Keep track of the time," he said as he jumped out of bed.

The twenty-four-hour emergency number was by the phone. Tim turned on the light and squinted at it, trying to get his eyes to adjust. In a few minutes he got the doctor on the line and told him about the contraction just as Sara moaned again.

"I think she's having another one."

"How long between contractions?" the doctor asked.

"How long between?" Tim asked Sara.

"That was about eight minutes," she said, rubbing her stomach.

Tim relayed the time to the doctor.

"I'll call the hospital and meet you down there," the doctor told him.

Tim took charge. "I'll get your mother, and she can help you get ready while I get the car." He started out the door.

"Tim!" Sara called, laughing. "You'd better get dressed first. Unless you want Mother to see more of you than she wants to."

Tim looked down at his naked body and snickered. "Nerves."

They got Sara to the hospital, and while her mother started calling relatives, Tim stayed and coached Sara's breathing. Finally, in a few hours, the orderly wheeled her into the delivery room, where Tim watched their daughter's birth. The nurse handed him the bundle after the baby was cleaned up, and with tears in his eyes, he went to his wife and gave her their daughter.

"I love you both so much," he said, his voice hoarse. He pushed back from her forehead the paper cap that had protected Sara's hair, and kissed her.

She smiled tiredly as he stood up again. "I love you, too. Merry Christmas," she said as she hugged the little girl.

Chapter 14

One morning in September of 1984, Teri made an announcement to her family at the breakfast table. "Since Marcy started kindergarten this year, I'm going to get a job in real estate."

David stared at her curiously. "Teri, we don't need the extra money. You don't have to work."

"David, I want to. I've done the stay-at-home-mom bit, and now I want to try something different. Besides, Bobbie has been running her printing business for over a year now, and Don doesn't seem to complain."

"Sounds like women's lib talking. I guess I'd be a pig if I said no."

Dave Junior, better known as DJ, looked up hopefully. "Does that mean you won't be home after school?"

Teri gave him her best mother face. "No, mister, that's the beauty of being a realtor. I can work when I want to and be home when I want, also."

Thirteen-year-old Katie didn't seem to be listening to any of this. Teri reached over and rapped her on the forehead. "Katie, how many times have I asked you not to wear the Walkman to the table?"

"Oh, Mom, please! I wasn't hurting anything."

David said firmly, "Take that thing off!"

"Okay! I was just listening to an oldie station. They had a rad song on there called 'Taking On' by a group called Virgin Ram."

Teri sucked in a breath.

"Mom, what's wrong?"

Teri glanced at David, who had an unreadable expression. She managed a little chuckle. "I used to know the members of that group."

DJ seemed impressed. "Dad, did you know them too?"

Staring steadily at Teri, David shook his head. "No, not really."

Katie asked, "How well did you know them?"

David raised an eyebrow at Teri.

Thinking fast, she turned to her daughter. "I was very good friends with them at one time, but when they got famous, I lost touch." She couldn't tell her teenage daughter she'd lost her virginity to one of them.

Katie and DJ reacted with new respect and said, "Wow."

Changing the subject, much to Teri's relief, Katie continued, "By the way, Mom, when are we going to see the Barneses again?"

"We're planning a trip next weekend to California."

"Oh, cool, I can see Kevin again. He's so hunky."

DJ made a face and said, "Gross me out!" while Teri and David laughed.

****

The next few years went well for Tim, Sara, and their daughter, Melissa. At first, Sara's television work kept her in Los Angeles, so she could take care of Melissa. After a couple of years, her movie work started again and took her out of California. Then Tim would take over. With help from his mother, sister, and sister-in-law, Melissa got quality parent care. Whenever he could, he took Melissa with him when he traveled, and they became inseparable pals.

Sara burned up phone lines to stay in Tim's and Melissa's lives. She was sometimes gone for months at a time, but she always showered Tim with "I love you" and "I miss you greatly." Coming back to joyful homecomings, Tim and Sara would have sex to make up for lost time. The little family couldn't be happier.

One evening in 1985, Sara answered an insistent ring of the telephone. After she hung up, she came into the den, where Tim was busy with a score he was writing. She sat on the piano bench next to him. "That was my agent. He has a fantastic movie deal that would have me starring with the popular Karl Graham in New York." She sighed. "The only problem is that it would take me away from you both for eight months."

"You can't pass this one up, darling. If you do, you'll regret it. Melissa and I will be fine and looking forward to your calls." Tim kissed her.

"Could you come with me?" She squeezed his hand.

Tim shook his head. "I've got too much work right now." So when the time came to go, she kissed her loving husband and four-year-old daughter goodbye.

Sara started communicating almost immediately, but gradually her calls became fewer. Melissa crawled onto Tim's lap after dinner during this time. "Daddy, when is Mommy going to call? I haven't talked to her in ages."

Tim stroked her hair and kissed her on the forehead. "Mommy is probably real busy with the film. She'll call when she can." He felt his stomach tighten, but he didn't want to worry the child.

Tim took Melissa with him to the supermarket. They were standing in the checkout line when she tugged his hand. "Isn't that Mommy?" She pointed at a *National Enquirer*. On the front page was a picture of Sara and Karl, his arm around her, walking down a street in New York. The caption read "Sara James and Karl Graham seem to be getting very close on and off the film set." Tim felt like someone had clubbed him in the chest. He was grateful Melissa couldn't read yet.

Tim looked at his daughter. "Yes, that's a picture of Mommy and her co-star."

"Can we buy it?"

"No, Lissa, we have some better pictures of Mommy in our *Newsweek*. We don't need this one." The last sentence came out with an edge to it, but it seemed to satisfy the child. Tim went home with a rock in his stomach.

That evening, Tim tried to call Sara at her hotel in New York. The special operator answered. "Can you ring Sara James' room? This is her husband."

"I'm sorry, Sara James asked not to be disturbed tonight. Is this an emergency?"

The rock turned into a boulder and rose to choke him. "No, I'll call another time."

A couple of days later, Tim and Melissa were invited to a weekend in Palm Springs with Roy and Linda and their three girls. On Saturday night, after the children were in bed, Tim, Roy, and Linda were having a beer by the pool on a cool desert night.

"Have you heard from Sara lately?" Linda asked.

Tim was quiet for a moment and stared at his glass. "I heard from her a couple of weeks ago."

"Is something wrong?"

Tim looked at Linda and sighed. "I've been bothered for a few days. I saw a *National Enquirer* with a picture of her and Karl on it."

Linda looked down. "Oh, yeah, I saw that one too. Tim, you know their reporting isn't always the truth."

"I know that, but I tried to call Sara that night, and the hotel operator told me she'd asked not to be disturbed." A strange look appeared on Linda's face. "Linda, do you know something?"

"It's not about that—" She sat back and looked off toward the horizon.

"What is it?" he pressed.

"It sounds like what happened to Teri. You may as well know. After she got out of the hospital, David asked her to marry him, but she wanted to talk to you first, so she called me up and asked me to bring the hotel list over. She called the hotel in Scotland while I was there, and she got the same statement from the operator as you did."

"You never told me Teri tried to call."

"I'd forgotten about it by the time you got home. I guess she assumed you didn't want to talk to her."

"Well, that's all water under the bridge now." Underneath, he was churning. *Maybe it wasn't just Dana that chased her off. I must have lost her because of my carelessness. Damn. And I was on a year's fling. Is Sara on a fling, too?*

Sunday evening, Tim tried to call again. This time he got through to Sara's room.

"Hello?" she answered.

"Hi, darling, I thought I'd call since I was gone over the weekend."

"Oh, Tim, hi. I wasn't expecting to hear from you."

Was it his imagination or did she sound distracted? "Lissa and I went over to the Gardners' for the weekend, and I thought I'd let you know, in case you'd tried to call."

"No, not much has been happening around here. I've been busy working on the movie. Where is Melissa? I'd like to talk to her."

"Just a minute." Tim called his daughter to the phone, and she talked to her mother for ten minutes.

"Would you like to talk to Daddy again?...Okay, bye, Mommy, love you too." Melissa hung up the phone. She crawled onto Tim's lap. "I really miss her."

"I do too, pumpkin," he said as he kissed her on the head. He didn't want Melissa to know how much Sara not wanting to talk to him caused hurt and anger. *Are my suspicions correct? Oh, Sara, what have you done to us?*

Toward the end of the eight months, Sara had trouble talking to Tim and talked to Melissa most of the time. Then the last call came.

"Tim?" Sara said when he answered. "We have to talk when I get home." She started sobbing. "I never meant for this to happen."

Tim felt like his heart dropped to the floor. "Sara, what is it?"

"I'd rather talk to you face to face. See you tomorrow."

The next day as the limo came through the security gates, Melissa was looking out the window and she ran out of the house, yelling, "Mommy's home!"

Tim watched from the foyer window and saw Sara talk to the driver, then hug Melissa. Mother and daughter came into the house hand in hand. Sara kissed her and said, "Why don't you go to your room and watch TV for a while and let me talk to Daddy."

Tim went into the living room ahead of Sara and stood next to the fireplace. He had a lump in his throat, but managed to say around it, "What happened, Sara?"

She took a deep breath and closed her eyes. "Tim, I fell in love with Karl when we were making the movie." She opened them and looked at Tim, who remained silent. "I'm going to take some of my things and move in with him today. I'll come back for the rest later." She took another breath. "And I'm going to take Melissa with me."

"No, Mommy!" cried a small voice behind her. Melissa ran across the room and attached herself firmly to Tim's legs. He picked her up and she buried her face in his neck. That moved him to tears.

When he caught his voice, he pushed Melissa back and looked her in the eye. "You know that was wrong to listen at the door. Now go to your room and let me talk to Mommy, okay?"

She slowly nodded and went down the hall.

He turned back to Sara, who was wringing her hands. "You're not even going to talk about trying to come back to me?"

"Tim," she said, her eyes lowered, "I'm carrying Karl's baby." She sobbed, "I'm sorry. I'm so sorry. I never meant to hurt you like this."

He gazed at her steadily. "Sara, I want custody of Melissa. I don't want to lose another child to divorce."

"But can you take care of her?"

"I can and have, all these times you were gone making movies. Sara, listen. My job keeps me here most of the year. You can have Melissa as much as you want when you're in town." He added bitterly, "And besides, you'll have another child to keep you busy."

Sara came over and put her hand on his shoulder. "I'm not going to ask for alimony, and as much as it hurts, you're right about custody. I'll go pack."

Tim turned to the bar and poured himself a drink. Staring at the glass and the bottle, he took them to the kitchen and poured them both down the sink. *I have to be responsible for Melissa now. It's time to get help for my drinking problem so I can take care of my daughter.*

Chapter 15

Teri was delighted when her parents decided to move to a senior community near her when her father retired from air flight instruction in 1984. Now she could see them more often than just four or five times a year. They were planning to sell the house in Alhambra and go on an around-the-world trip.

With the Kelseys' help in moving, they arrived at the senior community the following spring. David and his father-in-law spent much of David's rare time off playing golf at the country club. Teri and her mother had a standing date once a week for lunch. Her parents were happy to spend more time with their grandchildren, too. They had seen quite a bit of Laura's two children in California but had missed much of Teri's children through the years. Now they had time to make up for that.

About a year after her parents moved to Arizona, David came in one Saturday after playing golf with Teri's dad. "Teri, I'm a little concerned about your father. When we were out on the course, he seemed to be in some pain, and he looked pale."

"Did he say anything to you about it?"

"I asked him, and he said he was just getting old."

Teri's stomach clenched. "I wonder if Mom knows about that."

She called her mother and told her what David had

said.

"Teri, I've noticed that too. I made an appointment with the doctor so your father can get a check-up."

A few days later, her mother called back in tears.

"Mom, what's wrong?"

"Sweetheart, we got back the tests from the doctor. Your father has pancreatic cancer and it's spread. I don't know what to do."

Teri's heart was in her throat and she didn't know what to say. "Oh, Mom! How is he feeling?"

Her mother made an effort to steady herself. "He's in the hospital now, but he will be allowed to come home after the doctor tries some treatments. Keep both him and me in your prayers."

Teri and Laura took turns helping their parents through several painful months. Finally, her father had enough of the treatments and requested the doctor to let him go home. He was given a couple of weeks to live. The family took turns sitting with him.

It was Teri's turn one day, and her father said to her, "Teri, I have to tell you, before I go, how proud I am of you."

"Dad, don't—"

"Please. I need to tell you this. Come over here." She came over and sat on the bed, and he took her hand. "I was so worried about you when you ran off after high school, but since then you have become a fine wife and mother. I'm in awe of how you turned yourself around. Tell me, Teri, what kind of hold did Tim have over you?" The question surprised her, and at first she didn't know what to say. Her father had always been angry when he spoke of Tim, but now he sounded curious.

Iris Rainbow

"Dad, I can't explain it, but every time I saw him, I had to be with him. It was a love, but different from what I have with David. I love him very much, yet it isn't that strong pull I had with Tim."

He squeezed her hand. "Your mother told me she spoke to you about my friend Mike, the man she was engaged to before the war. I know she doesn't love me as much as she did him, so I understand David's position. He has told me he knows, too. Honey, you can't change how you feel, and I'm glad you stayed with David. He's a good man and he loves you very much."

Daddy does understand, or is trying to. Oh, why does he have to die? It isn't fair. Teri put her other hand on top of his and tried to smile through her tears. "I love you so much, Daddy."

Two days later, her father died.

****

As the years went by, Katie's interest in Kevin Barnes turned into a long-distance love affair and both families had to put up with big phone bills. In 1992, Teri found herself planning a big wedding for fall, and the families were happy with the arrangement. Evie and Teri would be related now.

The wedding was wonderful. Katie and Kevin were married in the Kelseys' church in Tucson, and family and friends from both sides were able to attend. David beamed when he walked Katie down the aisle. Teri noticed he had aged in the past year since he took over as area manager of the corporation. He made money, but the stress level was rising, and David's sandy hair was turning white. *This wedding is just the thing to take his mind off work for a while.*

At the reception, held at David's country club, Teri felt a pang of déjà vu. How far they all had come over the years. Evie seemed aged hardly at all, while Ken was getting iron-gray hair and wore glasses. Teri had to admit she herself was looking older, with her hair starting to go gray, but for her age she didn't look bad.

She glanced across the table at her mother, who was now in her seventies and had moved into the senior community apartments after Teri's father died. *It hurts that he couldn't be around to see this. I still miss him so much.*

"Teri, where are you?" Evie nudged her.

"Sorry, Evie, I was lost in thought. It's hard to believe all we've been through."

"And now we really are family. Who would have thought?" They giggled as of old.

The deejay they'd hired to play music at the reception was getting ready to start. "For our first number, I want the bride and groom on the dance floor first, then the parents. The number is a request from the bride. She wants to dedicate it to her mother, who, she informed me, was friends with this particular group, Virgin Ram. So here is their song "Beloved.""

Then Teri heard Tim's voice. "I didn't realize when I saw you that day, Beloved..." She smiled sadly. "That was the song he wrote for me."

Evie studied her. "Are you all right?"

"I'm okay. Let's go dance."

David expressed his concern when he took Teri onto the dance floor. "I don't think Katie realized what that song was to you."

Teri drew him close. "Let's just enjoy this dance."

The rest of the reception went beautifully. Late that

night, David drove back home with thirteen-year-old Marcy asleep in the back. As he pulled into the driveway, he shut off the engine and turned to Teri.

"Did you ever regret never having a wedding like that?"

"Maybe a little, at the time, but I haven't thought about it since. Why, do you regret it?"

"Sometimes, but I love being married to you. Even though I know I don't have your whole heart."

"David, I—"

"Stop, Teri. I know what you're going to say. I know you love me too. That's what keeps me going." David kissed her. "I just wanted to let you know, I understand." They got out of the car, and David woke up Marcy and half-carried her into the house. Teri noticed he was pale and breathing hard, so she sent Marcy to her room.

"David, are you sick?"

He glanced at her and shook his head. "Just exhausted from today. I'll be fine after a good night's sleep. Come on, let's go to bed."

"If you're not, I'm calling the doctor tomorrow." *I don't want to lose you.* The next day he seemed all right, so she let it go, but she expressed her concern to Bobbie.

"I'm worried about David working so hard. He went very pale and was out of breath when we got home from the wedding."

"Teri, I'd keep an eye on him. I've realized, since we've known you, he's a workaholic."

"I've asked him to slow down, but he can't seem to. He's very dedicated to his job." She tried to not worry but wasn't very successful.

****

Four years had passed since Katie's wedding, and she made David and Teri grandparents when she had a son the third year of her marriage. Teri was delighted with her new role as a grandma and swore she was going to spoil little Michael Barnes. Evie was equally happy with their new bond. In the meantime, DJ moved in with his girlfriend, Stacy. He was on the race car circuit, which Teri thought was a dangerous occupation. He was doing what he loved, so she lived with her doubts. Marcy was in her senior year in high school and planning to study law at a university in Phoenix.

David was still a worry to her. He handled more and more stress at work and was away from home for days at a time in high-powered meetings with other corporate heads. The last time he came home from one of those meetings, he was very pale and drawn. Teri begged him to slow down, but he didn't.

One day, in the fall of 1996, Teri came home from closing a deal on a house. As she went in her front door, her cell phone went off. It was David's secretary, Barb. "Teri, get down to the hospital as soon as you can. David's had a heart attack."

"Oh, Barb, thank you for calling." *Oh, my god, no. Oh, please don't take David yet, I need him.*

She left a note for Marcy, then flew out of the house and into her car. The drive to the hospital seemed to take a very long time. She ran through the emergency entrance and asked about David Kelsey.

The nurse took her to a waiting room, and a few minutes later a doctor appeared. "Mrs. Kelsey?"

Teri nodded.

"I'm Dr. Peterson. Your husband has had a

massive heart attack. We have him stabilized, so we are going to take him in for a bypass. I'll let you see him."

Teri felt lightheaded. "Thank you, Doctor."

She was led to a small room near the doors to the OR. David was barely awake when she took his hand and kissed it. "I'm here, Tiger." She forced a smile through her tears.

David regarded her and, in a very weak voice, he said, "I love you, Sweet Stuff."

The orderly came to move him to the operating room, and Teri gave David's hand a squeeze. "I'll be waiting for you."

The nurse showed her to the waiting room. Teri took her cell phone out and called Katie and DJ, and then Marcy came in. In a couple of hours, the whole family sat, praying and waiting.

Dr. Peterson came in with a grim look on his face. "I'm sorry, Mrs. Kelsey, but the damage was too great. We couldn't save him."

Teri and her family sat for a moment, stunned, then they dissolved into tears. Teri put her hand on the doctor's shoulder. "I'm sure you did all you could. Thank you."

The next day, Teri was curled in her mother's arms, sobbing. "How did you find strength when Daddy died?"

Her mother took her by the shoulders and looked her in the eye. "This is the hardest thing you are ever going to do, but I know you can do it. This is a part of life, to have to face the death of someone you love." She wiped her own eyes with a tissue. "When Mike died, I thought my life was over, but your father came to fill it. You will be happy again, but David will always be with you, right here." She put her hand over Teri's heart.

After the funeral, Teri realized she had to go on alone. She was making enough money in real estate to support herself, plus there were pension checks from David's company. She figured she would be all right. Bobbie told her to come to her and Don if she needed anything.

Teri was grateful for their friendship.

****

In January of 1997, Tim was working on a deal in his executive suite at the recording company. He was now the vice president in charge of production. The president, Mr. Louden, called Tim to his office.

Tim greeted Darlene, Louden's secretary. "What's up, Darlene?"

"I think you'll enjoy this idea," she said, as she waved him into the office.

Inside, he recognized the three other men with Mr. Louden. Tim gave a shout and they all embraced, while Louden looked amused. There was John Simon, whom he still saw often, but Luke Knoll and Roy Gardner he hadn't seen in many years. They settled in the chairs facing the president.

Louden began, "I have an idea to put before you. There has been an upsurge of interest in music from the Sixties. We re-released your old albums on CDs, along with those of several other artists, and the sales were surprising. I wondered if the four of you would consider doing a three-month reunion tour of the United States?"

John shook his head. "But we haven't played together in years."

"We would give you five months to shake the rust

out. You can use the facilities here to practice. What do you say? The tour will be next summer. That would be thirty years since your first one."

Luke snorted. "God, I feel old after hearing that."

Tim slapped him on the back. "You are!" Luke made a face while the others laughed.

They looked at each other, then at Louden. "All right!"

Within the next month, they got their music out and listened to it countless times. Tim hadn't played a bass in years, so he almost had to re-learn it. He still got a catch in his throat when he heard the song "Beloved."

One evening before the tour, John was at Tim's house. Tim handed him a soda and sat across from him at the kitchen table.

"This is dredging up a lot of memories for me. My life hasn't been ideal for the past thirty years. Melissa is sixteen now, and she's worried about going to college in a couple of years and leaving me alone in this big house. My own daughter feels sorry for me." Tim put his head in his hands.

John cleared his throat. "There might be someone else out there for you. You might even meet her on this tour. You've been cooped up in that office too long. You can't meet anyone there."

"I wonder if she thinks about me after all these years."

"Who?"

"Teri. I should have married her before we left on that damn tour. I probably wouldn't have had all these heartaches since."

"You don't know that."

"I know she's out there, John. I can almost feel her.

Maybe I'll find her this time."

John looked sadly at him.

"Some people get second chances, don't they?"

John nodded. "Some people do."

Chapter 16

A year after David's death, Teri was steeling herself, knowing that for the first time she would be living all alone in the house.

The day before, she, DJ, and Stacey had helped Marcy move most of her things into her dorm room after she registered. Marcy had come back with Teri to pack her clothes and personal items. She was officially moving into her room this evening, and had started getting her things together after lunch. It was now three o'clock.

"Marcy, do you need any help with your packing?" Teri called from the dining room.

"No, thanks, Mom. I have it under control. I'm almost finished."

Marcy, her baby, was leaving for college in Phoenix. Teri looked out the window at the mountains and desert of Tucson and wished David could be here to see Marcy off. She still missed him.

Teri picked up the morning paper and sat at the table. She'd turned several pages when an article caught her eye. "The Sixties rock group Virgin Ram is here in Tucson for a concert on their reunion tour," it said. "The group consists of members Luke Knoll, Roy Gardner, John Simon, and Tim Olson..." Teri couldn't read any further, because her eyes were full of tears.

Marcy came in the room with her suitcases and set

them down. "Mom, what's wrong?"

Teri had her hand over her mouth, tear running down her face. She turned the paper in Marcy's direction and pointed to the article.

"Isn't that the group you said you knew in the Sixties?"

Teri nodded. "I never told you everything. Not even your father knew everything that happened then." She glanced at her daughter. "It has a lot to do with the drug problems I had. Remember the talks I had with all of you about staying away from drugs? I knew about it firsthand."

"Mom, if you want to talk about it, I'll listen." Marcy sat across the table from Teri and watched intently.

Teri got up and poured them each a cup of coffee. Then she sat back down at the table and told Marcy her story, from going to the press party at the record company to going through drug withdrawal in the hospital. She made it sound as horrible as possible. *Maybe I can prevent Marcy from getting caught up in the party atmosphere at college. I don't want her going through what I went through.*

Marcy was speechless. "Oh, god, Mother, I never would've thought you'd done everything you warned us against."

"I nearly killed myself, and I never wanted you to go through the same thing. I prayed that all of you would avoid it, and I think you did."

"After that story, I won't ever touch drugs." Marcy glanced at the article again, then jumped up from her chair. "Mom, help me get the suitcases out to the car."

"You don't have to leave yet, do you?"

Marcy pointed to the newspaper. "The band is signing autographs at Music World right now. Come on, or we'll be late!" Teri stood there, unmoving, so Marcy grabbed her arm. "Come on, Mom!"

Do I want to do this? Numb, she took a couple of suitcases in hand and locked the door behind her.

The crowd was beginning to thin out when they reached Music World. It was fifteen minutes to closing. Marcy and Teri walked into the store and stood behind a group of people. She saw the band at a desk still signing a few autographs. *After thirty years, of course, they've aged.* Roy had white hair, and Luke had aged well, but he had a rugged look. John's hair was very short and she didn't recognize him at first. There at the end of the desk sat Tim. Her heart skipped a beat, and those old feelings welled up in her. *I haven't stopped loving him. Just remember how he walked out on you.* Outside of short, thinner, gray hair, he was still very handsome. Teri glanced at her own image in the security mirror. She saw a woman with a fairly nice figure and short gray hair with red streaks. In fact, David had given her the nickname of "Rusty" before he died. Teri turned her attention to the band members. John looked up and nudged Tim. She smiled when she noticed they were looking in Marcy's direction. Of course. Her daughter resembled Teri at that age. She walked beside her daughter and put a hand on Marcy's shoulder. As Teri waved, Tim's reaction was startling—he jumped up and grabbed Teri in an embrace.

"Teri! Oh, my god! Teri!" he shouted. He turned to the manager. "Can we borrow your office?" The surprised man motioned them in.

Teri's emotions ran rampant. She wondered if she should open the door she'd shut so long ago. Should she open old wounds? But how wonderful to be held in his arms again. *I can't look him in the eyes or I'll be lost.* Teri said firmly, "I'm glad we got the chance to finally say goodbye."

"Goodbye? Teri, I just found you again. Don't say goodbye! Are you still married?"

"David died last year. I have three children, and Marcy, who is with me today, is the youngest. She's on her way to college this evening. How about you?"

"Married twice, divorced twice. I have a son who is estranged from me and a daughter I'm raising. Teri, did you love David?"

"He was a good man. He loved me very much and I loved him, too." *But he wasn't you.*

"Teri, why didn't you wait for me? I promised you I'd find you when I returned, and I told you I loved you. I don't say that unless I mean it. When I came back and found you were married, that was a pain I can't describe."

This was something she hadn't considered before. "I went through hell when you left. I got more and more involved with drugs and liquor, and after Carol died, I nearly killed myself. I haven't touched that stuff since. How about you?"

"I've been clean and sober for twelve years."

"When I got out of the hospital after detox, I saw a newspaper column about you dating a German girl, and it said you might be engaged. Are you telling me you didn't have sex when you were on tour?"

"I wasn't strong enough to resist it, so, yes, I did, but I was never serious about any of those girls. You can't say you didn't have sex while I was gone, can you?" He gazed at her steadily.

Teri lowered her eyes. "No, I can't, not in the drug scene." She sighed deeply. "It's been good to see you again. Goodbye, Tim."

"One kiss first. Please?"

Teri hesitated, then gave in, and the kiss was electric. She felt it all the way down to her toes. *David never did that to me.* Their bodies were blending into one when she broke away. "I have to go." She rushed out to where Marcy waited. "Come on. Let's go."

Tim was right behind her. "Teri, please wait." He wrote something on a piece of paper. "I put the name of our hotel, and the room phone number, if you change your mind. I'll be in town for two days." He put his hand on her cheek. "You felt that kiss as much as I did."

Marcy put out her hand to Tim. "I'm Marcy Kelsey, Teri's daughter. Pleased to meet you, Mr. Olson."

Tim took her hand and his eyes misted. "You look just like your mother." He turned to Teri. "Kelsey is your last name?"

Teri nodded. Then she did what she had been avoiding and looked deep into his eyes. A strong wave of love and tenderness came over her. She became lost in those beautiful green eyes. Reaching up, she caressed his cheek, wiping a tear away. Suddenly, the pain she'd felt after he left returned, but she realized Marcy was watching intently. "Marcy, come on. Let's go," she said with a rasp.

"But, Mom…"

"Let's go!" They dashed out of the store and went

home in silence.

Marcy pulled her old red Mustang into the driveway, and they got out of the car and sat on the low wall next to the house. "Mom, you know I loved Daddy very much and I still miss him."

Teri nodded.

Marcy looked her straight in the eye. "But I never saw you and Daddy look at each other like you and Tim did. You never forgave Tim for leaving you to go on that tour, did you?"

"I guess not."

"Don't be a fool, Mother, forgive him. Most people only dream of a love like that."

"He did say I hurt him badly when I didn't wait for him."

"That's what I mean. Mom, you shouldn't go on hurting each other. Call him and give him another chance. Forgive him."

"I'll think about it. You'd better get going." They hugged and kissed goodbye, and then Marcy got back in her car.

"Mom, you've got a second chance. Don't blow it! Besides," Marcy said with a wicked grin, "it would be way cool to have a rock star as a stepfather."

Teri smiled and smacked the side of the car. "Get out of here!" She watched her youngest drive off down the street.

Unlocking the door, she went into the now-empty house. She put her purse on the sofa and got another cup of coffee. Sitting down, she set her cup on the coffee table and stared out the picture window at the desert and the mountains.

Teri knew how she had yearned to be at the top of

the food chain. No parents telling her what to do, no husband to come to a compromise with, and no more children to take care of. Even her job in real estate was flexible. She could work when she wanted.

Taking a sip of the coffee, Teri sat back and gazed outside. As she looked, desert and mountains dissolved and she found herself by another window a lifetime ago, looking out over the lights of Los Angeles. *Talk to me, Teri, what should I do?* She felt a tug at her heart. *Tim was as hurt by me as I was by him, but he seems to want me back. He can forgive me. Can I forgive him? Talk to me, Teri.* She felt another tug. Then she heard Marcy's voice: D*on't blow your second chance.* All of a sudden, being on top of the food chain seemed more lonely than she wanted to be. Teri could still feel Tim's kiss.

Glancing at her purse, she saw a piece of paper had fallen out. Teri opened it and read, *To my Iris Rainbow, I still love you. I'll be waiting for your call. Tim.* There was the name of the hotel, with the room number at the bottom. She stared at the piece of paper for a moment. *There's one more person I owe an apology to.* She pulled her cell phone from her purse, but a second later, put it back.

****

Tim slid into the sleek black limo taking them to the hotel and stared bleakly out the window as the others piled in. John turned to him. "Well, do you think Teri will call?"

Tim shook his head sadly. "So much time has gone by, I don't know if she feels the same about me."

Luke clapped him on the shoulder. "I wish my wife had stayed that good-looking. Teri is still beautiful for her age."

Roy laughed. "Spoken like a true insensitive male. Well, Tim, it's five o'clock now. We have three hours until the show. Good luck."

The limo rolled into the parking lot, and the four friends went to their respective rooms. On the way, Tim gave Teri's name to the desk and told them he wanted any call from her to be put through immediately. An hour went by as Tim tried to take his mind off the silent telephone. He'd just decided it was time to get ready for the show when he heard the ring. Closing his eyes with a silent prayer, he picked up the receiver. "Hello?"

"Hello, Tim. This is Teri, and I wanted to apologize for the way I acted this afternoon. I didn't want your visit to Tucson to end on a sour note."

Tim almost sobbed. "Please forgive me for everything. If I hadn't been so stupid in my youth, we would've been together all these years. Of course, I forgive you."

Teri was silent for a moment. "Tim, open your door."

"Why?"

"I want to see you."

He flew across the room and opened the door. Teri stood there, cell phone in hand, and then she slowly turned it off and put it in her purse. Tim held out his arm, she took it, and he escorted her inside, closing the door behind her.

Chapter 17

The love she had for him welled up. It was like a dam breaking and overflowing. They stood in a deep kiss and embrace, two halves finally completing each other.

Tim started to unbutton his shirt and Teri stopped him with her hand. "Allow me," she said, slowly undressing him. "I remember what you like." She rubbed his chest and stomach, down to his erection.

As Teri's clothes fell away, he kissed each breast tenderly. "You are still incredibly beautiful, baby." He swept her up into his arms and carried her to the bed.

"Let me feel you inside me again," she half-sobbed, and he entered her, stroking to the depths. After they both came in a massive orgasm, they lay embraced for some time, sobbing in each other's arms.

Tim glanced at the clock. "I have to get ready for the concert. Teri, you were my first love and my last. I want you forever to be mine and to stand with me. Marry me, please?"

Teri thought of that warm night in the trailer at the music festival, when Tim had first opened her, and the intervening years fell away. *Love that is eternal will not be denied.* She gazed at him through her tears, seeing the humor in the fact he proposed while lying naked on top of her, buried deep. She laughed and cried. "From the position I'm in, how could I possibly say no?" Her voice cracked as she put her arms around his shoulders, and he kissed her tenderly.

When they were dressed and headed to the door, Tim held out his hand. "You're going with me. I'm not letting you go again."

Teri kissed him. "I'm not going anywhere, mister, except with you."

They went out the door arm in arm, and waiting in the hallway were John, Luke, and Roy.

John held his arms out. "Welcome back, Teri. Somehow I knew you couldn't stay away. It's good to see you again," he said, hugging her.

She went to Roy next. "It's good to see you too, Roy."

"Been a long time."

She turned to Luke, then stopped, and Luke smiled sheepishly. "I won't try to rape you, I promise." Teri hugged him, too. "But can I have a date?"

Teri patted him on the cheek. "I told you a long time ago I wasn't interested."

"Anyway, we're engaged," Tim said as he drew her back.

John laughed. "That didn't take you long. Congratulations, you two."

"Just thirty years," Tim replied. "Thank you." The others shook his hand and hugged Teri again.

John started moving them toward the elevator. "Come on, the limo's waiting."

Tim took Teri by the shoulders. "Are you coming to the theater?"

"I didn't buy a ticket."

"I'll talk to our manager. I'm sure he can arrange something. I want you with me."

She went down with them to meet their manager, Kevin Powers, and the entourage in the lobby. Tim went directly to Kevin, with Teri right behind.

"Kevin, this is Teri Kelsey, my fiancée. Can you get Teri on the backstage guest list? I'd like to get her a seat in the theater, too. Can you arrange it on your cell phone?"

Kevin looked at him with his mouth open. "Fiancée? Why haven't I seen her before? When did you meet?"

Tim smiled at Teri tenderly. "A long time ago, but we were apart for too long. I'm going to right that."

Kevin sighed and shook his head. "Okay, Tim, I'll take care of it. We'd better get in the limo."

All the way to the theater, Teri's inner voice kept chiding her. *What's the matter with you? You're letting him get to you again. Haven't you learned anything?* She glanced at Tim, who beamed, his arm around her. *Yes, I have. I found I still love him and can't say no to him, so I said yes.*

At the theater, they got out of the limo and were hustled into the backstage area. A young man, well dressed in a business suit, came up to Teri. "Are you Teri Kelsey?"

She said, "Yes."

"I have a special seat for you. Will you follow me, please?"

Kevin came over. "I'll arrange to let you backstage again. Come back before the last number, okay?"

Teri nodded and quickly kissed Tim. "Break a leg, love."

She followed the young man into the theater to a front row seat toward the right of the stage.

The lights went down and the announcement came: "Ladies and gentlemen, please welcome Virgin Ram!" A cheer went up, and Teri had the strangest feeling of déjà vu. She scanned the crowd, amazed. There were original fans, like herself, but there were many younger fans, as well.

She enjoyed the show and sang along with all the songs, as the whole audience did. It was like a big party. Then Tim took over the microphone. "Our next song is very special to me, because I wrote it for a very special girl. Those of you who have been fans from the start might remember the beautiful redhead I dated before we went on our first tour thirty years ago. I didn't realize it then, but she was the love of my life, and we went our separate ways. Today, I found her again and she has agreed to be my wife." A cheer came from the audience. "I dedicate this song to my Iris Rainbow. Here's to you, babe. It's called "Beloved.""

Teri dissolved into tears.

The next morning, Teri and Tim were blissfully entwined under the sheet with the early morning sun shining through the hotel window. Teri kissed him tenderly. "What time do you have to leave for the flight to Las Vegas? It's eight o'clock now."

Tim stretched and yawned. "Not until eleven-thirty." He chuckled. "We've been acting like two teenagers instead of two middle-aged people."

Something about that bothered her as she sat up in bed. Younger women were attracted to rock stars. Maybe he would find someone he liked better. *I can't compete with those supermodel types.* "You know, you could have your pick of any younger woman. You don't have to settle for me."

"What are you talking about?" He eyed her with a puzzled expression.

"Look at me. I'm not the eighteen-year-old you fell in love with. I've got gray in my hair, cellulite in my thighs, and nipples that point straight to the ground. When you really see me, you won't want me." Tears came to her eyes. "I couldn't take it if you walked out on me again."

He sat up and moved around on the bed to face her. "I didn't walk out on you. Anyway, take me. I have gray, thinning hair and droopy jowls. I'm aging too." Tim got up on his knees and cupped her chin in both hands. "Teri, I've dated younger women. They've had great bodies, yes, but they didn't have something very important." He pointed his index finger between her eyes. "They didn't have Teri inside. I've had a hole in my heart that didn't heal until yesterday." He took her in an embrace, cradling her body next to his. "You're the only woman I want and need. I'll never leave you." He buried his face in her hair and sighed happily. After a few minutes, they got up and dressed.

As Tim was packing his suitcase, he glanced at Teri, who sat on the edge of the bed. "Teri, tell me, why do you think I walked out on you?"

She stared at her hands. "It was something your old girlfriend told Carol and me."

An angry edge passed over his eyes. "Dana? What did she tell you?"

"She said when you got tired of me, you would tell me you loved me and walk out forever. I was crushed when you left, because all she told me seemed to be true. I self-destructed in San Francisco, and when I came back, I saw news releases that showed you very close with that German girl, so I resigned myself that I'd lost you. Dana told Carol that John would do that to her, too."

Tim whirled around. "Is that why Carol went with you to San Francisco?"

"Yes. She probably wouldn't have gone if John had said something. Especially after Linda called Carol and told her Roy proposed."

"Looks like Dana screwed up a lot of lives." He closed the suitcase and sat next to her. "Dana is a very selfish woman who wants things all her way. She confessed a few of those things to me before the divorce."

"Divorce?"

"She was my first wife, I'm ashamed to say. She found out where we lived by following us home from my parents. Remember when we had dinner over there? She followed you to work, too. Do you remember your co-worker, Barb?"

"The one who almost got me raped? Yes."

"That was Dana's younger sister, who owed her a favor."

Suddenly Teri remembered something. "That must be the reason she didn't want to meet you. You would've recognized her. Why did you marry Dana?"

"I was still in a blue funk after I returned from the tour and found you were married. I started dating Dana again on the rebound. Well…" He looked a little embarrassed. "When I was going with her before, she always practiced birth control, and I assumed she still did. I was wrong and she got pregnant. The band was on tour in Europe when I got an angry call from her. I promised to marry her when I got home, and believe me, that was the marriage made in hell. We got divorced two years later, and after that she turned my son against me. I haven't seen him in years."

"What happened with your daughter's mother?"

"Sara? She was a lot like you when I met her. She was acting in a movie with Luke, and I was writing the soundtrack. We were very happy for a few years, but she fell in love with her co-star in a movie. I got custody of Melissa." He looked down. "Now you know the whole sad story of my life."

"Do you think you could stay married to me? You've been divorced twice. How do I know you won't leave me, too?"

"Oh, Teri, ever since I met you I never wanted to be married to anyone else. Dana and I should have never married. We couldn't stop fighting. If she hadn't got pregnant, I wouldn't have stayed with her. Sara reminded me of you, but she was younger and was the one who left me. I would have stayed with her. She hurt me, but in a way I still care about her."

She put her arms around him. "I love you, Tim. I'll never leave you, I promise."

He returned the embrace. "I'm just happy to have my Teri back. I didn't realize how much I loved you until I lost you." He pulled back and gripped her shoulders. "Let's get married in Vegas. Hell, come with me on the rest of the tour."

She hesitated. "No, David and I got married in Vegas. I've got a few things to take care of here before I go. When do you end the tour?"

"We have San Francisco and Los Angeles left after Vegas."

"How about the first weekend in October? I could

go to Los Angeles and get it arranged. We could have just family and friends. You can call when you get off the tour. Here, I'll give you my sister Laura's phone number, just in case I have my cell phone off." She took a piece of the hotel stationary and wrote it down, then added, "And here's my cell phone number."

"I'll call my mother and have her get the family together. I'll give her your phone number and you can give her the information." The phone in the room rang and he picked it up. "Okay, I'll be right down." He turned to Teri. "That was John. The limo for the airport is here, and I have to leave." He picked up his suitcase, and Teri took her purse and followed him to the lobby, where the chauffeur took the suitcase and put it in the trunk. Members of the press were milling around as well, but she didn't think anything about that. Tim hugged Teri and kissed her. "I'll keep in touch. I love you."

She walked with him to the limo. "Love you too." She blew a kiss and waved as the limo pulled out of the parking lot, then got into her car for home.

She took a deep breath when she entered the house. *It feels like years since I was here.* She picked up the coffee cups from the table and rinsed them out. Pouring some milk over cereal, she took the home phone to the table and punched in Laura's number while taking a bite of cereal.

"Hello?" Laura answered.

"Laura, this is Teri. I need a favor. I want to plan a wedding."

"I thought Marcy and Pete were going to wait until after college. What happened?"

Teri laughed. "It's not Marcy, it's me."

There was silence on the other end. "I didn't know you were dating anyone."

Teri was enjoying this. "Oh, it was a guy I met yesterday."

"What? Have you lost your mind? Marrying someone you don't know?"

"I know him very well, and so do you. You met him a long time ago." She stirred her cereal with the spoon absentmindedly.

"Oh, my god! Do you mean Tim?"

"He was here in Tucson on the reunion tour, and we got back together. Long story, but now we're engaged."

"Sis, it was because of him you got involved in drugs. Should you go back to him and fall into that trap again?"

"I asked him about that. He said he's been clean and sober for twelve years, and I believe him."

"I hope you're right. What was the favor you wanted?"

"I don't know how long I have to be a resident of California to get a marriage license, so could I give them your address if there's a problem?"

"I suppose so. You can come and stay with me in Burbank. Since Kyle and I divorced and the children left, I'm in this house by myself. It'll be nice to have some company."

"I'll be over in a couple of days. I have to get things wrapped up here. Thanks, Laura."

"I hope you're making the right decision. See you."

Teri made a mental list of everything to do before she left. *First, I need to quit my job.* She would call her co-worker, Luis Rialto, and give him her listings and clients. She had trained him, and he was a good friend. "Luis? Would you meet me at my desk in twenty minutes at the office?"

"Teri, what's up?"

"I'll tell you when I get there."

Teri finished her cereal and put the bowl and all the dirty dishes into the dishwasher. Then she went to the desk in the den and removed all her work folders.

At the realty office downtown, Teri parked in the lot and hurried in. In one of the client chairs at her desk was Luis, and she handed him the folders. "I'm quitting my job as of today. I want you to have the listings in my computer. You can access them with the password 'rainbow.' I will write my letter of resignation, and you can have the clients."

Luis sat there with his mouth open. "Why are you quitting? This is awful sudden. Did something happen?"

Teri smiled. "I'm moving to Los Angeles and getting married in a few weeks." She whipped off a letter and printed it out. "It's all yours, and good luck to you. I want you to list my house in a week or two. I'll get the papers set up and find someone to take care of it."

He held out his hand to her. "I'll miss you. Good luck, and thanks." She set the letter on the owner's desk and walked out to find a graying, black-haired woman, dressed in a blue tailored skirt and jacket, standing next to her car.

"Hello, are you Teri Kelsey?"

"Who wants to know?"

"I'm Nancy Blake, of the Tucson Review." She pulled out a picture from a folder. "Is this you?" It was a picture of Teri hugging Tim next to the limo.

"Yes, but…"

"Then you're the mysterious Iris Rainbow."

Teri took a few steps around the reporter and got into her car. Before Nancy Blake could do anything, Teri backed out and left. *I shouldn't have gone with him to the limo.* She'd forgotten about avoiding the press. Teri drove back and put her car in the garage.

As she went into the house, the phone was ringing and Bobbie was on the other end. "Teri, can I come over?"

"Sure." In a minute or two, there was a knock, and Teri opened the door. "What's wrong, Bobbie?"

"Some news people were snooping around, asking questions about you, but I didn't tell them anything. What's going on?" Bobbie looked at her curiously. The phone rang and it was Teri's mother.

"Teri, turn on the Tucson Review now." Teri dashed to the television.

Nancy Blake was saying, "It looks like the mysterious Iris Rainbow, engaged to rocker Tim Olson of Virgin Ram, is Tucson resident Teri Kelsey. She was confronted at her realty office and admitted this picture is of her with Olson at his hotel." The picture she'd seen in the parking lot was shown on the television. Teri turned off the set and picked up the phone.

"Mom?" she said, her cheeks burning.

"Teri, this is clearly true. How could you have messed up so badly?"

"I'm sorry, Mom, but everything happened so fast, I wasn't thinking. I'm going to marry him in a few weeks. And before you say anything, yes, I was going to tell you."

"Why are you doing this? You know what happened last time you were with him. I don't think you should get involved again."

"He's off the booze and drugs, and I still love him. You can accept this or not, but I want you at the wedding. I hope you trust my judgment after all these years. Give him a chance, please." Teri's mother hung up abruptly. Teri took a deep breath and slowly put the receiver on its cradle. *Damn, I just feel angry. Mother is treating me like a child again. She'd better get used to the idea that I'm marrying Tim.* Teri sighed and turned to Bobbie, who stood there with her mouth open.

"Teri, there are clearly a few things I don't know about you. How long have you known Tim Olson?"

"I lived with him thirty years ago."

"Really!"

"I guess the subject never came up in our conversations." The phone rang again, and Teri answered it.

"Hello, this is Sean Holmes of the Nightly News. Is Teri Kelsey there?"

"No," Teri said and hung up fast. She switched on the answering machine just as another call came in. "Thank goodness for these machines."

Bobbie pointed outside. "There are some reporters coming up the walk."

"They weren't outside when you came over, were they?"

Bobbie shook her head.

"Good, let's go in the back rooms away from the windows. I'm glad I put away the car. It'll look like nobody's home."

They went to the family room and Teri pulled the

drapes over the patio doors. "There. No one at home for a while. Let me get some sodas from the kitchen." She heard the doorbell and knocking as she brought out the two frosty cans. The phone was ringing every ten minutes while the two women stretched out on the couch.

Bobbie laughed as she pushed in the tab on her can. "I almost feel like a fugitive. What are you going to do?"

Teri thought for a moment. "Bobbie, can you help me pack? Maybe I can leave tonight." She went to her purse and pulled out her cell and phone book. "Let's see, I'll call to have the paper stopped. I've got slips for the change of address that I give clients. Could you take that to the post office for me tomorrow?"

"Sure, I can. What about the food in here?"

"Take what you want and give anything else to the food pantry." Teri stopped. "I hate to put all this on you."

Bobbie waved her hand. "You've helped me out many times. I'll get started on your packing. Where are the suitcases?"

Teri showed her and then started calling to get things fixed up. She called Laura and told her she would be there around eight tomorrow morning. After they finished putting her clothes and toiletries together, they went out the door from the kitchen into the garage and loaded the car.

"You still have the key to our house, don't you?"

Bobbie nodded.

"Good. Would you look after the house? I'll be back for everything else when things cool down."

Bobbie went to the window in the living room. "I'll

take care of things for you. It looks like the reporters are gone and I can get back home now. Be careful, Teri, and, oh, I'm going to miss you."

"I'm going to miss you and Don, too. You'll have to come visit Tim and me." The two friends embraced. "I'll call and give you my address and phone number when I settle."

Bobbie left, and Teri's cell phone went off. It was Tim. "Hey, babe, what happened? We were being interviewed on a radio talk show here in Vegas and they asked me about you by name."

"We were photographed coming out of the hotel this morning. It's been a living hell since then, but I've managed to avoid the reporters. I'm leaving for Laura's tonight and should be in Burbank by tomorrow."

"Take it easy. I've got to get ready for the concert. I'll call you at Laura's. I love you, babe."

"Love you too. Bye." Teri smiled as she dropped the phone into her purse. *Yes, it's worth it.* She went to bed and set the alarm for midnight. When it went off, she got something to eat and some food to take along with her. Teri stopped before she left and gazed at her home. She'd raised a family in this house and had been very happy with David. He was still in everything she saw. "Are you happy for me, Tiger? I was able to be with the two loves of my life. I love Tim, but you'll always be in my heart too." Teri blew a kiss and locked the door. Getting into her white Lexus, she started the long journey.

The sun rose over the desert near Palm Springs as Teri decided to stop for breakfast. Everything was cast in a golden glow as the sun peeked over the horizon. At a roadside café, she slid into a booth by the window and the stuffed seat squeaked. Teri checked her watch. It was six o'clock, more than enough time. Teri ate her eggs and sausage and took off again, but she'd forgotten about rush hour. She called Laura from the stalled freeway, saying she would be there when she could. It was four hours later before she got to her sister's house. Teri pulled her car into the driveway, and Laura came out to greet her with a hug.

"Come on in, I have a ton of phone calls for you," Laura said, as she helped Teri unload the trunk, putting the suitcases in one of the empty bedrooms. Teri followed Laura to the family room, where Laura picked up a piece of paper off her desk. "Have a seat and I'll get some coffee," Laura said, indicating the chair and handing Teri the paper. Teri sat in the green swivel office chair and checked what Laura had given her, until her sister came in with two steaming coffee mugs.

"I wonder why they didn't call me on my cell phone?"

"I don't think they wanted to call while you were driving. Anyway, Mom said she was coming in tonight with your son and Stacy. She wants to talk to you and didn't sound happy. Dave is racing here this weekend, and I told her everyone could stay with me, but Dave had already reserved a hotel room for him and Stacy. Mom will stay here. Then Tim called, and he was on his way to San Francisco. He called his mother and gave her our phone numbers. Eileen Olson called, and she and Dan will come over tomorrow after lunch. They're going to bring Melissa over to meet you. Tim told her about you."

Teri laughed. "You make a good secretary. Do you mind if I call Evie, Marcy, and Katie?"

"Unless you want me to do it for you, boss." Laura saluted.

Teri took a sip of coffee and called Evie. "Well, it's about time you called me back," Evie said when she answered. "I've left several messages on your machine."

"I'm not at home. I'm at Laura's house. Evie, guess what—"

"You're engaged to Tim Olson."

"How did you know that?"

"Oh, I saw a picture of you leaving a hotel with him yesterday morning on *Entertainment Tonight*. Looks like you got caught with your hands in Tim's cookie jar." Evie laughed.

"Can you come over tomorrow? I'll give you Laura's address. She lives in Burbank too." Teri's cheeks were warm, and she was grateful Evie couldn't see her. Then she called Marcy and Katie. Marcy said she could come for the wedding on the first weekend of October, and she wasn't surprised. Katie was, and chided her mother for being impetuous, but she was happy for her.

Later that day, Teri's mother showed up with Dave and Stacy. Teri greeted the young couple before they took off to the hotel with the promise they would be back at Laura's for lunch. As soon as they left, her mother turned to Teri sharply.

"What is the matter with you? Why are you letting him back in your life again? He ruined your health and thought nothing of you."

"Mom, that was a long time ago. We've both matured since then. He realized long ago how he messed up, and he's apologized. Give him a chance, please. He was hurt, too, and he's a good man. Imagine if somehow Mike, the man you were engaged to first, could come back into your life since Daddy died. Don't you think you would still love him? That's how I feel about Tim."

She gazed at Teri for a moment. "Okay, I'll give him a chance, but he'd better not hurt you again."

The next day an assembly of family met at Laura's house—Teri and her mother, Dave and Stacy, Evie, Ken, Katie, Kevin, and baby Mike. The doorbell rang after lunch, and Laura answered it. Eileen, Dan, and Tim's daughter Melissa appeared, and Teri went to greet them. Although Tim's parents had aged quite a bit, they were still the handsome couple she remembered from years ago, and she hugged them. They introduced her to Melissa, and Teri instantly liked her. She was very much like Marcy. "I'm so glad all of you could come."

Eileen Olson put her hand on Teri's cheek. "I'm happy Tim found you again. You're just what he needs."

Dan got a sly look. "Teri, we brought a surprise for you." He opened the front door and Tim stepped in. Teri cried out and was in his arms in an instant.

When she regained her senses, she asked, "But, how—"

"Our last concert is here in Los Angeles tonight, and I came in early, that's all." He gave her a kiss, then introductions were made all around as they gathered in Laura's spacious living room.

"I've been thinking," Tim started. "Instead of trying to rent a hall at this late date, Teri and I could have a garden wedding at my house, and the reception could be there, as well. We can let a caterer take care of the set-up and clean-up. I can hire a band and have the reception in the courtyard. I'll take care of all the expenses. What do you say?"

Teri saw her mother purse her lips, but she didn't say anything. Everyone else thought that was a great idea. Tim knelt in front of Teri where she sat in an overstuffed chair. "Baby, I thought I'd do this officially in front of our families." He pulled a small box out of his pocket and opened it. "Teri, I never stopped loving you since I met you. I want you with me for the rest of my life. Please say you'll be my wife."

Teri looked at him with tears misting her eyes. "Oh, yes, yes, yes!" He put the ring on her finger, and it was a perfect fit. She stood, drawing him up with her, and threw her arms around him while everyone applauded.

An hour went by. Tim and Teri managed to slip out into the backyard to get away from the others for a few minutes. As they sat on a bench on the lawn Tim leaned in close.

"I want to tell you about this ring. I bought it for you in San Francisco when we were there on the end of our first tour. The last few months of that long year, I couldn't think of anyone but you. When I found out you were married, I put this ring away in a drawer. I thought about giving it to Dana, and then to Sara, but somehow I couldn't give your ring to someone else. That was a little bit of you I kept. Now I give it to you with all my heart."

She was so full of love for this man that she couldn't speak. Tears ran down her face as she held him close. Finally they went back in to their families.

Later, when everyone had gone, Teri's mother drew her aside. "Teri, I talked to Tim's parents and to his daughter. They seem like fine people. I learned he has raised Melissa himself. I'll give him a chance for your sake. I just want you to be happy."

She hugged her mother. "I am happy, Mom. Very happy."

The morning of the wedding, Teri stared into the mirror while her sister did her hair. *What is it? Why does Tim have such a hold on you?* She remembered the strong pull to him even before she met him. Seeing him at the Scene in Alhambra seemed like a million years ago.

She couldn't say no to him... And the way she'd defied her parents and moved in with him... *I should hate him for the pain he put me through, but when I saw him a few weeks ago, all I could feel was joy.* She looked deep into the reflection of her eyes in the glass.

"Teri! I said, what do you think of your hair?" Laura stood back, her hands on her hips.

"I'm sorry. I was lost in thought. You did a beautiful job." Her hair was once again her younger shade of auburn, and it curled in ringlets around her face. "This will look great with the pearl cap."

After lunch, the bride's party, consisting of her mother, her children and their partners, and Evie and her family, assembled at Laura's house. They drove in several cars to Tim's.

At the security gates, Teri rang the bell. "Ah! Mrs. Kelsey, you are here. Come on up," came the voice of Rosa, the housekeeper. The gates opened and Rosa met them at the front of the house. "I will show you to the guest room on the far end."

Her mother, Laura, and Evie helped her into the pale blue silk dress with the beading on the bodice. The cap of pearls gave it just the right touch. Her mother gripped her shoulders and drew her aside.

"Teri, I want you to wear this necklace." She clasped it around her neck. "This was the last gift Mike gave me before he was killed. I've kept it all these years. I want this to be a symbol that I understand your love for Tim."

Teri looked at it in the mirror. It was an outline of a heart set with tiny diamonds. "It's beautiful. Thank you, Mom, for everything."

A knock came at the door. It was Rosa. "They're ready for you. My dear, you look lovely."

"Thank you." Teri sighed nervously and walked into the hall with her family.

****

"Mr. Olson, it's seven-thirty and the banquet staff is here," was the announcement accompanying the knock on Tim's bedroom door.

"Thank you, Rosa. Please show them where to set up and where things are in the kitchen." Mrs. Rosa Calini had been his head of staff since his divorce from Sara. Rosa was a small wiry Italian woman with iron-gray hair. She was a blessing to him when he was away during the early years. She took care of Melissa when he couldn't take her with him and family wasn't available. Now she was seventy-six and planning to move into a senior apartment near her son's house in North Hollywood. Rosa would stay until Teri and he returned from their honeymoon in Paris. Tim sighed happily; this was the last night he would be in bed alone. He and Teri had agreed not to live together until after the wedding, because Teri thought that would make it special. The image of Teri in his mind's eye sent a tingling through his body. *Not now. I've got things to do.*

Tim got out of bed, took a shower, and slipped on a pair of jeans and a sweatshirt. Hurrying to the kitchen for breakfast, he greeted his daughter, who was already sitting at the kitchen table. "Morning, Lissa." He kissed her on the head and sat across from her while Rosa worked busily at the stove.

"Hi, Dad." A mischievous smile crossed her face. "Nervous?"

Tim grinned. "Yes, very. Do you like Teri?"

"Yes, I do. She's a lot like Mom, isn't she? I like her family, too. I have how many step-siblings now?"

"Well, you met Katie and Dave. Marcy is in college, but she'll be here today. She's eighteen, not much older than you. I met her in Arizona, and she looks a little like you, except she has blue eyes instead of green."

Rosa brought two plates of pancakes and two steaming hot cups of coffee to the table. "Eat hearty, you two. It's going to be a long day."

Tim looked at her. "I'm going to miss you, Rosa. Are you sure I can't convince you to stay?"

"With Mrs. Kelsey here, you won't need me. I introduced her last week to the cleaning, gardening, and pool staff. I'm sure she'll do fine. Then I showed her around the kitchen, and she sounds like she loves to cook."

"She's a very good cook. Almost as good as you."

"Eat! Your breakfast is getting cold," she said firmly, but her eyes were misty.

After breakfast, Tim walked out into the large courtyard to check on the progress of the banquet crew. Bordered on three sides by the house, the courtyard was all red slate, with a blue ceramic fountain in the middle that echoed the one in the circle drive out front. The ceremony would take place in the garden on the other side of the swimming pool, where the crew was busily setting up chairs and decorations. The courtyard would be set up later.

The foreman came over and shook Tim's hand. "We'll have everything the way you want it by three o'clock, Mr. Olson," he said confidently. "It's a beautiful day for a wedding." He waved his hand to the unusually clear blue sky.

"Thank you, Ed. I knew I could trust you."

An hour before the wedding found Tim pacing in circles in his bedroom, watched with amusement by John, his best man. Ensconced in the chairs by the large sunny window and also keeping a good-humored eye on Tim were his father and his brother Mike. A knock came at the door and Tim answered it.

Rosa stood there. "Mrs. Kelsey is here. I showed her to the far bedroom."

"Rosa, I want to see her."

"Mr. Olson! You know very well you can't see the bride before the ceremony. It's bad luck!" A laugh erupted from the three men as Tim closed the door.

Tim shook his head. "Sometimes Rosa acts more like my mother than my housekeeper. Oh, by the way, I told Teri she could redo the house any way she wants, since she's in charge now."

"Most women would drool over that prospect," said Mike. "It's a good thing you have enough money."

Tim was fighting with his bowtie while looking in the mirror and getting frustrated. "Dad, could you do this for me?" He pointed to the offending piece of material. After his father did a masterful job, Tim leaned over the back of one of the chairs. "Am I doing the right thing? Are Teri and I the same people we were?"

John pointed his finger at him. "No, thank goodness, you're not the same people. You have both finally matured into thinking adults. Remember what you said about getting another chance with Teri before we left on the reunion tour? From what I can see, Teri loves you very much, and you got your second chance."

Another knock at the door proved to be Melissa. "They're ready for you, Dad. Come on."

Tim looked at the three most important men in his life and sighed. *I need Charlie here too. Where are you?* They all hugged and backslapped and then set off with Melissa.

The entrance to the garden had a white trellis set up, with red, orange, and gold flowers attached with white ribbons. Most of the guests were seated on the chairs set out in rows. He scanned the people and saw Teri's family and his, plus Luke and his wife Suzanne, and Roy and Linda. Tim noticed a pretty red-haired teen standing to one side of the trellis with a handsome dark-haired young man. "Marcy, is that you?" he called.

She turned and smiled. "Hello, Tim!" She came over with the young man in tow.

Tim grinned. "I hear I have you to thank."

"Just started the ball rolling." She motioned to the young man. "Peter, this is Tim Olson, soon to be my stepdad. Tim, this is Peter Kingston, my boyfriend." The two men shook hands.

"Pleased to meet you, Peter." He put his hand on his daughter's shoulder. "Marcy, this is my daughter, Melissa. Melissa, this is your new stepsister Marcy." The girls smiled and shook hands. John thumped Tim on the back and pointed to where the minister waited. When the two men took their places, the string quartet began playing. Evie, the matron of honor, came down the center aisle between the chairs first. Tim restlessly shifted his feet from side to side and sighed deeply. Then Teri came into view, and he was riveted.

Teri wore a blue gown of a soft material, its loose sleeves billowing in the afternoon breeze. Any nervousness or doubt flew away in the sunny California sky, and Tim had eyes for no one except her.

Teri came down the aisle on the arm of a tall young man with light reddish-brown hair. Her handsome son Dave was giving her away. There were tears in his eyes when he shook Tim's hand, and then Teri and Tim faced the minister and the ceremony began.

They had written their own vows. When the time came, Tim had to find his voice over the lump in his throat. "Teri, the time we were apart made me appreciate you more. I promise to care for you and love you for the rest of my life." He couldn't say anymore.

Teri looked at him with tears running down her face. "Tim, I have loved you since I met you. There was an empty place inside me when we parted. Now I promise with all my heart to be at your side, no matter what happens, and to love you forever." Their kiss at the end of the ceremony was spectacular.

After a sumptuous dinner, everyone went to the

courtyard, where decorations included colorful lanterns and streamers, and where a small band was stationed in one corner. Tim slipped the bandleader a piece of paper.

The bandleader tapped on the microphone. "May I have your attention, please? For the first dance, with the bride and groom, we have a special request by the groom. Ladies and gentlemen, Mr. and Mrs. Tim Olson will dance to 'Moonlight Serenade.' " As Tim and Teri held each other, the music started and they got lost in each other's eyes.

By three o'clock the next morning, the guests, banquet crew, and band had left. Tim carried his bride to their bedroom, and in the soft glow of a dozen candles they undressed each other and embraced tenderly. When Tim swept Teri up in his arms again, the lovers kissed deeply before he laid her on the bed.

Tim kissed down her neck and traced her nipples with his tongue and she moaned. Teri sat up and took his organ in her hands and stroked it gently, setting up a tingling throughout his body. God, he wanted her. He almost lost control and pulled back for a couple of seconds.

He rubbed her slit, and she was wet and ready for him. Tim raised up over her and entered, starting a rhythmic thrusting. Teri cried out and he felt her contract around his shaft, letting the sweet release take him, and they held each other in the warm afterglow.

Mr. and Mrs. Olson were finally at home.

Chapter 18

Teri slowly opened one eye. The sun was up. She ventured a glance at the clock radio. Thursday, February twelve, eight o'clock. *Damn, I overslept!* Two days ago, she'd caught the flu or something and was sick after she arose. She'd felt better yesterday, but she still wasn't a hundred percent. Rolling over, she felt the other side of the bed. Tim wasn't there. Easing herself up, she felt a little dizzy, but that passed. Teri heard the door open and glanced up as Tim brought in a tray. "Good, you're up. I brought you some buttered toast and mint tea."

"I'm sorry, I guess I didn't hear the radio go off."

Tim sat down beside her. "I got up earlier and turned it off. Don't worry, I got Lissa off to school on time. I've got to leave this afternoon for New York, with the others, for the *David Letterman Show*. I'll be back on Saturday."

"Melissa told me last night that her mother is picking her up tomorrow afternoon and she wants to meet me." Teri moved her hands around the warm cup and took a sip of the fragrant liquid. She felt a little more nervous than she let on.

Tim kissed her on the head. "Sara won't bite. We've stayed friends, though mostly for Melissa's sake. Sara just got back from making a film in Italy."

"Don't kiss me. I don't want you coming down

with something. You'd end up puking on TV."

Tim laughed and kissed her again. "They would remember me. Didn't you go to the doctor on Tuesday?"

Teri took a bite of toast. "I'll get the results of the tests tomorrow. Until then, I'm quarantined."

Tim started to pack while Teri put on a robe and took the tray to the kitchen. There, she finished the toast and tea, then put things away.

Virgin Ram was going on a three-month tour of Europe, starting the last week in February. Tim had asked her to come with him this time, maybe to make up for the fiasco of the last time they were together and he went on tour. They'd gone to Paris for their honeymoon, but she wanted to see more countries, so she said yes.

Tim brought his suitcase out and put it by the door, while Teri went back to the bedroom and got dressed. They spent the rest of the time talking together in the courtyard until the limo came.

"Call me when you get to New York. I love you." Teri put her arms around him.

He kissed her on the forehead. "I will. I love you too."

She waved as the limo took off down the driveway, and then she pushed the button to close the security gate.

The next morning, Teri felt better, and she was able to get up to see Melissa off to school. She was dressing when the phone rang.

"Mrs. Olson?" said a voice on the other end.

"Yes?"

"This is Dr. Stevens, I have your test results. You

may want to sit down for this."

She suddenly was scared. "What is it?"

"You're pregnant. I think about two months along."

"What? I was starting to go through menopause. I thought I couldn't get pregnant."

"If you still have eggs, you can get pregnant. I want you to set up a time for your next appointment." He transferred her to the desk and a date was set.

Teri stayed on the bed a full half hour, stunned to the core. *A baby? At forty-eight? Oh, my, do I really want this child? I felt so free when Marcy went off to college, and Tim's daughter is a year away from leaving home. All the diapers and messes, school headaches, and being stuck at home again.* Deep down she was ashamed. *This child didn't ask to be brought into existence, and now that it has, it deserves a chance. Maybe it won't be so bad. This is Tim's baby. I hope it'll be all right. I've heard of problems for older mothers.* She mused for a while longer, letting the information sink in. *I've got a hell of a good Valentine gift for Tim when he gets home on Saturday.*

The phone rang again, early that afternoon. "Hello? This is Sara Matisse. You must be Teri," said the voice on the other end.

"Yes, I am. When are you coming over for Melissa today?"

"I'd like to come over around two-thirty. That should give us time to talk."

"Fine, I'll see you then." Teri was a little nervous. She'd never dealt with ex-wives before. When she let Sara through the security gate, she wished Melissa were there to act as a buffer, but Melissa wouldn't be home from school for another half hour. She met Sara at the door. "Hello, Sara. I'm Teri." She held out her hand.

Sara looked a little hesitant but took it. "Hello, Teri. I'm glad I got to meet you. Even when we were married, Tim told me many stories about you." She studied Teri's face. "Oh, that's all right. I always knew how much he loved you. I'm glad he found you," she said, a slight edge to her voice.

"I've got some fresh lemonade out in the courtyard. Would you like some?"

"Yes, thank you."

Teri poured the lemonade into two frosty glasses, and they sat on the padded iron chairs next to the decorative matching table under its blue umbrella. There was an uncomfortable silence between them.

"Teri, I love what you've done to the house. It looks beautiful," Sara said, but Teri didn't think she meant it.

"Thank you. I've really enjoyed myself, redecorating."

Sara took a drink of the lemonade and was quiet. Her mood seemed to change. "You are very lucky. Tim is a wonderful man. I regret hurting him so much. What did he tell you about me?"

"That you were very happy for a while, and then you divorced."

She looked very sad. "I was working on a movie with Karl Graham. You've heard of him?"

"My daughter Katie had a crush on him."

"Well, I did too. At first, I resisted any advances he made to me, because of Tim and Melissa, but he was so charming, I fell under his spell. We were in New York for eight months, and I was sure I was in love with him.

Then the last month, I found out I was pregnant. I know I hurt Tim terribly. I even let him take custody of Melissa because I felt so guilty."

"You know, you don't have to tell me this."

"Please, Teri, I want you to realize how much you mean to him. Anyway, I moved in with Karl, and we lived together for five years. We had two children during that time, and I was pressing him to get married. Well, a new girl caught his eye and he moved out on me. I was hurt and sought out Tim for comfort. I wanted to come back to him, but he wouldn't have me. He told me the only woman he wanted was you. If he couldn't have you, he wouldn't get married again."

Teri pondered this over her glass. *Now I know he never stopped loving me.* "You did find someone else, obviously. Your last name is different."

"Yes. He's Lou Matisse, a photographer. We met on a movie I was making four years ago. He accepted my other children and we have a one-year-old of our own. I love him very much." Sara smiled and seemed more relaxed. Teri found herself more at ease.

"I was worried about meeting you, but I was wrong. Thank you for telling me this."

"I knew Tim was still in love with you even when we were married, and I resented you for it, but I can see why he was fond of you. I like you too. I think you'll be a good stepmother for Melissa."

"She's a nice girl. You and Tim have done a wonderful job with her."

"I think Tim deserves the most thanks. He's a great dad."

"Hmm, that's good to know…"

Sara looked at her curiously. Then Melissa joined

them in the courtyard. "Hi, Mom! Welcome home. I'm ready to go when you are." Sara and Melissa embraced.

"I'm happy to see you again, sweetie. My word, you've grown."

"Mother, please. I haven't grown that much since you last saw me." They both laughed.

"We'd better get going." Sara turned to Teri and held her hand out. "It was nice meeting you."

Teri took the offered hand. "Good meeting you too."

Melissa touched Teri on the shoulder. "Tell Dad I'll be back before he leaves." Then she looked at her mother and Teri standing together. "Dad was right— you two do look alike."

"I'll let him know you'll be here. Goodbye, Melissa." She saw them to the door and waved as the car disappeared down the driveway. *I'm glad that went well. Sara's nothing like Dana, thank goodness.*

Saturday morning was Valentine's Day. Teri was having coffee in the kitchen, thinking here she was married to Tim and he wasn't with her. A buzz came from the security gates. She went to the video screen and switched it on. From the camera, she saw three delivery trucks waiting outside. A young man in a uniform stood in plain sight.

"Mrs. Olson?"

"Yes."

"I'm from Chatsworth Florist." He held his ID card by the camera. "I'm here to make a delivery."

He did remember. She hit the security gate button. "Come on up." She went out the front door and stood on the steps, shading her eyes. "Three trucks?" she asked the delivery man.

He tapped his pen on a clipboard. "Where do you want these flowers? I have ten free-standing vases with three dozen roses each."

Teri gasped. "That's thirty dozen roses! Um—put them in the living room."

She watched, amazed, as the men filled up the room with the fragrant scarlet flowers. The delivery man handed her a card and the clipboard to sign, and she gave him a fifty-dollar tip.

"Thank you, ma'am. Happy Valentine's Day." He and the other men left.

She opened the card and read, "Happy Valentine's Day, babe. I made up for lost time."

Teri made a special dinner of grilled porterhouse steaks and baked potatoes. She had just poured the non-alcoholic wine when she heard the limo. The door burst open, and Tim came in with another dozen roses. Her heart swelled and her eyes filled with tears. He set down the flowers and swung her around in an embrace.

"It's been thirty-one years since we met. I got a dozen roses for every year." She saw such joy in his eyes as she kissed him.

"That was a wonderful surprise. I've got a surprise for you too."

He looked around. "Where is it?"

She put her lips close to his ear. "Tim, I'm pregnant."

A myriad of expressions crossed his face, among them surprise, tenderness, and amusement. Then a suspicious look rested there. "Heh-heh. Teri, you've always been one for practical jokes. That was a good one, I almost believed you."

Teri felt a strange pull of amusement and anger.

She wanted both to laugh and to kill him. "It's true, you crazy idiot. I'm due in September."

The shocked expression was priceless. "A baby? At our age?"

"Yes, you Casanova, you finally knocked me up." They embraced, laughing and crying at the same time.

Tim turned serious. "Do you realize how old we'll be when this child graduates from high school? We may not even be around. I'll be fifty-five this year. Let's see, that will make me seventy-three. You would be sixty-seven."

Teri felt a stab at her heart. "Yes, I've thought about that, but we don't have a whole lot of choices. We can keep it and raise it for as long as we can, or we could give it up for adoption. There is a third alternative…"

"No abortion." He put his hand on her stomach. "This is a product of our love. I lost a son to divorce. I don't want to lose another child." He kissed her tenderly. "I love you, babe. We'll find a way to deal with having a baby."

"What about all the genetic problems connected with older parents? Down's Syndrome and such."

Tim held her close. "We'll have all the tests done, and we can deal with any problems down the line."

Teri served the dinner, and Tim raised his glass to her. "Here's to the love of my life and the mother of my child, Teri." Then he kissed her.

"I love you so much." Teri gazed into his eyes.

After dinner, they took lemonade out to the courtyard.

Tim sat musing. "I never thought I would have any more children. This almost makes it perfect…" His voice trailed off.

"Something wrong?" Teri asked, concerned.

"Hearing the news made me wish I could have kept connected with Charlie."

"You know, you could try to find him. He might have realized by now what his mother did to him."

Tim's fist slowly started striking the iron patio table. Tears threatened when he looked at her. "Leave it alone, Teri," he said angrily. He stalked back into the house.

He's really hurting. I wonder what I can do to help?

Teri received some bad news when she went for her appointment. "I don't think you should go on this tour of Europe with your husband," Dr. Stevens said seriously. "You have slightly elevated blood pressure, and I want to keep an eye on you."

"But we've been planning this, and I want to be with him."

"Mrs. Olson, this could be a threat to the health of your child. What's more important?"

Teri sighed. "You're right, of course. I guess there will be other chances." But she didn't feel that at all. She was angry while she got dressed. *Why did this baby have to come now? Damn the timing. Can I trust Tim to be faithful to me? Does he really love me?* All the old fears and doubts came flooding back. This was too close to what had happened thirty years ago.

Wait a minute. You are married to him and he shows you love every day. Do what you asked your mom to do. Give him a chance.

She thought about that on the way home. *Since I'm going to be here while he's away, I wonder if I could find Charlie. I have to learn how to track someone down.*

The following Tuesday was her weekly get-together with Sandy Simon, John's wife, and Evie Barnes. The three of them got together to talk and relax for a while in each other's company. This week, they were meeting at the Simons' spacious home by the ocean.

Teri stood grinning while Sandy and Evie looked incredulously at her. A suspicious edge came over Evie's face. "Teri, I should shoot you. You almost had me believing you were pregnant. Sandy, she always plays pranks like this."

Teri started tapping her foot. "I'm not kidding. I'm two months along. Why doesn't anyone think I'm telling the truth?"

"Because you've been known to suck me into these things and make me look like a fool."

Sandy smiled. "Well, congratulations about the little one. I hope that's what you wanted."

"It surprised me too." Teri nodded.

"What was Tim's reaction?" Evie asked.

Teri sat on one of the patio chairs. "Same as yours. He didn't believe me at first."

Just then Jeff Simon, Sandy's youngest son, came out the french doors. "Hi, Teri, is Melissa at home?"

"No, she's with her mother for a while. You can call her there."

"Good. There's a dance at school, and I wanted to invite her. Thanks, Teri."

"Anytime, Jeff." She watched him go back into the house, then winked at Sandy. "Those two seem to be sweet on each other."

Sandy laughed. "For so many years they couldn't stand each other. Then the hormones kicked in."

Teri turned serious. "Sandy, what do you know about Charlie?"

"Not a whole lot. Tim and Dana had their final break-up after they left our wedding. I know Charlie was hard on Tim and Sara. After Melissa was born, he stopped coming to see Tim altogether. He refused to take any calls and all of Tim's letters were returned. Of course, that may have been Dana's doing."

"I want to see if I can find him."

"You may want to talk to Tim's mother. I think she had all the information, since Tim's visitations were always at his parents' house."

"Please don't tell John I'm going to do this. He might tell Tim."

"I'll keep your secret if you want. Are you going looking while they're in Europe?"

"I plan to." Teri was busy hatching a search. "If I find him and he wants nothing to do with Tim, it won't hurt Tim if he doesn't know. If Charlie wants to be back in Tim's life, I can arrange that."

"Just be careful you don't open old wounds," Evie said.

"I'll be a diplomat, I promise." *I hope I can find him.*

And they went back to enjoying the lazy afternoon.

****

Later in February, Teri found herself experiencing the same sadness she'd felt when Tim was going on tour for the first time. She remembered thinking he didn't love her enough. She put her hand on her stomach. *I have assurance of that this time.* Sitting on the loveseat in the foyer, she watched the security screen as the limo pulled up.

"Tim, it's here!" she called toward the bedroom.

"I'm ready," came the reply.

Melissa joined Teri just as Tim hurried up the hall. He pushed the button for the gate and turned to his daughter. "Be good, sweetheart. I'll call as much as I can."

She put her arms around him. "I know, Dad. I love you. Take care of yourself."

He went to Teri and held her tenderly. "I'm going to miss you terribly." He put both hands on her stomach. "Take care of our little one. I love both of you." Tears were on his cheek as he kissed her.

Teri put her arm around Melissa as they watched the limo drive away.

A few days later, Teri visited her mother-in-law in a senior apartment complex in Palos Verdes. Mrs. Olson studied her carefully. "Why do you want to find Charlie?"

"I think Tim's really hurting inside. I thought I'd try searching for him, and if Charlie wants nothing to do with Tim, he can tell me and I'll leave well enough alone. But I have to try." Teri nervously tapped her fingers on the arm of the blue overstuffed couch in the sunny apartment living room. "Do you know where I can find him?"

Mrs. Olson sighed. "I haven't been in touch with him since he cut himself off from us when Melissa was born. Both we and Tim tried to keep communication going, but he wouldn't respond."

"Can you give me anything to go on?"

"I'll give you the last known address and phone

number. Dana was married to a Baxter. Um, Martin Baxter, I believe. I think he worked for the sheriff's department. I don't know what branch." She went into the bedroom and brought out an old address book. "Here, I'll give you the information I have." She found the page and wrote it down.

"Thanks, Mother Olson. I'll let you know what happens."

"Teri, I miss my grandson too," she said as she hugged her. "You take care of yourself and don't overdo. Remember, you have one of our grandchildren in progress."

Teri smiled. "I promise I'll take care of this one."

Teri went home and tried the phone number. It wasn't Dana's anymore. She drove to the last known address, and the person didn't know the Baxters. These people had moved in about three years ago.

It's too bad this won't be easy. I do know Martin Baxter worked for the sheriff's department. Maybe I could find him. She tried several branches in the San Fernando Valley until she hit pay dirt.

"Yes, Captain Martin Baxter works here," said the woman who answered.

"Can I make an appointment to see him?"

"What is this in regard to?"

"I'd like to ask him a few questions about his stepson, Charlie."

"One minute, please."

Soon a gruff voice came on the line. "Who is this? This is Captain Baxter."

"My name is Teri Olson. I'm Tim's wife. I would like to find Charlie and talk to him."

"Why do you want to do that?"

"Tim regrets not staying in contact, and I want to try and find Charlie. I'm looking for anyone who can assist me."

"I don't know if I can help much, but I'll give you what information I have. Can you come over in an hour? I get off work then. Meet me outside the main door."

"Thank you. I'll be there." Her hands were sweating as she slipped the phone into her purse.

An hour later as she parked her car by the building he'd specified, Teri saw a rugged, gray-haired man of medium build standing next to the wall by the door. Teri walked up to him. "Captain Baxter?" He nodded. "I'm Teri Olson. Thank you for taking time to talk to me."

He pointed to a coffee shop across the street. "Let's go in there." They ordered two coffees and sat at a corner table. "What do you want to know about Charlie? Hasn't your husband told you anything?"

"I want to know where I can find him. I'd like to talk to him. Can you help me?"

He looked down at his cup and took a sip. "I don't know if I can tell you where he is. Dana and I were only married seven years, and then we divorced. She is a hard woman to get along with. Anyway, Charlie was a troubled sixteen-year-old when I last saw him. Dana and I didn't keep up with each other after that. Why do you want to find him?"

"I wanted to try to get Charlie to talk to his dad. Tim still is upset about losing touch with him."

"That was mostly Dana's doing. I think I was wrong in judging Tim so harshly. Dana seemed to do everything in her power to make anybody miserable if they crossed her. I know. That's why we divorced."

"You said he was sixteen when you left. How old would he be now?"

"Let's see. I haven't seen them for maybe about thirteen years, so he would be, hmm, around twenty-nine."

"That's close to my oldest daughter's age. What high school did he go to?"

"It was Van Nuys High School. You know, you would have made a good detective."

"I'm playing that by ear right now. Thank you, Captain Baxter." She shook his hand as he got up to leave.

"I'm sorry I couldn't be of more help. Good luck, Teri."

She went home and tried to get an address from the high school alumni files, but she ran into a dead end there, too. Next, she looked for any Stanleys living in Encino. No luck there either.

After two months of dead ends, Teri sat at the computer, searching for a Charlie T. Olson, when Evie called.

"Evie, I've just about run out of ideas. I've been at the computer for days, searching for Charlie Olson, but I haven't hit any information yet."

"Teri, you aren't much of a Sherlock Holmes, are you?" Evie laughed. "Why haven't you been looking under his given name of Charles?"

Teri immediately felt stupid. "I guess I didn't think of that. Thanks for jogging my brain."

"That's why they pay me the big money. Good luck."

The next couple of days, Teri searched the Internet

for Charles T. Olson. Late one Saturday morning, she gave a shout. On one of the results, she found a news story of an arrest in Santa Ana by a patrolman named Charles T. Olson, and it gave the station where he worked. Could this be Charlie? Could he have gone into law enforcement like his stepfather? She looked at the date of the story and it was only a few months earlier.

Teri heard a knock at the door of the study. "Are you all right?" It was Melissa.

"I'm sorry, I just found something on the Net."

Melissa came in. "What is it?"

"If you promise not to tell your father, I'll tell you."

"This isn't going to hurt Dad, is it?"

"Honey, I would never hurt your father. I've been trying to find your brother for him. I know he's bothered by losing touch with Charlie, so I've been looking for him. See what I found."

She read the news blurb. "Do you think Charlie went to work for the police department?"

"It's possible his stepfather, Martin, inspired him to work on the force. When I talked to Martin Baxter, he told me he and Dana divorced when Charlie was sixteen. From what I learned from your father, Charlie admired Martin. I want to ask Charlie if he would at least meet with his father."

"I hope you're right. I promise I won't tell Dad."

The next day, Teri called the station in Santa Ana and asked if Patrolman Charles Olson still worked there.

"Yes, he does, but he's on duty right now. Would you like to leave a message?"

"I would, but you may think this sounds strange. If

his father was named Tim and his mother was Dana, I want to talk to him. I'm Teri Olson, and I would be his stepmother." She gave the phone number.

A few hours later, the phone rang. Teri gripped the instrument tight as she answered.

"Is this Teri Olson?" said a man on the other end. "This is Charlie Olson." He sounded as nervous as she was.

For a moment, she couldn't talk. Then she cleared her throat and said, "Charlie, I would like to talk to you about your father. Where and when could I meet you?"

There was silence on the other end, and Teri prayed that he wouldn't hang up. "Why do you want to talk to me about Dad?"

"He told me that he regrets not keeping in touch with you. He still cares about you. Can you meet with me, please?" There was more silence.

Then he spoke. "I'm off tomorrow. Could you meet me on the Santa Monica Pier? All the way on the end. I like to go down there to watch the waves."

"How will I know you?"

"I'll be in a Def Leppard T-shirt and a pair of cut-off jeans. I'll wear my dark blue visor. Be there at ten tomorrow morning."

"See you tomorrow." Teri felt crazy butterflies in her stomach. She wanted to shout and tell everybody. *I'm going to have trouble talking to Tim this evening.*

The next day was warm and sunny as the breeze whipped at her hair. The greasy hot dog smells and loud rap music attacked her senses. As she walked on the boardwalk, she remembered her own trips to the beach when she was young. How far away that was, but how near to her memories. She saw a young man sitting at the end of the pier. Tears threatened, because he looked very much like his father had so long ago. Teri composed herself. "Hello. Are you Charlie Olson?" She seated herself beside him.

He looked at her guardedly. "Yes, I am. You must be Teri. Are you the same Teri Darden that my dad dated before he married my mom?"

"Yes. You've heard of me?"

"You were the subject of many of my parents' fights."

"Oh, I'm sorry."

"No, it's not your fault. My mother confessed a lot of things to me before she died."

Teri felt the blood drain from her face. "When did she die?"

He shifted uncomfortably. "It was two years ago. She died of breast cancer. She told me all about the break-up with Dad and how she manipulated to get rid of you. It was her plan to marry him and make his life a living hell for dumping her. That was before he ever met you. I realized then how she'd swayed my opinion of Dad, and I'm ashamed of everything I put him through. I wanted to get in touch with him, but I didn't know what to say." He put his face in his hands.

Teri put her hand on his shoulder. "He's talked about you only a little, but I know he regrets not having you in his life. I wanted to find you and see if you would at least talk to him."

When he glanced at her again, there were tears in his eyes. "There was another thing that happened that changed how I feel. I just got a divorce myself, and I miss my three kids. Oh, I see them on weekends, but it's not the same. I know I really hurt Dad with the way

I acted. I didn't know if he would even want to see me again." When his voice cracked, Teri put her arms around him.

Oh, Charlie, he wants to see you. "He'll be back in two weeks. I want to plan a surprise get-together to welcome him home. Will you come?"

"In front of a bunch of people? I don't know."

"All those people will be family and friends. *Your* family and friends. Your grandparents, aunts, and uncles. All their children, too. And your half-sister, Melissa. I know they all want to reunite with you. You can bring your children to meet their relatives."

He looked at her with his deep brown eyes. "You win. I'll come."

Teri gave him the address and directions for the house. She stood to leave and looked back at him. "Oh, and Charlie, lose the Def Leppard T-shirt."

He saluted her. "Yes, ma'am!" She could hear him laughing as she strolled back along the pier.

****

Tim shifted restlessly in the limo coming from the airport. John stared out the window, seemingly lost in thought.

"I wish Teri hadn't decided to throw a welcome home party today. I just wanted to get home and stretch out," Tim pouted.

John regarded him. "She said it won't last any longer than necessary and the whole family was going to be there. That includes my family, apparently."

Tim's security gates opened as they turned in, and he noticed cars were parked up to the house. Teri stood by the fountain on the circle drive, waiting for him. Her body was already blossoming with the new life within, and Tim forgot all his complaints when he saw her. She was the most welcoming and beautiful sight ever, with her dazzling smile. Tim flew out of the limo and into her arms. He put his hands on her belly. "I missed you so much," he said as he kissed her.

She clasped his hand. "I missed you too." She made a motion to John to follow them. "Come on in, both of you. We're all here to welcome you home."

At the door, Melissa stood with John's son, Jeff. Tim hugged his daughter and gave a sidelong glance at John. "You better keep a handle on your son."

John laughed and slapped Jeff on the back. "He's as much a gentleman as I am."

"That's what I'm afraid of."

From the house, they heard the cry, "John!" and Sandy ran out and into his arms.

Teri guided Tim inside. As he greeted his parents, he thought his mother looked like she'd been crying. He glanced around, and all of Teri's children and families were there. He shook hands with Ken and kissed Evie on the cheek. They continued into the living room, and he waved to Teri's mother, who waved back. She was seated with Laura and her children. His brother Mike and their sister Colleen were gathered around the fireplace with their families. Teri led him to the other end of the room.

A young man with dark brown hair and eyes stood as they approached. Three children were on the floor beside him. Tim studied him carefully before finally choking out, "Charlie!"

Charlie's eyes filled. "Oh, Dad, I'm so sorry." And the two latched onto each other like they wouldn't let go. Tim's emotions ran wild. All he cared about in that moment was his son.

Tim pulled back and gripped Charlie by the shoulders. "How? Why?" was all he could say.

Charlie glanced down. "Teri found me and asked if I would see you. I just went through a divorce and missed having my children. Mom died two years ago of breast cancer and confessed how she turned me against you. I realized how awful I'd been to you and wanted to say I was sorry." He gulped, an agonized look on his face, before he continued, "I want you back in my life, Dad, if you'll have me." His voice broke, and Tim took him in his arms again.

"I love you, son."

"Dad, I want you to meet your grandchildren." Charlie stepped back as the children stood at his urging, and he put his hand on the oldest one's shoulder. "This is my eight-year-old son Austin." He pulled the older girl over. "This is five-year-old Kelly." He picked up the toddler. "And this is two-year-old Emily."

Austin and Emily watched him shyly, but Kelly stepped right up to Tim. "Are you really my grandpa?" she asked with her hands on her hips.

Tim smiled at the child. "Yes, I am, Kelly."

"Then I want a hug and a kiss."

Tim swept her up and kissed her. She put her small arms around his neck and hugged him tight, and Tim melted. *How can you fall in love so fast? I have grandchildren and I love it.* The other two slowly approached him and greeted him as well.

Tim turned and everybody was there, moved by the scene of reunion and discovery.

He gave Kelly back to Charlie and went to Teri, putting his arms around her. "Thank you for giving me my family back."

She gazed at him through her tears. "I'd do anything for you, my love."

He held her with a deep love he had for no other.

Epilogue

A month before the baby was due, Dr. Stevens put Teri in the hospital; her blood pressure was dangerously high. All of her other tests had come back fine, and the baby was a normal healthy fetus, but things could change in an instant. The doctor wanted her where he could keep an eye on her.

Teri spent many an evening gripping Tim's hand. "Oh, god, could I die?" Then she would cry and he would try to calm her down.

One evening, Tim walked into her room and gingerly eased down into the chair. He took her hand and squeezed it. "Babe, I decided I don't want to lose you and I do want to continue to make love to you, so I got snipped. I figured it was easier for me, and you've been through enough all ready."

Teri didn't know what to say. "But then you can't have any more children."

"You're more important to me. Besides," he said with a smile, "we're getting too old for this."

"Does it hurt much?"

"I'll have to sit on an ice pack for a day or two."

Teri gazed at this man she adored. He was willing to go through pain for her. "I love you so much." And she squeezed his hand back.

Dr. Stevens decided to do a caesarian. He said it would be dangerous for both Teri and the baby if they waited any longer.

On September tenth, Teri delivered a healthy baby boy. They had previously discussed a name, and Teri wanted to name him after her father, so Theodore Darden Olson came to be.

Six months later, Teri found Tim standing over the crib, watching their sleeping son. She came up behind Tim and put her arms around him. "I wondered where you were. He looks so peaceful now, doesn't he?" she said with her voice lowered.

Tim nodded. "Teddy can be quite a handful at times."

"He looks a lot like my dad's baby pictures. He had red-gold hair most of his life. But Teddy got your beautiful green eyes."

Tim turned and kissed her on the forehead. "And your dazzling smile. He's going to be a heartbreaker someday."

They stood for some time, watching their miracle.

A word about the author...

Ilona Fridl still lives in Wisconsin with her mate, Mark. This was the first book she wrote, and she felt it was important for Teri and Tim's story to get out.

Talk with Ilona at her website:

http://www.ilonafridl.com